I0830373

SHATTERED ECHOES

THE MORNING LANDS

By M.R. deSamson

To my wife—my anchor in the storm,

and to our three children, whose laughter lights every shadow.

To Papa and Mama, who taught me to keep going.

And to my brother and sisters, who've walked this path with me in

their own ways.

Contents

ACKNOWLEDGEMENTS

I want to acknowledge the team at American Publishers Inc., who helped me bring this book to life. I also want to thank the readers who will give my story a chance. And to those who are suffering from grief and depression—this is for you.

CHAPTER 1

The fluorescent lights buzzed overhead as Butch logged his final inventory count into the ancient warehouse computer. His fingers flew across the keyboard with unexpected precision, muscle memory from years spent gaming in internet cafes back home. The screen's green text reflected off his glasses while the dot-matrix printer churned out his end-of-shift report.

"Hey Tito, heading out?" Manuel from receiving waved from behind a stack of boxes.

"Yeah, just wrapping up." Butch stretched, his back cracking from eight hours of lifting and checking pallets. The warehouse had emptied out, most workers gone home an hour ago.

He grabbed his worn leather bag from his locker, pulled out his keys. The metal jangled as he walked through the empty aisles toward the exit, his footsteps echoing off concrete floors and corrugated metal walls.

The Southern California evening hit him with a blast of warm air as he pushed through the heavy door. His '89 Civic sat alone in the far corner of the lot, paint faded from endless sun. The door creaked as he opened it, the sound familiar as an old friend's voice.

"Just you and me again, girl." Butch patted the steering wheel. The engine coughed twice before turning over, the old car shuddering to life beneath him. The radio crackled with static before finding its signal-some pop song he didn't recognize.

He adjusted the rearview mirror, caught his own tired reflection. Gray streaked his temples now, lines around his eyes deeper than when he'd first come to America. Five years in San Francisco, now here in Fullerton-not the life he'd planned, but it paid the bills.

The Civic's headlights cut through gathering dusk as he pulled out of the lot. Tomorrow would bring another shift, more inventory, more boxes. But for now, the road home stretched before him, empty and waiting.

The next evening, Butch scanned boxes in aisle seven while Jesse, one of the college-age workers, stacked cleaning supplies nearby.

"Tito, how come you always take the evening shift?" Jesse balanced a box of bleach on his hip.

"Less people watching me mess up." Butch winked, tapping his scanner against a case of Banana Ketchup. "Plus, traffic's better. Not that my car could go fast anyway."

"Man, my cousin said this area used to be popping back in the day." Jesse set down his load. "Like, Florentine Gardens-type crazy. Clubs everywhere, people lined up around the block."

"Before my time." Butch typed numbers into his handheld. "Now the most exciting thing is watching security chase raccoons out of the dumpster."

"For real, though. My cousin said Thursday nights, you couldn't even find parking. Now look at it." Jesse gestured toward the window, where empty storefronts lined the street. "Everything's closed by nine except the Circle K."

"Hey, Circle K has great coffee." Butch patted his stomach. "And donuts. Maybe too good."

"You're not that old, Tito. Bet you could still party."

"Only party I know now is packing party." Butch lifted another box. "Besides, young people's music gives me a headache. Too much..." He made exaggerated bass-thumping motions with his hands.

Jesse laughed. "You sound just like my dad."

"See? Already practicing to be a grumpy old man." Butch checked his watch. "Speaking of old, these invoices won't file themselves. Your turn to chase raccoons if they show up."

"Man, those things are fearless now. One of them tried to steal my lunch yesterday."

"Smart raccoon. Your mom makes the best adobo in town."

During his break, Butch settled into the worn pleather chair in the break room. The overhead fluorescent light flickered, casting uneven shadows across the empty space. He pulled out his wallet,

3

weathered brown leather cracked at the edges, and extracted a faded photograph.

His father smiled back at him from behind thick-rimmed glasses, arm thrown around a teenage Butch's shoulders at their old home in Iloilo. The photo's edges had softened, white creases marking where he'd carried it across an ocean.

"Miss you, Pa." Butch traced his thumb across the image. The familiar ache spread through his chest, years of distance doing nothing to dull the pain.

His phone buzzed-a message from his mother. She'd sent a photo of her garden, proud purple eggplants hanging heavy on the vine. The sight brought a slight smile to his face. At least she was doing well, keeping busy with her vegetables and the neighborhood gossip she loved to share.

"Kumusta, Ma?" He typed back, adding a heart emoji. She'd learned to use those faster than he had.

The break room's ancient coffee maker sputtered and dripped, filling the silence. Butch carefully tucked the photo back into his wallet, between his driver's license and Social Security card. The leather folded with practiced ease, edges worn smooth from countless openings.

His mother replied with more emojis-flowers, hearts, and a smiling face. "Miss you, toto," she wrote. "Come visit soon?"

"Soon," he typed back, though they both knew it might be months before he could afford the trip. The warehouse paid decent wages, but international flights weren't cheap.

The break room door creaked. Butch quickly pocketed his phone, straightened in his chair. Time to get back to work, back to counting boxes and scanning barcodes. The photo of his father stayed close, tucked against his heart in his wallet pocket.

Butch's key ring jingled as he locked up the warehouse's side entrance. The parking lot stretched empty before him, painted lines fading into shadow beyond the security lights' reach. A police siren wailed somewhere in the distance, its cry echoing off buildings before fading into the night.

He paused, head tilted. Another siren joined the first, then a third-their overlapping wails drifting from the direction of Harbor Boulevard.

"Just another crazy night in the O.C." Butch shrugged, adjusting the strap of his bag across his shoulder. The sound was familiar enough after years in Southern California-probably someone running a red light or teenagers racing their parents' cars again.

His Civic waited in its usual spot, hood still warm from the day's sun. The driver's side door protested with its familiar creak as he slid behind the wheel. More sirens joined the chorus, their pitch rising and falling like mechanical coyotes.

"Getting busy out there tonight." Butch turned his key in the ignition. The engine coughed once, twice, before settling into its usual rough idle. He flicked on the headlights, casting twin beams across empty asphalt.

The radio came to life with static before finding its signal. The music cut out mid-song, replaced by an emergency broadcast tone that made him wince. Butch reached to change the station, but every frequency carried the same piercing sound.

Through his open window, the sirens grew louder, more urgent. Red and blue lights painted the buildings in strobing colors as emergency vehicles raced past on the main road. Butch counted five police cars, then two fire trucks, all heading north with lights flashing.

"Must be some party." He put the car in drive, pulled out of his spot. The emergency broadcast tone finally ended, replaced by regular programming. Whatever was happening, it wasn't his problem. He had leftover pancit for dinner and a new episode of his favorite show waiting at home.

The radio crackled again, the late-night DJ's voice cutting in and out through bursts of static. Fragments of words overlapped- multiple stations bleeding together through the aging speakers.

"...emergency protocols..." came a stern voice, fading into "...beautiful night for..." before dissolving into Spanish music that lasted three seconds.

Butch reached for the dial but pulled his hand back. The jumble of sounds formed an oddly hypnotic rhythm-talk shows merging with music, news reports, and what might have been a religious sermon.

"Always the weirdos this time of night," he muttered, drumming his fingers on the steering wheel. The Civic's engine hummed beneath him as he turned onto Harbor Boulevard, away from the direction the emergency vehicles had gone.

The radio's chaos continued. A woman's laugh cut through the static, followed by what sounded like a weather report for a city he'd never heard of. Numbers rattled off in sequence, reminding him of those old spy station broadcasts he used to pick up late at night back home.

He left it playing, the strange audio symphony keeping him company as he drove. Maybe the heat was messing with the signals, or some kid with a pirate radio setup was having fun. Either way, it beat the usual late-night commercials.

***

Jin peered at his phone screen, brow furrowed as he compared the bubbling pot to the recipe photo. "That doesn't look right."

"Because you didn't slice the rice cakes thin enough." Mina hip-checked him away from the stove, taking control of the wooden spatula. "Mom would cry if she saw what you're doing to her tteokbokki recipe."

"Hey, I followed it exactly." Jin held up his phone as evidence. The sauce splattered, leaving red dots across the kitchen counter.

"You're supposed to stir it constantly." Mina demonstrated with quick, practiced motions. "See how the sauce is getting thicker? That's what we want."

Jin crossed his arms. "When did you become the cooking expert?"

"Someone had to learn after you nearly burned down the kitchen trying to make ramyeon last year." Mina tasted the sauce, adding a splash of fish sauce. "Hand me the green onions."

"That was one time." Jin grabbed the cutting board, sliding the chopped vegetables her way. "And the fire alarm was oversensitive."

"The neighbors called 911."

"Because they're nosy." Jin stole a rice cake from the pot, juggling it between his hands as steam rose from the chewy surface. "But this is actually good."

Mina swatted his hand with the spatula. "Stop eating it before it's done! Go set the table or something."

"Yes, chef." Jin gave an exaggerated bow, dodging another swat. He pulled bowls from the cabinet, arranging them on their small dining table. "Remember when we were kids and Mom would only let us help by setting the table?"

"Because you'd try to 'experiment' with the ingredients." Mina turned off the heat, giving the sauce one final stir. "Like putting chocolate in the kimchi jjigae."

"I was ahead of my time. Sweet and spicy is totally a thing now."

"You're still weird." Mina carried the pot to the table, the rich aroma of gochugaru and fish cake filling their apartment. "But at least you've learned to follow a recipe."

"Mostly." Jin grinned, already reaching for another rice cake.

The front door clicked open. Their father stepped inside, his dress shoes scuffing against the welcome mat. His tie hung loose around his neck, collar unbuttoned after another long day at the county office.

"Appa!" Mina called from the kitchen. "We made tteokbokki."

He crossed the living room in measured steps, briefcase still clutched in one hand. The leather was worn at the edges, the same briefcase he'd carried for the past decade of project meetings and municipal planning sessions.

Jin watched his father's face, searching for hints of the day's weight. Dark circles shadowed his eyes, deeper than usual. His shoulders slumped beneath his navy suit jacket.

Their father set down his briefcase and moved behind their chairs. His hand found Jin's head first, rough palm resting there for a moment before shifting to Mina's hair. The familiar gesture carried years of unspoken affection.

"The sauce came out perfect this time." Mina pushed a bowl toward his empty seat. "Jin actually followed the recipe."

Their father's lips twitched-almost a smile. He sank into his chair, loosening his tie further.

Jin ladled more rice cakes into his father's bowl. "How was work?"

The question hung in the air. Their father picked up his chopsticks, stirring the red sauce without answering. His silence filled the kitchen like another presence at the table.

"There's fish cake too," Mina added softly, sliding the plate closer.

Their father nodded, patting her head once more before taking his first bite. The quiet stretched between bites, broken only by the soft clink of metal against ceramic.

Jin pushed his empty bowl away, patting his stomach. "Worth every penny I didn't have."

"The ingredients were from Mom's last grocery run." Mina rolled her eyes. "You didn't spend anything."

"Hey, my time is valuable." Jin stretched in his chair. "I could've been doing important things instead of cooking."

"Like what? Playing League of Legends in your pajamas?"

Their father's chopsticks paused halfway to his mouth, his eyes crinkling at the corners.

"I'll have you know I made it to Gold this season." Jin puffed out his chest. "That's practically professional."

"Wow." Mina's voice dripped with sarcasm. "Maybe you can pay rent with your ranking."

"At least I didn't spend thirty dollars on bubble tea last week."

"That was a study group!" Mina's cheeks flushed. "And it was only twenty-five."

"Children." Their father's quiet voice cut through their bickering. A hint of amusement softened his tired features. "The food is good."

Jin and Mina exchanged glances, years of shared understanding passing between them. Their father's praise, rare as desert rain, warmed the kitchen more than any spicy sauce.

"Next time I'll teach Jin how to make japchae." Mina gathered the empty bowls. "If he promises not to add chocolate."

"That was ten years ago!" Jin threw his hands up. "Let it go!"

"Never." Mina stuck out her tongue. "It's my duty as your sister to remember all your cooking disasters."

Jin scraped the last bits of sauce from his bowl. "Remember that camping trip you promised us, Appa? The one to Crystal Lake?"

Their father's shoulders tensed. He set down his chopsticks with deliberate care.

"Oh yeah!" Mina's eyes lit up as she rinsed dishes in the sink. "You said we'd go when I turned sixteen. That was like, what, three years ago?"

"Three and a half," Jin corrected. "You kept showing me pictures of the lake. Said we'd see actual stars instead of just smog."

Their father's gaze dropped to the table. His fingers traced invisible patterns on the wooden surface.

"We should still go." Mina dried her hands on a dish towel. "After finals next month. The weather will be perfect." She perched on the edge of her chair, leaning toward their father. "I checked online. They have these new cabins with real bathrooms. Not like those gross pit toilets you were worried about."

"The pit toilets were an excuse." Jin smirked. "He just didn't want to admit he's scared of bears."

"I am not scared of bears." Their father's voice carried a hint of indignation. The familiar argument sparked life back into his tired eyes.

"Then we should go!" Mina clapped her hands together. "I'll be done with finals by the fifteenth. Jin can take time off from his very important gaming career-"

"Hey!"

"-and we can finally use that tent that's been collecting dust in the garage." She bounced in her seat. "Please, Appa? You promised."

Their father looked between his children-Jin's teasing grin, Mina's hopeful expression. His shoulders relaxed fractionally.

"Perhaps." He pushed back from the table. "We will discuss it later."

"That means yes." Jin stage-whispered to Mina. "He always says 'perhaps' when he means yes."

"I can still hear you." Their father picked up his briefcase, the ghost of a smile tugging at his mouth. "And you are not always right."

"But I am this time." Jin winked at Mina. "Start packing your bear spray."

"I am not scared of bears," their father repeated, heading toward his room. But his voice carried the warmth of old memories and shared jokes, softening the edges of his earlier silence.

***

Butch eased his '89 Civic between a rusty pickup and a minivan, two blocks from his apartment. The dashboard clock blinked 11:47 PM, late enough that the good spots near his building had filled up with other night shift workers and their vehicles.

He grabbed his lunch bag from the passenger seat and killed the engine. The radio cut off mid-sentence, leaving him in the quiet of the suburban night. Crickets chirped from behind chain link fences. A dog barked three houses down.

"Every damn night." He stepped onto the cracked sidewalk, keys jingling. "Two streetlights away. Like clockwork."

The walk home wasn't bad-just annoying after eight hours of warehouse work. His boots scraped against concrete as he passed under the first sodium light. The orange glow cast strange shadows across browning lawns and empty driveways.

The stench hit him mid-step, sharp, metallic, sour. Butch froze. In an instant, he was face-down in the jungle, cheek pressed to damp earth, heart thudding against the ground. The air, thick with heat and the copper sting of blood-not his. Something unseen sliced the space above. He didn't breathe.

A shiver crawled down his spine. He jerked his head, once, twice-like shaking off a dream-and blinked himself back to now.

He drew in a slow breath. Steady inhales, measured. He'd buried those memories deep, locked them where they couldn't reach him. It had been years since they'd clawed their way out. Why now? Why tonight?

He glanced around. The street looked normal enough, just houses and parked cars stretching into darkness. Yet that smell lingered, coating the back of his throat.

"Getting paranoid in your old age, Lolo," he muttered to himself, using the Filipino phrase for Grandpa. Still, his pace quickened as he walked toward the smell.

A gust of wind whipped around the corner, scattering dried leaves across Butch's path. The air pressure shifted-wrong for this time of night, wrong for Southern California. Paper trash and debris skittered across empty driveways.

Above him, a flock of crows burst from a telephone wire, their wings beating against the dark sky. More birds joined them, abandoning trees and rooftops in a chaos of feathers and harsh cries.

Pain stabbed behind Butch's eyes. He stumbled, catching himself against a parked car. The pressure built inside his skull like someone had stuffed it with cotton and kept pushing more in. His vision blurred.

"Susmaryosep." The Visayan curse slipped out as he pressed his palm against his temple. The headache pulsed in time with his heartbeat, each throb worse than the last.

He fumbled for his phone, squinting at the bright screen. The display flickered, numbers and letters scrambling before settling back into place. 11:52 PM.

The wind died as suddenly as it had started. The birds vanished into the night sky. But the pressure in Butch's head remained, a weight that made his teeth ache and his sinuses burn.

He'd had migraines before-long nights and high stress from his old job, a thought he quickly pushed away-but this felt different. Foreign. Like his brain was trying to sonically vibrate inside his skull.

"Earthquake weather," Butch muttered, though the words felt hollow in his mouth. The night air hung thick and static, like the moments before a storm, except storms rarely visited Southern California this time of year.

His feet carried him forward despite the warning signals firing in his brain. Each step brought that metallic scent closer, sharper. The smell mixed with childhood memories of hiding under blankets, convinced monsters lurked in dark corners of his family's old house in Iloilo.

His father had always laughed it off. "Wala man dira, anak." Nothing there, son. But sometimes, in the deep night when the house creaked and the wind whispered through banana leaves, Butch had sensed something watching. Waiting.

That same feeling crawled up his spine now. His skin prickled beneath his work shirt, damp with cooling sweat. The pressure in his head throbbed in time with his steps.

A cat yowled somewhere in the darkness, the sound distorted and wrong, like audio played through broken speakers. Butch's hand tightened around his keys until the metal bit into his palm.

"Just tired," he whispered in Bisayan. "Like Papa used to say- your imagination makes the monsters."

But his father wasn't here to chase away the monsters anymore. And that metallic scent grew stronger with each reluctant step, pulling him forward like a fish caught on an invisible line.

CHAPTER 2

The dishes clinked as Jin stacked them in the sink. His father settled into his usual spot on the couch, newspaper rustling. Mina wiped down the table, humming a K-pop song under her breath.

A low vibration shook the apartment windows. The glass rattled in its frame, making the blinds dance. Jin's hands froze mid-scrub.

"Did you feel that?" Mina's voice wavered.

Their father looked up from his paper. "Probably a truck passing by."

The hum grew deeper, resonating through the walls. The water in Jin's glass rippled like a scene from Jurassic Park. Pictures rattled on the walls - family photos from happier times, their mother's smile frozen behind shaking glass.

"That's not a truck." Jin dried his hands on his jeans.

The vibration intensified. Their father stood up, newspaper forgotten. The building groaned around them as if under immense pressure.

"Get away from the windows," their father commanded, his project manager voice taking over.

Mina backed toward the kitchen, eyes wide. "Maybe it's an earthquake?"

But Jin had lived through California earthquakes before. This felt different. Wrong. The hum burrowed into his bones, making his teeth ache.

Their father's phone buzzed. He pulled it out, frowning at the screen. "Emergency alert. But it's just garbled-"

The lights flickered once, twice. Static crackled through their father's phone speaker, a harsh sound that made them all wince. The hum peaked, rattling dishes in the cupboards and sending the cat scrambling under the couch.

"Appa..." Mina reached for their father's arm.

The vibration seemed to compress the air in the room. Jin's ears popped. Through the window, he caught glimpses of other apartment lights blinking out across the complex. Car alarms began wailing in the parking lot below.

Mina doubled over, palms pressed against her ears. Her face contorted in pain. Jin lunged toward his sister, but his movements felt sluggish, like wading through a pool of water.

Through the living room window, the street split open. The asphalt cracked and peeled back, revealing a violent gash of deep purple light. The tear stretched wider, its edges crackling with energy that looked like burning paper, curling and disintegrating into the night air.

The world plunged into absolute silence. Jin's mouth moved, calling Mina's name, but no sound emerged. Their father reached for them both, his shoes scraping across the carpet in mute friction. The quiet pressed against Jin's eardrums like a physical weight, reminding him of diving too deep in a pool - that suspended moment of pressure and isolation.

Mina's eyes went wide, her hands still clamped over her ears. The purple light from outside painted her face in alien shadows. Their father's grip tightened on Jin's shoulder.

Pop.

Sound rushed back like a breaking wave. Car alarms blared. Dogs barked. Glass shattered somewhere down the street. Mina gasped, dropping her hands from her ears.

"What's happening?" Her voice shook.

The tear in the street pulsed, sending waves of purple light across the apartment walls. Their father pulled them both away from the window, his fingers digging into Jin's arm.

Their father yanked the front door open, his keys jangling in his grip. Jin followed close behind, heart hammering against his ribs. The hallway carpet muffled their footsteps as they raced past closed apartment doors.

"Stay behind me." Their father's voice carried an edge Jin had never heard before.

They burst through the building's main entrance into chaos. The night air hit Jin's face, thick with that burning paper smell. Purple light pulsed across parked cars and dumpsters, casting double shadows that twisted and merged with each movement. The tear in the street had grown wider, its edges now tall enough to swallow a bus.

A woman stumbled past them, mascara streaked down her face. Her high heels clattered against the pavement as she ran. More people emerged from nearby condos - some in pajamas, all wearing the same shocked expressions.

The first scream cut through the night like broken glass. It came from the direction of the tear, raw and desperate. More voices joined in - a chorus of terror that made Jin's blood run cold.

Their father grabbed Jin's wrist. "We need to get back inside-"

Another scream, closer this time. A man in a business suit sprinted past them, his tie flapping over his shoulder. "They're coming through!" His voice cracked with panic. "Oh god, they're coming through!"

The purple light flared brighter. Jin squinted against the glare, raising his free hand to shield his eyes. Dark shapes moved within the tear, angular and wrong, like broken pieces of machinery reassembling themselves.

More screams erupted from different directions. The sound of running feet and slamming doors filled the night air. Car engines revved as people tried to flee.

"Jin!" His father's grip tightened. "We need to get Mina and-"

The screams grew louder.

***

The metallic scent grew stronger as Butch rounded the corner. His headache pulsed in time with his steps, each throb more intense than the last. The street ahead warped like a mirage, but instead of heat waves rising from asphalt, purple light rippled through the air.

A crack formed in reality itself - a jagged tear that hovered three feet above the ground. The edges glowed violent shades of violet, curling inward like burning photographs. Static electricity raised the hair on Butch's arms. The tear widened, its borders crackling with energy that reminded him of the old TV back home when the antenna lost signal.

His mind searched for comparisons, anything familiar to make sense of what he saw. Like someone had taken scissors to the night sky. Like lightning frozen in reverse. But nothing quite fit.

The pressure in his head peaked. Sound drained from the world, leaving behind a vacuum that made his ears strain for input. The silence felt absolute - no cars, no wind, no distant sirens. Just the quiet of deep space or ocean depths.

Pop.

His ears cleared like stepping off an airplane. Sound crashed back in waves - car alarms, dogs barking, glass breaking. Then came the screams. High-pitched wails of terror cut through the night, multiplying as more voices joined the chorus. Running footsteps pounded against pavement.

Butch's legs locked in place. The old survival instincts from his youth screamed at him to run, but his body refused to move. He could only watch as the tear pulsed wider, its purple glow painting the street in alien light.

Dark shapes poured from the tear like oil spreading across water. Small, hunched figures with leathery skin moved in jerky, predatory motions. Their bodies were covered in patches of coarse, matted fur that looked more like quills than hair. Yellow eyes reflected the portal's light, set deep in reptilian faces with jutting jaws full of needle-sharp teeth.

They moved with a primal intelligence, spreading out in coordinated groups of three or four. Their clawed hands gripped crude spears and clubs wrapped in rusted metal. The creatures communicated through clicks and guttural sounds that made Butch's skin crawl - not quite animal, not quite human, but something ancient and wrong.

More emerged from the portal. Dozens now. Their heights varied from child-size to just below his shoulder, but all shared the same twisted features - scaled skin stretched over wiry muscle, elongated ears that twitched at every sound, and that same predatory grace that spoke of hunting instinct.

A larger one emerged, its presence causing the others to drop into submissive crouches. This one stood straighter, wore crude metal armor, and carried what looked like a sharpened machine part as a sword. Its face bore ritual scars that formed intricate patterns across its scaled hide.

The sound of their movement reminded Butch of lizards scuttling across dry leaves, but the way they organized themselves showed disturbing intelligence. They formed rough ranks behind their leader, brandishing their weapons with practiced ease.

The armored one raised its blade and let out a shrieking war cry that set off every car alarm on the block. The others answered with their own howls - a sound that mixed hyena laughter with reptile hisses.

Butch's legs moved before his mind caught up. Not away from danger, but toward it. Each footfall carried him closer to the creatures, driven by an instinct he hadn't felt in decades.

His heart hammered against his ribs - a rhythm he knew too well. Fear mixed with purpose, coating his tongue with a copper taste that transported him back to another life. Back to mud-soaked nights in dense jungle, where right and wrong blurred into simple survival. Where ideology meant nothing against the raw need to act, to fight, to live.

The familiar weight of terror settled in his gut. But terror wasn't new - it was an old acquaintance that had taught him how to move, how to breathe, how to focus when everything else scattered to chaos. His hands remembered what to do even as his mind raced with doubt.

Sweat trickled down his back as he pressed against a parked car, using its bulk as cover. The creatures hadn't spotted him yet. Their clicks and hisses filled the air with alien music that somehow echoed the war cries of his past. Different sounds, same meaning - the prelude to violence.

His fingers trembled, but not from fear. Adrenaline coursed through his veins, sharpening his senses. The streetlights cast sharp shadows that danced across cracked pavement. Every detail burned into his mind with crystal clarity - the way the creatures moved, the gaps in their formations, the weak points in their makeshift armor.

Butch drew in a deep breath. The fear didn't leave, but it transformed into something useful - a tool he'd wielded before when choices vanished and only action remained. His muscles coiled, ready to spring. The old instincts awakened, rising from wherever he'd buried them beneath years of quiet living.

He wasn't fighting for a cause this time either. Just the raw, human need to push back against something. To face the fear head-on until it broke against his will like waves against stone, or it breaks him.

***

Jin watched in horror as more scaled creatures flooded from the violet tear, their quilled bodies moving with predatory grace across the darkened street. Their yellow eyes caught the portal's light, reflecting like cats' eyes in headlights. They spread through parked cars and front yards with military precision, their crude weapons held ready.

His father burst back through their front door, gripping something long and metallic. The moonlight caught the shaft of a golf club - a seven iron from the set Mom had given him on their last anniversary together. His knuckles whitened around the grip, the same way they'd tighten when he'd practice his swing in the backyard on quiet Sunday mornings.

"Stay behind me." His father's voice carried a steel Jin had never heard before. Gone was the tired project manager who barely spoke at dinner. In his place stood someone else - someone who moved with decisive purpose, who held the golf club like he'd wielded weapons before.

The creatures' chittering grew louder as they approached, their scaled feet scraping against concrete. Jin's father adjusted his stance, placing himself between Jin and the advancing horde. The seven iron trembled slightly in his grip - not from fear, but from contained energy ready to explode.

"Dad-" Jin started.

"I said stay back." His father's eyes never left the approaching threat. His voice dropped lower, carried an edge that brooked no argument. "Get ready to run when I tell you."

The nearest creature turned its reptilian head toward them, needle teeth bared in what might have been a grin. Its claws flexed around a rust-covered spear as it clicked something to its companions. More yellow eyes swiveled in their direction.

Jin's father raised the golf club to his shoulder, muscle memory from countless driving range visits transforming the casual motion into something deadly. His breathing steadied, like he was preparing for a crucial putt rather than facing monsters from another world.

The first terrifying creature lunged. Jin's father's swing connected with a sickening crack, sending the creature sprawling across the pavement. Another rushed forward, spear thrust out - but the seven iron caught it under the jaw, snapping its head back with bone-crushing force.

"Run!" His father's voice cracked through the chaos.

More shapes emerged from the darkness. Three, six, a dozen - their scaled bodies flowing like a tide of leather and quills. Jin stumbled backward as his father fought with desperate precision, each swing finding its mark. But for every creature he dropped, two more appeared.

A high-pitched scream pierced the night. Jin's blood turned to ice.

"Mina!"

He spun toward their house door just as three hunched figures in jagged armor dragged his sister onto the street. Her kicks thudded uselessly against their plated hides as she thrashed in their grasp.

Jin lunged forward, but something hard slammed into his ribs. The world tilted sideways as he crashed into the apartment's stucco wall. His vision blurred, head ringing from the impact. Through the haze, he watched his father try to fight through the swarm toward Mina.

"Let her go!" His father's golf club cracked across one creature's skull. His voice, raw and furious, held a rage Jin had never heard before. But there were too many now. They moved like a single organism, surrounding him, overwhelming him with sheer numbers.

Mina's screams grew fainter as the creatures pulled her toward the portal. Jin tried to push himself up, but his limbs wouldn't respond. The world spun violently. Through double vision, he saw his sister's terrified face disappear into the violet tear in reality.

His father's desperate roar cut through the chittering swarm. The seven iron flashed again, and again, and again, and then once more in the purple light - then vanished beneath a wave of scaled bodies and rusted weapons.

Jin's vision swam as he struggled to focus on the chaos before him. His father disappeared under the writhing mass of scaled bodies, the golf club's arc becoming slower, more desperate with each swing. Blood sprayed across stucco. A goblin's neck snapped. Another took its place.

"Dad!" The word tore from Jin's throat, raw and primal.

His father's arm broke through the swarm, still gripping the bent seven iron. The creatures dragged him down again. Metal clanged against concrete. Jin caught a glimpse of his father's face - bloodied but defiant, fearless, lips pulled back in a snarl as he fought to reach where Mina had vanished.

"Mina!" Jin tried pushing himself up, but his legs buckled. The world tilted sideways. Purple light pulsed at the edges of his vision, making his stomach lurch. "MINA!"

His father's voice cut through the chittering swarm one last time - not a scream of pain, but a name. "Jin-"

The sound snapped off. Darkness crept in from the corners of Jin's eyes, eating away at his consciousness. He fought against it, clawing at the stucco wall, trying to stand. His father's shape blurred, fractured, merged with the mass of scaled bodies.

"Dad... Mi-"

The words died in his throat as everything went black.

***

Butch crouched behind a parked car, tracking the creatures' movements. A Ford Explorer caught his eye - its back end crushed, liftgate hanging open like a broken jaw. Years of experience had taught him to spot useful tools in chaos.

He darted forward, keeping low. Glass crunched under his feet as he reached the Explorer's cargo area. The metallic stink grew stronger here, mixing with leaked gasoline and burned rubber. His hands moved through scattered belongings - reusable grocery bags, a child's baseball mitt, fast food wrappers.

The tire iron's dull chrome handle glinted in the portal's purple light. Butch wrapped his fingers around the cold metal, testing its weight. Not his first choice of weapon, but the L-shaped tool felt solid, balanced. Better than nothing against whatever hell had opened up in front of him.

A screech pierced the air behind him. He spun, tire iron raised. One of the smaller creatures had spotted him, its yellow eyes fixed on his position. It called to its pack with a series of clicks and growls.

Butch tightened his grip on the tire iron. His palms were sweating, but his hands didn't shake. The weight of the tool brought back memories he'd rather forget - nights in the jungle when any weapon meant survival.

Butch snatched a pink Hello Kitty sweater from the Explorer's debris, muscle memory driving his movements. He wrapped the cotton sleeve around his forearm, creating a makeshift shield. The fabric felt flimsy, but he knew from experience that even thin protection could deflect a blade.

The first creature lunged. Butch pivoted, slower than he wanted but precise. The tire iron connected with its skull - a wet crack followed by a spray of dark fluid. The thing dropped, twitching.

Three more rushed him. Their crude spears jabbed forward in a coordinated attack. Butch blocked one thrust with his wrapped arm, the metal tip catching in the sweater's fabric. He yanked, pulling the creature off balance. The tire iron swung in a brutal arc, crushing its throat.

Pain flared across his shoulder as claws raked his shirt. Butch rolled with the blow, using his attacker's momentum to slam it into the Explorer's frame. The impact knocked loose its weapon. He finished it with a sharp strike to the base of its skull.

The last one circled, more cautious now. Its yellow eyes tracked Butch's movements, assessing. Smart. These weren't mindless beasts. The thing feinted left, testing his defense. Butch didn't bite. He'd seen that trick before, paid for the lesson in blood.

It charged right instead, exactly as he'd expected. Butch met the attack with the tire iron's hooked end, catching the creature under its jaw. One savage pull and twist later, it lay still.

Butch's muscles burned. His breath came in heavy gasps. Not as young as he used to be, but still standing. He checked himself quickly - scratches on his shoulder, bruises forming, but nothing deep. The Hello Kitty sweater hung in tatters from his arm, stained dark with alien blood.

More shrieks echoed from nearby streets. This fight was just the beginning.

Through gaps between houses, Butch caught flashes of movement - hunched figures dragging screaming shapes across lawns and driveways. His stomach turned as he realized they only grabbed females - teens from bedroom windows, mothers from doorways, girls from parked cars.

The creatures moved like a frenzied pack, spreading through the neighborhood in waves. They bounced between houses, communicating in guttural barks and shrieks. No formation, no discipline - just savage purpose as they smashed windows and kicked down doors.

A high-pitched scream cut through the chaos. Two houses down, a young woman in pajamas fought against three of the scaled hunters. They had her by the arms, pulling her toward the pulsing portal.

Butch charged forward, tire iron ready. His legs felt heavy, each stride burning with effort. Age slowed him down, but rage and memory fueled his advance.

He caught the first creature across its spine, feeling vertebrae crack under the blow. The second turned to face him, baring yellowed fangs. Butch drove the tire iron's hook into its throat, ripping sideways. Dark blood sprayed across the manicured lawn.

The third released the woman, brandishing a crude spear. "Run!" Butch shouted, keeping his eyes on the threat. The creature lunged, its weapon scraping his ribs as Butch twisted away. He countered with an upward swing that shattered its jaw.

More screams echoed from a nearby condo complex. Through a broken sliding door, Butch saw them dragging a teenage girl down carpeted stairs. Her mother lay motionless in the kitchen.

He started running again, pushing through the pain. The tire iron felt heavier with each step. But the memories that haunted his dreams - brutal fights, desperation - drove him forward.

Through the shattered windows of a ranch house, a child's cry pierced the night. Butch vaulted over a fallen trash can, his boots crunching broken glass. The front door hung off its hinges, splintered near the lock.

Inside, a small girl huddled beneath an overturned coffee table, her stuffed giraffe clutched tight against her chest. Two creatures stalked the living room, sniffing the air, their quilled backs scraping the ceiling. They hadn't spotted her yet.

Butch's tire iron caught the first one in the back of the knee. It buckled with a shriek, claws scrabbling against hardwood. The second whirled, spear thrusting. Butch deflected with the Hello Kitty sleeve, metal tip glancing off his forearm. He stepped inside its guard and drove the iron's hook up through its throat.

The wounded one lunged for the coffee table. Butch grabbed its quills, ignoring the barbs that cut into his palm, and smashed its head against the wall. Once. Twice. The creature went limp.

"Hey there, little one." Butch kept his voice soft, crouching by the table. "Let's get you somewhere safe."

The girl's eyes were wide, fixed on the dead creatures. She couldn't have been more than six.

"My mommy-"

"We'll find her." Butch scooped her up, giraffe and all. "Hold tight."

Outside, a couple sprinted past - the man carrying a baseball bat, the woman with car keys jingling in her grip. Butch recognized them from the apartment complex.

"Wait!" He caught up in three strides. "Take her. Get out of the city."

The woman's arms opened automatically as Butch passed the child over. The girl clung to her neck, face buried in the stuffed giraffe.

"What about you?" The man gripped his bat tighter.

"There are others." Butch turned back toward the sounds of fighting. More screams echoed from deeper in the neighborhood, mixed with inhuman shrieks and breaking glass. The portal's violet light pulsed stronger now, casting twisted shadows across suburban lawns.

The couple hesitated for a moment, then ran for their car. Butch adjusted his grip on the blood-slicked tire iron and pushed forward into the chaos.

***

A shrill whistle pierced the night - three ascending notes that cut through the chaos. The scaled creatures froze mid-attack, heads snapping toward the portal's violet glow. Their eyes gleamed with primitive intelligence.

As one, they abandoned their pursuits. Those empty-handed bounded toward the tear in reality while others dragged struggling captives - mothers, daughters, sisters - their claws digging into flesh as they retreated with terrifying precision. The coordination sent chills down Butch's spine. This wasn't random violence - it was organized hunting.

Butch sprinted toward the girl's desperate screams, but a wave of gray-skinned creatures swarmed him. Stone clubs and sharpened flint struck his leather armor. He rolled with the impacts, deflecting what he could with his forearms.

His fist connected with a misshapen jaw. Bone cracked. Another attacker crumpled from his boot to the chest. The creatures pressed in, their rancid breath hot on his face. Their stone weapons battered him from all sides.

He dropped and swept his leg, knocking three down. A fourth leaped at his throat - he caught it midair and slammed it into the ground. His muscles burned as he fought to stand.

Something massive struck him from the shadows. The impact lifted him off his feet and sent him flying. His shoulder hit packed earth, knocking the wind from his lungs. Stars burst behind his eyes.

Butch staggered up, head spinning. Through blurred vision, he watched the portal's light fade. The girl's screams grew distant, then silent. His legs gave out and he dropped to his knees. Too late. He'd failed her.

***

The portal loomed like a wound in reality, its jagged edges crackling with violet energy. Butch's hands trembled, sticky with blood that wasn't his own. The tire iron lay forgotten at his feet as he stared into the otherworldly tear. Through its shimmering surface, impossible geometries twisted and writhed.

His chest burned with each breath. Sweat and blood matted his clothes to his skin. The sounds around him - sirens, screams, sobbing - faded against the portal's electric hum. It pulsed with a rhythm that felt almost alive, like the breath of some vast, alien thing.

Fifty yards away, Jin Park swayed on his feet. Blood trickled down his temple where he'd hit the wall. His vision blurred, but he couldn't look away from the portal's hypnotic glow. Every pulse of light sent daggers through his skull.

"Mina," he whispered, voice cracking. His sister's final scream echoed in his mind, her terrified face disappearing into that violet maw. The creatures had dragged her through, along with countless others. Now the portal just... waited.

Emergency vehicles crowded the street. Red and blue lights painted the scene in surreal colors. Paramedics rushed between victims. Police erected barriers. But no one approached the portal itself. They gave it wide berth, as if sensing its wrongness.

Jin's legs buckled. He caught himself against a car, leaving bloody handprints on its door. His head throbbed where he'd been thrown. He needed to find his father. Needed to know if... but he couldn't tear his eyes from the portal. Knowing his sister might be there, beyond there.

The portal breathed. Waiting. For what, neither man knew. But its presence felt deliberate. Patient. As if this was only the beginning.

The thrum of helicopter rotors cut through the night, searchlights sweeping across broken windows and scattered debris. Jin pressed his palms against his ears as the aircraft circled lower, their beams catching the portal's violet glow.

"Do not approach the anomaly. Evacuate the area immediately." The voice boomed from mounted speakers, echoing off empty houses. "This is a mandatory evacuation. Clear the area now."

Police cruisers blocked off intersections. Officers in tactical gear herded shell-shocked residents away from the portal, their voices sharp with urgency. Radios crackled with codes and coordinates.

Butch watched an ambulance speed past, its siren wailing. His muscles ached, each breath burning in his chest. The tire iron hung loose in his grip, blood dripping from its curved edge. Around him, dazed survivors stumbled through the chaos - a woman clutching a photo frame, an old man in pajamas leading two children by the hand.

"Sir, you need to move back." An officer approached Butch, hand raised. "This area isn't safe."

More helicopters appeared, their searchlights crisscrossing the street. The loudspeaker repeated its warning, competing with police radios and distant screams. Emergency response teams deployed barriers and flares, creating a perimeter around the portal.

Jin slumped against the car, his vision swimming. The helicopters' downdraft whipped debris across the pavement. Through the chaos, he spotted a golf club lying in a pool of blood - his father's last stand. His throat closed up.

"Move! Move! Move!" Officers shouted, pushing the crowd back. Armored vehicles rolled in, their heavy tires crushing broken glass. Men in hazmat suits emerged, carrying strange equipment that beeped and flashed.

The portal pulsed, sending ripples through the air. The helicopters' searchlights caught its crystalline edges, casting fractured shadows across evacuating crowds. Its hum grew louder, drowning out even the aircraft overhead.

"Final warning," the loudspeaker blared. "Clear the area immediately. This is a mandatory evacuation."

Butch wiped sweat from his forehead with the sleeve of his navy work shirt, the company logo now stained dark with blood. His steel-toed boots crunched over broken glass as he backed away from the portal's pulsing light. The cargo pants he'd worn for his warehouse shift were torn at the knee, spattered with evidence of the night's violence.

"What the hell are we dealing with?" The words escaped in a whisper, his Filipino accent thickening with exhaustion.

The hazmat teams looked just as lost as everyone else, their instruments giving contradictory readings or no readings at all. One device sparked and died when pointed at the portal. Another spun in useless circles. The technicians' confusion was visible even through their sealed masks - this defied every protocol, every contingency they'd trained for.

A general emerged from a tactical vehicle, barking orders into multiple phones. His face shifted from anger to disbelief as subordinates presumably failed to provide answers. The military's arrival should have felt reassuring, but their obvious bewilderment only heightened the sense of unreality.

The portal's violet light caught the safety reflectors on Butch's work shirt, making them glow an impossible color. He'd started his shift expecting nothing more dramatic than inventory counts and pallet jack repairs. Now he stood in a war zone, watching the world's most advanced military scratch their heads at a hole in reality.

The general slammed his phone shut and shouted at a subordinate, "What do you mean the satellites can't see it? It's right there!"

Butch's grip tightened on the tire iron. The blood coating it had begun to dry, flaking off in dark patches. His arms trembled with fatigue, but he couldn't bring himself to drop the makeshift weapon. Not while that tear in the world still pulsed with alien light. Not while those creatures might return.

CHAPTER 3

Jin's eyes fluttered open to fluorescent lights and the sharp smell of antiseptic. Canvas walls rippled around him, medical equipment casting strange shadows across worried faces. His skull throbbed where bandages wrapped tight, and each breath sent pain that tore through his ribs, but it was nothing compared to the panic clawing at his chest.

"Mina?" The name caught in his throat. "Where's my sister?"

A nurse moved between cots, checking IVs and bandages. Her eyes skipped past him like he was invisible. Other patients lay groaning - some wrapped in gauze, others staring vacant-eyed at nothing.

Memories crashed back: the portal's violet light, his father's last stand, Mina's screams as they dragged her away. The same screams he'd heard when she'd fallen off her bike at seven, when she'd burned her hand cooking at twelve. He'd always been there to help, to fix things, to be the big brother she needed.

But not this time.

"Please, my sister - someone has to know where they took her." His voice cracked. "She's only seventeen. She was wearing a blue sweater. Someone must have seen-"

The nurse turned away, shoulders tense. A soldier stood rigid at the tent's entrance, rifle across his chest, jaw set beneath his helmet.

Jin's heart hammered. He couldn't lie here while Mina was gone. She'd be terrified, alone, waiting for him to save her like he always had. He swung his legs off the cot, ignoring the pain that shot through his body.

"Sir, stay in bed." The soldier's voice was flat, practiced.

"Get out of my way." Jin stumbled forward. "I have to find her."

The soldier's arm blocked his path. Something snapped in Jin's mind - the fear, the guilt, the helplessness crystallizing into blind rage. His fist connected with the soldier's jaw before he could think.

Hands grabbed him from behind. A needle pricked his arm. The world tilted sideways as darkness crept in from the edges.

***

The detective slid a cup of lukewarm coffee across the folding table. "Witnesses say you saved at least four people. Maybe more."

Butch shifted, uneasy. His English, touched by a Filipino lilt, came out slow and careful. A decade in America hadn't erased the instinct. No matter what he'd done, who he'd been, the sight of uniforms always shrank him back into that quiet, uncertain immigrant. The same one who mumbled through his visa interview at the U.S. Embassy in Manila, hands clammy, throat dry, like everything depended on how he said his name.

"Sir, I just tried to help." His Filipino accent thickened with exhaustion. "Nothing special."

As soon as he said it, he regretted speaking at all. Some part of him - stubborn, irrational - still believed that drawing too much attention might get him sent back. Even with the little blue passport tucked in a drawer at home.

"Nothing special?" The detective - Williams, according to his badge - leaned forward. "People described you fighting like a trained soldier."

Butch let out a nervous laugh, eyes darting briefly to the floor. "Sir, too many action movie." Still afraid that even the wrong joke might be the wrong answer.

The lie tasted bitter. His muscles ached with memories of similar nights - different jungle, different enemies, same fear. The screams still echoed in his head: mothers calling for daughters, sisters crying out names that would never answer back. The creature's dying eyes haunted him, that final look of recognition...

Williams studied him but didn't push. "Well, whatever it is, you did good out there. Not many would've run toward that nightmare. You're a hero."

Butch gave a small nod, eyes downcast. But the word hero landed like a punch wrapped in kindness. It felt like a joke - one he wasn't allowed to laugh at. He let it hang there, said nothing, and hoped the silence would carry it away.

"Sir, sorry," he mumbled, massaging his skull. "Getting a migraine. Can I step outside for some air?"

Beyond the tent flaps, chaos continued to unfold. Parents clutched photos of missing children. News vans crowded the perimeter, reporters shoving microphones at shell-shocked survivors. Armed soldiers patrolled the edges, their weapons trained on the humming portal.

Butch stepped outside, hands trembling as he lit a cigarette. The smoke did nothing to calm his nerves, and the familiar scent only brought back darker memories he'd rather forget. He'd fought tonight not from courage but from muscle memory - his body remembering old battles while his mind screamed to run. His fingers traced old scars under his shirt, phantom wounds from another life. As adrenaline faded, the weight of what he'd seen crushed his shoulders with each breath. The portal's otherworldly hum behind him only made the cigarette taste more bitter on his tongue.

A woman sobbed nearby, clutching a small pink backpack to her chest. The sound cut through him like a blade.

***

Screens across Fullerton blazed with breaking news. In shop windows, on phones, in bars - every display showed the same footage on endless loop: violet light tearing through suburban streets, dark shapes moving with terrifying purpose.

"Officials confirm eighty-seven women and girls missing after the incident," a news anchor reported, her voice steady despite the horror in her eyes. "Ages range from seven to forty-two."

In an electronics store window, multiple TVs played different channels simultaneously. Military vehicles encircled the portal on CNN, while Fox showed a shaking witness and MSNBC displayed impact zones.

"The anomaly remains stable," a physicist explained on screen, pointing to readings. "But attempts to probe or interact with the energy field have yielded no results. It's as if the portal is... waiting."

Social media erupted with theories. Social media platforms and streamers analyzed grainy video footage frame by frame. Posts on X threads dissected every detail. YouTube channels went live 24/7, discussing possibilities ranging from government experiments to alien invasion.

Downtown Fullerton transformed into a military zone. Concrete barriers rose around the portal's perimeter. Armed personnel carriers rolled through streets where children once played. Helicopters circled endlessly, their searchlights cutting through purple-tinged darkness.

But at the heart of it all, the portal remained silent. Its surface rippled like dark water, offering no answers to the questions that multiplied by the hour. Only the low hum persisted - a sound that seemed to whisper of other worlds, other hungers, waiting in the void beyond.

***

Jin stepped into his home, feeling the weight of emptiness. The front door creaked on its hinges, the sound echoing in the silence that had replaced his family's laughter. The walls bore deep scratches, some stained with dark, dried blood. Furniture lay overturned, a silent testament to the chaos that had torn through this place.

His gaze drifted across the wreckage until it landed on something familiar amidst the debris - Mina's phone. It lay on the floor, its screen cracked but still recognizable. Jin's heart clenched as he picked it up with trembling fingers. The device felt cold and fragile in his hand, like a piece of her had been left behind in this broken world.

With a deep breath, he unlocked it and found a voicemail from a few days ago. Hesitation gripped him, but he pressed play.

Mina's laughter filled the space, bright and unburdened by the horrors that had since unfolded. "Hey Jin! Just calling to remind you about our movie night. Don't forget the popcorn! Love you, loser."

Her voice was a cruel reminder of what had been ripped away. It echoed through the broken room, mingling with the shadows and silence until it became unbearable.

Jin fell to his knees in the hallway, unable to hold back the flood of grief any longer. He clutched the phone to his chest as if it could bring her back, tears streaming down his face. Sobs wracked his body, each one tearing at him like the claws that had marred their home.

In that moment, surrounded by the remnants of their life together, Jin felt utterly lost. The voicemail played on repeat in his mind-her laughter a haunting melody that only deepened his sorrow.

And so he knelt there, alone in the hollow shell of what once was their home, drowning in grief and clutching onto the last piece of Mina he had left.

***

Butch lay in his darkened apartment, the ceiling fan spinning lazy circles above his head. Sleep wouldn't come. Every time he closed his eyes, he saw them-those scaled bodies moving with predatory grace. Their movements haunted him, triggering memories of a nature documentary he'd watched years ago. Bonobo chimps, organized for war, their primitive tactics hiding a brutal intelligence.

He pushed himself up and grabbed his old laptop from the nightstand. The screen's harsh light made him squint as he typed. Conspiracy forums filled with wild theories offered nothing solid. Deep in archived news sites, he found a single paragraph about a Siberian village-population vanished overnight. The details matched: strange lights, metallic smell, silence. But the story died there, buried under newer headlines.

Hour after hour, he dug deeper. Scientific journals. Declassified files. Local news reports from remote places. Each lead dissolved into dead ends and speculation. His eyes burned from the screen's glare, but he couldn't stop searching.

Butch rubbed his temples, leaning back against the headboard. The laptop's glow cast harsh shadows across his weathered face. None of it added up. The patterns were there, but fragmented, like pieces from different puzzles forced together. His gut, honed by years of survival, told him these weren't old stories being repeated. This was something new.

He stared at the screen, watching the cursor blink. If this had happened before, where were the survivors? Where were the bodies? Where was the proof? The silence around these incidents felt too perfect, too complete.

***

The portal's violet glow cast long shadows across the gathered crowd. Protesters waved signs and chanted while news crews jockeyed for better angles. Military personnel formed a barrier, keeping everyone a hundred meters back from the shimmer.

The Army had tried to lock down the entire area, but Fullerton's residents pushed back hard. Cal State students staged sit-ins. City council members demanded transparency. Even the local police chief refused to cede complete control. After three days of mounting tension, they reached an uneasy compromise - the military would secure the immediate area while allowing controlled civilian access and oversight.

Jin shouldered his way through the crowd, ignoring the ache in his ribs. He spotted a familiar figure arguing with a soldier near the barrier - the man from that night, still carrying himself like a weapon despite his casual clothes.

"You were the one with the tire iron," Jin called out.

Butch barely glanced his way, still focused on the soldier.

"Please." Jin stepped closer. "My sister Mina - they took her through that thing. I need to find a way in. I'm not asking you to fight, just... help me get her back."

"That place eat people." Butch's accented voice was flat.

"Then let it eat me too." Jin's voice broke, raw and hollow. "I'm not leaving without her. My dad died trying to save her. She's all I have left."

Butch went still, jaw tight. He'd sworn not to get involved again- not after-but the raw desperation in Jin's voice cut deep. Something shifted behind his eyes - an old pain, a buried memory. He saw himself at seventeen, desperate and alone, begging for help while adults looked away. No one had listened then. No one had cared.

He studied Jin's face, saw that same raw desperation he'd once known.

"Meet me here tonight, 9 p.m."

***

The portal's glow painted harsh shadows across the containment zone. Military floodlights swept over razor wire and barricades while soldiers patrolled in pairs. Drones buzzed overhead like mechanical wasps, their red lights blinking in the darkness.

Butch crouched behind a wrecked sedan, muscles tense. A battered backpack sagged against his shoulders, and a crowbar hung in his grip, its weight familiar. He glanced at Jin beside him and handed it over.

"Hold this real quick," he whispered.

Jin took it and instinctively hooked it through a loop on his belt.

Butch pointed toward a section of broken fencing just ahead. "Wait there," he said firmly.

He then moved low and fast toward the abandoned delivery van. He jammed a brick against the accelerator and shifted it into neutral. A quick twist of the wrench against the battery terminals sparked once-then again. The engine coughed to life.

The van lurched forward, rolling down the slope until it crashed into a concrete divider. Alarms pierced the night. Soldiers rushed toward the commotion, boots pounding pavement as they radioed for backup.

Jin flinched as the van exploded into the divider, the crash echoing through the night. Alarms wailed. He crouched lower behind the fencing, heart pounding in his ears. He couldn't move-legs frozen, breath shallow. The chaos pulled at something primal, screaming at him to stay down, to hide.

Then he saw Butch.

Charging back through the smoke and flickering streetlights, eyes locked on him.

"Now!" Butch yelled, voice cutting through the noise like a blade.

Jin hesitated for a half-second longer-then bolted. The crowbar clanked at his hip as he ran.

Shouts erupted behind them. Two soldiers broke from the chaos, boots pounding as they gave chase.

Jin sprinted toward the swirling light, heart in his throat.

Behind him, Butch turned to intercept. The first soldier swung a baton-Butch ducked under it, grabbed the man's belt, and drove him into the concrete with a bone-jarring slam.

The second came at him fast. Butch absorbed the hit on his shoulder, then twisted and delivered a brutal uppercut to the chin. The soldier's head snapped back, legs crumpling beneath him as he collapsed, out cold.

The first soldier lunged and caught hold of Butch's backpack strap. Butch twisted hard, yanking free and letting the bag fall behind him as he ran.

Chest heaving, muscles burning, he spotted Jin at the edge of the portal-waiting, just for a moment.

Butch pushed forward, sprinting toward him with everything he had left.

"Wait!" Butch shouted.

Jin paused for a heartbeat, then stepped through and vanished.

Butch instinctively looked right.

In the distance, two soldiers had rifles raised. Behind them, an officer stood motionless, watching.

He grit his teeth.

"O chit," he muttered.

The shots never came.

Butch kept running, each footfall jarring his bones. He was too old for this. Every step sent fire lancing through his knees, but he forced his body forward, refusing to fall. Wind whipped debris across the containment zone as floodlights caught his silhouette against the violet glow. His lungs burned, muscles screaming from age and abuse, but he pushed through the pain.

Next to the command tent, a weathered general watched the scene unfold. His uniform bore the dust of twelve hours in the field, arms crossed as he studied the two figures racing toward certain death. The boy's file sat heavy in his mind - Jin Park, student, orphaned when it all began. The general had seen too many faces like that, too many lives shattered by forces beyond comprehension.

But it was the older man who caught his eye. The way Butch had taken down the soldiers - clean, practiced movements born of hard experience. No wasted motion. No amateur fury. Just the cold efficiency of someone who'd done this before.

"Sir?" A soldier, rifle raised and ready, finger hovering near the trigger. The other followed suit, sights trained on Butch's back.

The general lifted one hand. "Stand down."

His men hesitated, exchanging glances.

"That kid's gonna need all the help he can get." The general's eyes narrowed as Butch's form grew smaller against the portal's light. "And that man?" A hint of recognition crossed his face. "He's something."

But Butch heard none of it. His world had narrowed to the pounding of his heart, the burn in his legs, the violet light growing brighter with each step. He saw Jin's form dissolve into the portal's surface like a stone into water.

Without slowing, without a moment's pause, Butch hurled himself after the boy. The portal swallowed him whole, leaving only empty air.

CHAPTER 4

The portal yanked them through with violent force, their bodies lurching as if caught in an invisible undertow. They stumbled onto alien ground, equilibrium shifting in ways that made their minds reel.

Jin sucked in a breath, then another. The air filled his lungs with startling clarity - pure, untainted, almost too clean. Each inhale felt deeper than physically possible, like his chest had extra space to expand.

Beside him, Butch rolled his shoulders with a puzzled expression. The constant ache in his joints had vanished. His movements felt unnaturally light, muscles responding with too little effort. The ground beneath their feet had an unsettling give, like compressed clay hiding something less solid underneath.

They stood under a pale blue sky that seemed familiar yet wrong. The sun hung overhead, but its light cast shadows that stretched too far, too sharp. Clouds drifted by with unnatural slowness. Around them, the forest rose in twisted patterns - massive ferns coiled like springs, tree trunks that rippled with slow, living movement. Giant insects drifted overhead on translucent wings that caught the light like oil slicks.

Behind them, the portal hung suspended an inch above the ground - a perfect circle of violet energy, humming steadily. It neither flickered nor faded but remained fixed in space as if it had always existed there.

"Shit," Butch muttered, patting his jacket. "Lost the supply pack wrestling with that guard."

He pulled out his phone and pressed the power button. The screen remained dark. He shook it, tried again. Nothing.

"Had a full charge too," he said, shoving it back into his pocket.

Jin took an unsteady step forward, scanning the horizon. The forest spread out in every direction with no clear path or marker. Just endless layers of ancient, alien growth that seemed to watch them with patient malice.

Butch surveyed their surroundings one more time and grunted. "This ain't Oz."

***

They walked in silence, the soft hum of the portal fading behind them. Each step felt lighter than it should, like their bodies weren't quite connected to the ground. The landscape stretched before them - familiar shapes twisted into alien forms, trees that bent at impossible angles, ferns that coiled and uncoiled in slow breaths.

Jin paused, drawing air deep into his lungs. The oxygen hit his blood like a drug, sharp and clean and almost too pure. His head spun with each breath.

Butch dropped to one knee near a gnarled tree trunk, brushing aside layers of damp vegetation. His hand closed around something long and dark. He pulled, and from the tangle of roots emerged a spear - sleek and deadly, its shaft gleaming like polished volcanic glass. The head tapered to a precise point, edges worked with intricate care. Not a crude weapon, but a masterwork of ancient craft.

"Doesn't look like an animal made this," Butch muttered, turning it in his hands. He held it out to Jin. "Here. Give me that back." He pointed to the crowbar.

Jin traded the crowbar, the spear feeling unnaturally balanced in his grip.

A few paces away, pressed into a patch of hardened earth, Butch found tracks. He crouched down, fingers tracing the distinct impressions. The footprints were narrow and precise, with a familiar arch and heel strike.

"These look like boot prints," he said. "But they're old. Really old."

Jin remained silent, attention fixed on something half-buried beneath a moss-covered boulder. There, carved deep into the stone's face, was a symbol - four skulls arranged in a cross pattern, the central one marked with strange, angular cuts around the eye sockets.

Jin moved closer, studying the crude artwork. "What the hell is this supposed to mean?"

Butch's gaze lingered on the central skull, his expression hardening. "If people came here before," he said, voice low, "they didn't leave happy. If they left at all."

***

The sun sank fast, plunging the twisted forest into deep purple shadows. Jin and Butch pressed against the trunk of a massive fern, its fronds curling away from their touch. The air grew thick with night sounds - clicks and whistles that echoed wrong in the too-pure atmosphere.

A sharp crack split the darkness. Butch's hand shot out, gripping Jin's arm. Through the undergrowth, five hunched figures emerged, their bodies covered in that same downy fur Jin remembered from the attack. Yellow eyes gleamed in the darkness as they dragged something heavy behind them.

Jin's breath caught. The net they pulled scraped across roots and stone, filled with sun-bleached bones that clinked together like wind chimes. Human bones.

These weren't just similar creatures - they were identical to the ones that had torn through their neighborhood, that had taken Mina. The same reptilian features, the same cruel intelligence in their movements. One wore crude armor hammered from scavenged metal, decorated with teeth and claws.

The patrol moved with purpose, communicating in low chirps and guttural sounds. Their weapons - spears tipped with that same black glass - swung ready at their sides. The largest one paused, nose lifting to the air, testing it. For a moment, its gaze swept across their hiding spot.

Jin's heart hammered against his ribs. Beside him, Butch's muscles coiled tight, ready to spring. The crowbar trembled in his white-knuckled grip.

The creature's head tilted, considering. Then it barked a command, and the patrol moved on, bones rattling in their wake.

A sharp chirp pierced the air. The patrol spun around, weapons raised. Their leader's yellow eyes locked onto Jin and Butch's position with predatory focus.

The creatures spread out in a practiced formation, their movements fluid and coordinated. The bone-net dropped with a clatter as they readied their glass-tipped spears.

Jin's legs turned to stone. His mind screamed to run, to fight, to do anything - but his body refused to respond. The memory of Mina's screams paralyzed him.

Butch exploded into action. The crowbar caught the first goblin under its jaw with a wet crack. The creature flew backward, its spear clattering against tree roots. The second lunged, but Butch had already pivoted. His elbow smashed into flesh, driving the air from its lungs.

The leader charged, its spear thrust forward in a deadly arc. Butch twisted, the blade slicing air where his throat had been. The crowbar swung down, catching the spear shaft. Wood splintered. Butch's boot connected with the creature's chest, sending it sprawling.

More chirps echoed through the trees - reinforcements approaching. Butch's breath came in controlled bursts as he faced the recovering patrol. Blood dripped from his crowbar, dark against the alien soil. His movements were heavy but precise, each strike calculated despite his age.

Jin watched, frozen, as Butch fought. The older man's face showed no fear, only grim focus. His Filipino accent thickened as he muttered under his breath, counting enemies, tracking movements. The practice of survival written in every line of his body.

The patrol regrouped, circling with raised weapons. Their chirps turned to snarls, yellow eyes gleaming with hatred. Shifting his hold on the crowbar, Butch positioned his body to shield Jin's immobile figure from the savage diminutive beings.

The patrol leader shrieked a command. Two of them rushed Butch from opposite sides, glass spears thrust forward. Butch dropped low, sweeping the crowbar in a wide arc. The weapon caught one creature's ankles with a crunch. The second spear grazed his shoulder as he rolled, tearing fabric but missing flesh.

Butch came up swinging. The crowbar connected with its skull - bone gave way beneath metal. Yellow eyes dulled as the creature crumpled. Another charged through its fallen companion. Butch caught the spear shaft, yanked hard. The creature stumbled forward into his waiting elbow. Its nose burst in a spray of dark blood.

The patrol leader circled, weapon raised. Its armor clinked with each step, teeth and bones rattling. The remaining subordinate flanked right, chirping signals. Both attacked at once.

Butch's muscles burned, but his body remembered. He sidestepped the leader's thrust, trapped the spear under his arm. The crowbar smashed down, shattering the subordinate's collarbone. Before it hit the ground, Butch twisted, using the leader's own momentum to drive it into a tree trunk. Leather armor crumpled. The creature howled.

Shifting his hold on the crowbar, Butch positioned his body to shield Jin's immobile figure from the savage diminutive beings.

The patrol leader staggered back, yellow eyes wide. Its confident snarls turned to whimpers. It cast one final hate-filled glance at Butch before fleeing into the twisted forest, leaving its dead behind.

Butch stood among the fallen creatures, chest heaving. His shirt was torn, bruises already forming beneath the fabric. He rolled his shoulder, testing for damage. Nothing serious.

The forest fell quiet again, broken only by Jin's shaky breathing and the distant sound of the patrol leader crashing through undergrowth.

Jin slumped against the tree trunk, his legs giving out. The memory of his father's last stand played against the sight of Butch's brutal efficiency. His hands shook as he pressed them against his face.

Butch knelt beside him, crowbar still dripping. "Hey. Look at me."

Jin's eyes stayed fixed on the fallen goblins, their bodies twisted in death. "I froze. Just like before. When they took Mina, when Dad-" His voice cracked.

"First time I saw combat?" Butch wiped blood from his weapon with a torn sleeve. "I pissed myself. Couldn't move. Thought I was gonna die right there."

Jin's head snapped up. Butch's face held no judgment, just quiet understanding.

"But I didn't die. And next time was different. That's how it works." Butch's hand found Jin's shoulder, steady and warm. "Fear's not weakness. It's what keeps us alive."

"You weren't afraid." Jin gestured at the carnage around them.

"Kid, I'm terrified." Butch's grip tightened. "But I've had practice being scared. You learn to move through it."

Jin wiped his eyes with the back of his hand. "I need to be stronger. For Mina."

"You crossed a portal into alien hell to find your sister. That's not weak." Butch helped Jin to his feet. "Being brave isn't about not feeling fear. It's about what you do with it."

Jin and Butch approached the fallen creatures, their boots crunching on twisted roots. The last rays of sunlight filtered through the canopy, casting long shadows across the carnage.

Jin crouched next to one of the bodies. Up close, the creature looked different from his first panicked glimpses during the attack. Its frame was small, child-sized, with a disproportionately large head. Yellowish-green skin stretched over lean muscles, covered in patches of fine, downy fuzz. The black eyes, now glazed in death, dominated its face above a flat, reptilian nose.

"Goblins." Jin traced his fingers through the air above the creature's features, not quite touching. His mind flashed to countless hours spent reading manga, watching anime, grinding through RPGs. "They're exactly like goblins from fantasy books and games."

Butch knelt beside him, crowbar resting across his knees. Blood dripped from its end, forming dark pools in the alien soil. "Goblins," he agreed, voice low. His eyes scanned the twisted forest around them. "Wonder what else is out here."

Butch lifted one of the fallen goblin's weapons, turning it over in his hands. Crude bindings held a jagged stone to a wooden shaft, strips of leather wrapped tight but uneven. Dark stains marked the binding - old blood, dried black against the pale wood.

"Look at this." He traced the edge of the stone blade. "Knapped flint. Stone Age work." His fingers found deep scratches in the wood, tribal markings carved with desperate tools. "Not like that glass spear you're holding."

Jin gripped the volcanic glass spear tighter, its polished surface catching the dying light. The difference was stark - where the goblin weapons showed desperate craftsmanship, this spoke of sophisticated knowledge. Purpose-built by steady hands.

Butch picked up a club next, testing its weight. Wood and stone married together roughly, effective but primitive. His eyes narrowed at the fresh marks along its edge. "These were used recently."

Jin's gaze fell to the scattered bones they'd been dragging. "They were hunting something." He crouched, examining the remains. "But what?"

"Us, maybe?" Butch shook his head, doubt creeping into his voice. "No. They seemed surprised to find us. This was something else." He gestured at the net of bones. "Something they hunt regular."

The bones clinked together as Jin shifted them with the glass spear's shaft. Fragments of skull and femur, some fresh, others bleached white by alien suns. But the size was wrong for humans - too small, too delicate. Whatever they hunted, it wasn't people.

"Different prey," Butch muttered, dropping the crude weapons. "Different weapons." His eyes swept the darkening forest. "Someone else made that spear you're holding. Someone with skill."

***

Butch rose from his crouch, muscles tensing as shadows lengthened across the forest floor. The alien sun dipped lower, casting purple-tinged light through the twisted canopy. His eyes tracked movement in the branches - something skittered, quick and dark.

"We need to move." He kicked dirt over the blood pools, obscuring their trail. "One that ran? He'll bring friends."

Jin's fingers tightened around the glass spear. "Which direction?"

"Away from their path." Butch pointed opposite the direction the goblins had come from. "They were dragging that net somewhere. Best we don't find out where."

The forest creaked around them, branches swaying without wind. Strange calls echoed through the trees - high-pitched whistles answered by guttural croaks. The familiar sounds of night creatures preparing to hunt, but wrong somehow. Alien.

Butch retrieved his crowbar, testing its weight. Blood had dried along its curve, flaking off in dark patches. "Stay close. Keep that spear ready." He gestured at the weapon in Jin's hands. "And remember - fear's okay. Just don't let it root you."

They moved through the twisted forest, stepping carefully over roots that seemed to pulse with inner life. The light faded faster now, shadows stretching impossible lengths across the ground. Something rustled in the underbrush ahead - both men froze, weapons raised. A creature like a giant millipede crossed their path, each segment glowing faintly blue.

"What the?!" Jin whispered.

"Keep moving." Butch nudged him forward. "We need shelter before full dark."

The forest grew denser, the spaces between trees narrowing. Phosphorescent fungi dotted the bark, casting eerie green light in the growing gloom.

A harmonic tone pierced the darkness - pure, crystalline, rising and falling in waves. Butch and Jin stopped dead in their tracks. The sound floated through the twisted trees, echoing off bark and stone until it seemed to come from everywhere at once.

"That's not them." Butch lowered into a defensive stance, crowbar ready. "Too clean. Too..." He searched for the word.

"Musical," Jin finished. The spear trembled in his grip.

The melody shifted, notes braiding together like silver threads. It pulled at something deep in their minds - not threatening, but alien. Ancient. The forest itself seemed to respond, the phosphorescent fungi pulsing in rhythm with the song.

"Look." Jin pointed to where the twisted trunks parted, revealing a faint blue glow in the distance. The harmonics grew stronger in that direction, each note precise and deliberate.

Butch's muscles coiled tight. This wasn't the guttural shrieking of the goblins or the chittering of forest creatures. This was language - complex, intentional. Something intelligent was calling into the night.

The song swelled again, closer now. Branches swayed without wind, keeping time with the melody. Even the air felt different, charged with potential.

Jin took an unconscious step toward the sound. "It's beautiful."

"Beautiful things kill you just as dead." Butch caught his arm. "We don't know what's making that noise."

The harmonics shifted once more - three distinct tones weaving together, then apart. A question hanging in the darkness, waiting for an answer.

Through the twisted trees, a figure emerged holding a torch that cast dancing shadows across the forest floor. Tall and elegant, she moved with fluid grace despite her leather armor. The firelight revealed features both familiar and alien - a pronounced brow ridge that swept up into a sloping forehead, ears that curved upward and back like sculpted shells, but flesh. Her eyes, a striking grey, were unmistakably human, and they studied them.

The spear in her free hand matched the craftsmanship of the one Jin held - volcanic glass worked with impossible precision. She stood tall, a head taller than Butch's 5'7". Her presence commanding yet not threatening.

Butch's grip loosened slightly on his crowbar. Years of combat had honed his instincts for danger, but something about her triggered no alarms. His muscles remained tense, ready, but the hair-raising dread that preceded violence was absent.

Jin shifted behind him, glass spear wavering. "Butch..." he whispered.

"Easy," Butch murmured back. His eyes never left the stranger, tracking her movements as she took another measured step forward. The harmonics that had drawn them here seemed to emanate from her very presence, though her lips remained slightly open and still.

She tilted her head, studying them with an almost clinical curiosity. The torch flames reflected in her grey eyes, giving them an otherworldly gleam. Despite some of her alien features, there was something achingly familiar in her.

The stranger approached with deliberate steps, each movement precise and controlled. Her leather armor, etched with intricate patterns, shifted soundlessly as she walked. The torch in her hand cast dancing shadows across her features, highlighting the alien sweep of her brow and the delicate curve of her ears.

She paused ten feet away, head tilted slightly as her grey eyes moved between Butch and Jin. Her gaze lingered on their weapons - Jin's glass spear, identical to her own, and Butch's blood-crusted crowbar. No disgust or approval crossed her face, just careful observation.

The harmonics continued to pulse through the air around her. Her lips lightly moved, but her throat seemed to vibrate. The sound seemed to resonate from within her.

Jin stared, not quite sure what he was seeing. She was tall, graceful, her skin patterned with faint markings that shimmered as she moved. Her features were sharp but not severe - eyes steady, movements precise. Something about her felt... familiar. Not from memory. From stories.

"You look like an elf," he said quietly, more to himself than anyone else.

Butch shot him a sideways glance.

Jin shrugged. "She does."

Ara said nothing. If she understood the word, she gave no sign.

Butch maintained his defensive stance but kept his crowbar lowered. Years of combat experience told him she could have attacked already if that was her intent. Jin shifted behind him, breathing quick and shallow.

Her stare fixed on them both in turn, studying their faces, their clothes, their postures. The calm scrutiny felt almost scientific, like a researcher examining unexpected specimens. The torch flames reflected in her eyes, turning the grey to liquid silver.

The forest fell silent around them, even the strange creatures seeming to pause and watch this meeting unfold. Only the harmonic tones continued, weaving through the twisted trees like threads of sound.

Butch raised his crowbar as the stranger approached, but she lifted her empty palm toward them. Her movements remained fluid, deliberate. The harmonics shifted to a softer tone as she closed the distance.

She stepped toward Jin, slow and deliberate, her eyes never leaving his. When she stood just a breath away, she raised one hand - palm open - then gently placed it against his cheek.

Before either man could react, her other hand cupped the opposite side of his face. She pulled him forward in one smooth motion until their foreheads touched.

Jin's body went rigid, eyes wide.

Images flooded his mind - a vast settlement woven through ancient trees, reaching impossible heights. Flashes of his home: the night sky split by floodlights and flame, black shapes descending on quiet neighborhoods. He saw his father swinging a golf club, the sound of impact sharp and final. His sister screaming, heels kicking against armored figures. The hiss of static, the bark of rifles, the helpless chaos. Then, symbols - carved into stone, shifting as he looked, older than language. Symbols that made his eyes burn, too vast, too alien.

Jin stumbled back, gasping. The stranger's grey eyes held his, filled with understanding.

"What the hell was that?" Butch's knuckles whitened around his weapon.

"You are not goblins," she said, her voice carrying that same harmonic quality. "You are... lost."

"Memory echo." She turned toward him. "Your thoughts... like picture."

"You speak English?" Butch's stance remained defensive, but curiosity crept into his voice.

"No." She shook her head. "You hear my thoughts." She tapped her forehead. "Only when we are this close, we can communicate. I let you hear mine." A slight smile touched her lips. "Your mind only perceives it as hearing."

The harmonics that had drawn them through the forest faded, leaving only the alien night sounds around them. She stood tall in the torchlight, neither threatening nor retreating, waiting for their response.

Ara turned and walked back the way they'd come, her torch casting long shadows through the twisted trees. Jin and Butch followed, watching her graceful movements as she traced their earlier path. Her feet made no sound on the forest floor.

At the site of their goblin encounter, she knelt beside the fallen creatures. A low hum vibrated from her throat, resonating through the air. Her fingers traced wounds and examined crude weapons with clinical precision.

"Too many. Their living god leads them." Her harmonics carried concern.

Jin saw the image of the living god. It looked like what a hobgoblin would look like, or close enough.

"What is a hobgoblin?" Butch stepped closer, still gripping his crowbar.

"Their god in flesh." Ara's grey eyes reflected torchlight. "When one is born, tribes unite. They raid."

Jin's voice cracked. "These things took my sister. Do you know where they took her, where they took everyone?"

Ara paused, her expression growing grave. She nodded slowly. "Taken to Wastes. North tribe. Breeding camps."

"You know the way?" Butch's question came sharp and quick.

Ara studied them both. "You came through the tear?"

"Yes," Jin answered. "Please, we have to find them."

"I do know the way." Ara stood, brushing dirt from her leather armor. "But my people... they fear your kind. You are... Echo of the Lost Flame."

"What does that mean?" Jin asked.

Ara didn't answer. She adjusted her grip on the torch, scanning the darkening forest. "Follow me. Before night finds us."

CHAPTER 5

The forest closed in around them as they followed Ara's silent footsteps. Jin noticed his legs felt lighter with each stride, like walking through shallow water. His breath came easier, deeper, filling his lungs with air that tasted pure and ancient.

"Something's different here." Jin flexed his fingers. "Like everything weighs less."

Butch rolled his shoulders, testing the weight of his crowbar. "Thought I was going crazy. Not as heavy as before." He took a deep breath. "Air's different too. Makes me want to run laps, but-" He patted his stomach. "Let's not get carried away."

Ahead, Ara navigated through massive ferns that curled away from her touch. Her movements flowed like water over stones, each step precise and measured. A soft melody rippled through the air - not quite sound, more like vibrations that brushed against Jin's thoughts.

Jin pressed his fingers to his temple. "You feel that? Like... music in your head?"

"Can't hear anything." Butch squinted at Ara's back. "But my hearing's shot anyway. Getting old sucks."

The forest floor sloped upward, covered in phosphorescent moss that pulsed with their footsteps. Twisted trees stretched toward a blue-violet sky, their bark rippling like muscle beneath skin. Everything felt alive, aware, watching their passage with ancient patience.

Ara paused at a ridge, her harmonics shifting to a lower tone. Jin caught fragments of meaning - danger, quiet, careful - floating through his mind like leaves on water. The sensation left him dizzy, but each pulse grew clearer, more distinct.

Butch noticed Jin's expression. "You okay, kid? Looking a bit green there."

"Yeah, just... different." Jin steadied himself against a tree trunk. "Like she's talking, but inside my head."

"Great." Butch adjusted his grip on the crowbar. "I can only hear her when she's next to me."

The group crested a rise, and there it stood - a colossal tree that pierced the canopy like a spear through flesh. Its trunk stretched wider than a house, bark blackened and twisted as if burned in some ancient fire. But what stopped Jin cold were the shapes fused into its base - bodies of something, dozens of them, their alien features frozen in eternal agony as the tree's flesh grew around them.

Jin's stomach lurched as a deep vibration crawled up his spine. The sound wasn't quite music - more like the hum of power lines crossed with whale song, but wrong. His teeth ached with each pulse.

"You hear that?" Jin backed away. "It's like... singing."

Butch walked right up to the trunk, running his hand over the gnarled surface. "Dead quiet to me. Just looks like a big ugly tree." He tapped the bark with his crowbar. "Solid though."

Ara stepped forward, her silver hair catching light that filtered through the canopy. She tilted her head back and released a series of melodic tones - not quite singing, not quite speaking. The sound rippled through the air like rings in water.

The tree's bark shuddered. Patterns of light raced through its surface like lightning under black glass. The embedded bodies seemed to twist deeper into the wood, their faces shifting in the shadows.

Jin pressed his palms against his ears, but the harmonics burrowed straight into his skull. "What is this place?"

"Some kind of marker maybe?" Butch squinted at the corpses. "Or a warning."

The tree's response to Ara's call grew stronger, its hum building to a fever pitch that set Jin's nerves on fire. Yet Butch stood there calm as ever, deaf to the otherworldly chorus playing out around him.

Beneath the twisted tree's shadow, weathered stone blocks formed a crude circle. Ancient glyphs covered their surfaces -

spiraling patterns that looked carved by claws rather than tools. Jin traced one with his finger, feeling rough edges beneath centuries of moss.

Ara stepped to the center stone. Her harmonics shifted to a deeper register, resonating through the ground. The glyphs flickered with pale light, pulsing in rhythm with her song.

Jin stumbled back as the vibrations crawled up his legs. "The stones - they're responding to her."

"Hm?" Butch cocked his head. "Just sounds like a kettle whistling." He knocked on the nearest stone with his crowbar. "Though these markings remind me of those Filipino cave paintings my father showed me once."

The glow intensified, casting strange shadows across Ara's face. She touched the central stone, her fingers tracing patterns Jin couldn't follow. Her mental projection brushed against his thoughts: The Hollow Line remembers. It remembers everything.

"What does that mean?" Jin stepped closer. "Have there been other humans here before? Is that why you called us 'Echo of the Lost Flame'?"

Ara's song faded. She turned away from the stones, her expression unreadable. The glyphs' light dimmed until only faint traces remained, like cooling embers beneath ash.

Jin waited for an answer, but Ara had already started walking, leaving his questions hanging in the air.

***

The group emerged into a circular clearing where mist clung to the ground like spilled milk. At its center stood a stone idol, worn smooth by countless seasons. Three faces merged from a single column of rock, each one blank and featureless, yet somehow watching. The pale stone seemed to absorb the violet light rather than reflect it.

Ara's harmonics cut off mid-note. Her silver hair fell still in the windless air as she backed away from the monument, her movements careful and measured.

Butch circled the idol, studying its weathered surface. His boot struck something that skittered across stone - a broken piece of the statue, no larger than his palm. He picked it up, turning it over. The fragment trembled against his skin like a living thing, its vibrations so subtle he might have imagined them. Without thinking, he slipped it into his pocket.

The piece pulsed once, strong enough to feel through his clothes. Butch's hand instinctively moved to touch it again, but Ara's fingers wrapped around his wrist. Her mental projection hit Jin with unusual force: No sound here. No words. Follow.

Jin opened his mouth to ask why, but Ara's grip on his shoulder stopped him. Her eyes held a warning that needed no translation. She gestured for them to leave, her usual fluid grace replaced by rigid caution.

They backed away from the idol, whose blank faces seemed to track their movement despite having no eyes. The shard in Butch's pocket continued its faint rhythm, like a tiny heartbeat against his leg.

Shadows flickered between twisted trunks. Silver-haired figures emerged from the forest depths, their crystalline armor catching violet light. The patrol moved with liquid grace, spears raised, faces obscured by mirror-smooth masks.

Their leader stepped forward. His chest piece pulsed with stored energy. A high-pitched tone pierced the air - not sound exactly, but pure resonance that bypassed the ears and struck directly at the mind.

Jin dropped to one knee, skull buzzing like it might split open. The world tilted sideways as waves of vertigo crashed through him. His stomach lurched.

Butch stood unmoved, tire iron ready. The resonance washed over him like a distant echo, present but powerless. His eyes narrowed, muscles coiled for action.

Ara's response came swift and sharp - a counter-harmony that cut through the leader's attack. The air itself seemed to shiver as their tones clashed and merged. She planted herself between the patrol and her companions, one hand raised in what might have been greeting or warning.

The patrol leader's mask tilted, considering. His resonance faded to silence.

Ara's gaze shifted to Butch, lingering on his steady stance. Her silver eyes held something unreadable - perhaps suspicion at his immunity, or curiosity about what other surprises this human might harbor. The shard in his pocket thrummed in response to her attention.

The patrol leader barked a command. An elf warrior lunged at Butch, crystal spear aimed at his chest. Butch pivoted, his weathered body moving with practiced efficiency. The spear thrust past him as he trapped the shaft under his arm. His elbow cracked against the elf's jaw. In one fluid motion, he twisted the weapon free and swept the elf's legs, sending them crashing to the ground.

More elves spread out in a practiced formation. Their voices rose in eerie harmony, the air rippling with sonic force. Jin clutched his head and crumpled, blood trickling from his nose. His eyes rolled back as the resonance overwhelmed his senses.

Butch remained standing, though the harmonics made his teeth ache. The fallen spear hummed in his grip, its crystal components vibrating in response to the elves' attack. His muscles tensed, ready for the next assault.

The patrol's song built to a crescendo that should have dropped him. Instead, Butch took a heavy step forward, tire iron raised alongside the captured spear. His immunity seemed to unsettle them - their perfect formation wavered.

Ara's voice cut through their chorus, her own harmonics clashing against theirs. But the damage was done. Jin lay unconscious at Butch's feet, blood still seeping from his nostrils.

The elven patrol's harmonics pulsed through the clearing, but Butch only felt a dull pressure behind his eyes. Their crystal-tipped spears glowed with stored resonance as they closed in.

Ara darted forward, her voice cutting through the air in sharp, focused bursts. The nearest warrior staggered back, losing grip on his weapon. She pressed closer, forcing them to break formation as her short-range attacks disrupted their concentration.

Butch moved with practiced restraint, blocking a spear thrust with his captured weapon. He stepped inside the elf's guard, using the shaft to sweep their legs while pulling his strikes. The warrior tumbled but rolled clear, eyes wide behind their mask.

Two more rushed him from opposite sides. Butch dropped and pivoted, hooking one's ankle while shoulder-checking the other. They crashed together in a tangle of limbs and armor. He could have finished them - a sharp twist here, a crushing blow there - but these weren't goblins. They were organized, intelligent. Killing them would only bring worse trouble.

Ara's harmonics crackled through the air as she forced another warrior back. At this range, her attacks left them gasping and disoriented. She fought smart, never letting them regroup or coordinate their songs.

"We're not here to fight," Butch grunted, deflecting another spear with his tire iron. The metal rang against crystal but held firm. He trapped the weapon under his arm and twisted, using the elf's momentum to throw them off balance. They sprawled but weren't seriously hurt.

The patrol's formation had completely broken down. Their coordinated harmonics scattered into discord as Ara and Butch pressed their advantage - she with precise sonic bursts, he with careful takedowns that left bruises rather than breaks.

The patrol warriors gathered their fallen weapons, backing away with wary glances at Butch. Their harmonics had failed against him - an impossibility that seemed to shake their confidence more than his fighting skills. They melted into the twisted forest, leaving only scattered crystal shards in their wake.

Ara knelt beside Jin, pressing her forehead to his. His eyes fluttered open as her resonance eased the lingering effects of the sonic assault.

"How did you resist their song?" Ara's mental voice carried an edge of fascination as she studied Butch. "Even untrained minds should collapse under such force."

Butch shrugged, wiping dirt from his crowbar. "Maybe I'm just dense. My ex-girlfriends always said so." His attempt at humor fell flat against Ara's intense silver gaze.

Butch asked, "What was that about?" Ara's only reply, "They test you."

She approached him slowly, head tilted like a bird examining a puzzle. Her hand reached toward his temple but stopped short of touching him. "There is... something different in your mind's pattern. A barrier perhaps, or..."

"What do you mean different?" Jin pushed himself up on shaky legs, one hand still pressed to his bleeding nose. "Is that why the harmonics don't affect him?"

Ara withdrew her hand, her expression closing off. "We should move." She turned away, effectively ending the conversation.

"That's not an answer," Jin pressed, but Ara had already started walking, her steps quick and purposeful through the misty undergrowth.

Butch helped Jin steady himself, the shard in his pocket pulsing with each step. Neither man spoke as they followed their guide deeper into the alien forest, but the weight of unasked questions hung between them like smoke.

***

The fire cast dancing shadows across their makeshift camp, flames burning with unusual intensity in the rich atmosphere. Ara sat cross-legged near the blaze, her silver eyes half-closed as she hummed. The sound wasn't quite music - more like wind through crystal, or water over stone. It resonated in the air, creating patterns that rippled outward into the darkness.

Jin dozed fitfully against a twisted trunk, dried blood still crusted beneath his nose. The patrol's harmonic attack had left him drained, though Ara's use of a healing plant and harmonic vocal vibration had eased the worst effects.

Butch cleaned his weapons by the firelight, methodically wiping goblin blood from the crowbar. The crystal shard in his pocket thrummed in response to Ara's harmonics, its vibrations syncing with her song. He felt its pulse against his leg but said nothing, watching their enigmatic guide through the flames.

Her humming shifted pitch, and the fire steadied to an unnaturally even burn. The surrounding forest seemed to lean in, drawn by her resonance. Even the bioluminescent fungi dotting the trees pulsed in time with her song.

The oxygen-heavy air amplified every note, carrying them further into the twisted woods than should have been possible. Yet instead of attracting attention, her harmonics seemed to create a bubble of calm around their camp - a sanctuary of sound in the alien night.

Butch pulled the crystal shard from his pocket, its surface cool against his calloused palm. The fragment pulsed with each note of Ara's song, like a tiny heartbeat answering her call. Purple light rippled through its faceted edges, matching the rhythm of her harmonics.

Jin shifted against the tree trunk, unable to find rest despite his exhaustion. He watched their guide through heavy-lidded eyes. Ara hadn't moved in hours, hadn't shown a hint of fatigue. Her silver gaze remained fixed on some distant point beyond the fire's reach, body perfectly still save for the subtle movements of her throat as she sang.

"She doesn't sleep," Jin whispered, voice rough from the day's ordeal. "Not since we met her."

"Different kind of being," Butch murmured, keeping his voice low. The crystal warmed in his grip, its glow intensifying with each passing moment. "Different rules."

Ara's song continued unbroken, weaving through the night air like silk. She showed no sign of acknowledging their conversation, though her melody shifted subtly - deeper, more resonant. The crystal in Butch's pocket responded with a surge of vibration that made his leg tingle.

"She doesn't stop," Butch agreed, rolling the crystal between his fingers. The shard's purple glow dimmed as Ara's harmonics faded into silence.

The night air hung thick around them, charged with lingering resonance. Tiny motes of light drifted up from the fungi-covered trees, dancing in patterns that mirrored Ara's fallen song. The forest seemed to hold its breath, waiting for the next note that didn't come.

The fire popped and crackled, throwing sparks into the heavy atmosphere where they hung suspended longer than they should have. In the strange gravity, even the smoke rose in slow, deliberate coils.

Jin's breathing had steadied into the rhythm of exhausted sleep, his body finally surrendering to the day's trauma. Blood still crusted his upper lip, a dark reminder of the sonic attack's intensity.

The charged silence pressed against their skin like a physical thing, dense with unspoken questions and the echo of Ara's song. Her silver eyes reflected the firelight as she sat motionless, her presence both alien and oddly familiar in the twisted landscape of their temporary refuge.

CHAPTER 6

Ara slowed at the canyon's edge and motioned for them to stop. "This place isn't like the rest," she said, voice low. "The pull changes here. It... twists."

Jin raised an eyebrow. "Gravity?"

She nodded. "We don't know why. It bends, sometimes too light, sometimes too heavy. No pattern. We only know to move carefully."

The descent into the canyon started with uncertain steps. Every step felt like guessing the weight of a ghost, sometimes barely there, sometimes crushing.

Jin grabbed a twisted root to steady himself, his body drifting longer than it should have between steps. The strange physics made distance hard to judge. What looked like a short hop became an awkward bound, while longer jumps fell short.

Ara moved with fluid grace ahead of them, her movements adapted to the shifting gravitational pull. Her feet found purchase where they struggled, dancing across the uneven terrain as if guided by an internal compass.

"Keep your center low," she projected into their minds. "The force changes with the minerals in the rock."

Butch caught himself as another step went wrong, his heel sliding on the crystalline surface. The crowbar strapped to his waist swung with delayed momentum, throwing off his balance. He compensated by widening his stance, learning to read the subtle variations in weight and resistance.

The canyon walls rose around them in impossible angles, layers of stone folded like paper. Crystalline formations jutted out at random intervals, their surfaces refracting the pale light into scattered rainbows. Each level they descended brought new challenges: patches where they practically floated, followed by sections of crushing weight that made their knees buckle.

Jin stumbled on a deceptive slope, his body carrying forward in a graceless arc. Butch reached for him but missed, his own balance compromised by the irregular gravity. Ara's hand shot out, catching Jin's wrist with precise timing. She pulled him back to stable ground, her movements perfectly calibrated to the strange physics of their environment.

"The stone speaks through its weight," she transmitted. "Listen with your feet."

They pressed on, learning to read the subtle signs: the way certain crystals meant lighter steps, how darker rock brought heavier gravity. Their bodies adapted slowly, finding rhythm in the chaos of competing forces.

Ara paused at a narrow ledge, her head tilted as if listening to voices in the stone. Her fingers traced patterns in the air, testing currents invisible to human eyes. Without hesitation, she stepped onto the precarious path.

Butch hung back, scanning the twisted rock formations. Something felt wrong. The air carried too much oxygen, making his thoughts race and his movements feel disconnected. Each breath filled his lungs with unnatural clarity.

"Wait." He grabbed Jin's sleeve before the younger man could follow Ara. "The rock's different here."

Ara turned, her ethereal features catching the scattered light. "Your instincts serve you well. The path shifts."

As if to prove her point, a section of crystal beneath her feet pulsed with faint luminescence. She adjusted her stance, compensating for changes they couldn't see.

Butch's muscles tensed. The oxygen rush made everything feel possible, dangerous. His experience screamed caution while his body urged him forward. He remembered mountain climbers who died feeling invincible at high altitudes, their judgment clouded by thin air. This was the opposite: too much oxygen, too much confidence.

"The air here plays tricks," he said, forcing himself to breathe slower. "Makes you think you're stronger than you are."

Jin nodded, his movements already showing signs of the air's influence: too quick, too certain. The high air masked the true difficulty of their descent.

Ara projected understanding into their minds. "Your bodies are not made for this abundance. Control your breath. Match my pace."

She demonstrated, her steps deliberate and measured despite the intoxicating atmosphere. Butch followed her example, fighting the false energy surging through his limbs. The crowbar on his waist felt lighter than it should, another warning sign.

The canyon's acoustics twisted reality. Jin's steady breathing echoed as if he stood right next to Butch, though he lagged several feet behind. Each scuff of boots against crystal multiplied, bouncing between the folded stone walls until direction lost meaning.

Butch's crowbar clinked against rock. The sound came from ahead, behind, above. He couldn't pinpoint its origin. A pebble tumbled down the slope, its impacts creating a cascade of phantom noises that circled the group like invisible birds.

"This ain't natural." Butch kept his voice low, but the words returned from multiple angles. "Place is built to screw with your head."

Jin's whisper arrived crystal clear. "Like being inside a spinning wheel."

"More than that." Butch tapped his crowbar deliberately against a crystal formation. The ring split and reformed, creating harmonics that set Jin's teeth on edge. "Sound shouldn't move like this."

Ara's projected thoughts cut through the acoustic chaos with arrow-straight precision. "The canyon was shaped by those who came before. They understood the arithmancy of sound."

Jin's breathing continued to ghost past Butch's ears, sometimes seeming to come from within his own chest. The unsettling intimacy of it made him want to hold his breath, but the oxygen-rich air demanded deep inhales.

"Getting real tired of this funhouse stuff," Butch muttered. His words fractured and reassembled, each echo carrying a different tone of his voice.

Jin kept his eyes on the path ahead, voice barely above a whisper. "Where are we going?"

Ara didn't look back. "To the Deep Fold," she said. "My home."

A beat passed before she added, quieter, "To ask for help."

Jin glanced sideways. "How many elves are there?"

Butch shook his head. "Really?"

Ara didn't miss a step. She gave a faint nod, almost amused. "Enough," she said.

Ara lifted her hand, releasing a brief melodic ping that rippled through the twisted canyon. The sound scattered and reformed, painting an acoustic map only she could fully interpret. Her features tensed with concentration as she processed the returning echoes.

Butch watched her work, noting how she kept the tones short and controlled, nothing like the sustained harmonics she'd used before. Each ping lasted barely a second, just enough to probe their surroundings without broadcasting their presence.

Jin steadied himself against a crystal formation, his body still adjusting to the irregular gravity. "Why so quiet?"

Ara's response filtered directly into their minds. "Sound travels far here. Others listen."

She released another careful ping, this one pitched slightly higher. The acoustic feedback revealed a stable path through a section where the gravity shifted unpredictably. She gestured for them to follow, her movements precise and economical.

The group advanced in near silence, guided by Ara's measured pings. Each brief tone mapped another segment of their route, showing drops in the path or unstable sections they needed to avoid. The sound-mapping created a strange rhythm: ping, move, pause, ping again.

Butch noticed how she timed the probing tones with natural sounds: a distant rockfall, the whisper of wind through crystals. She masked their acoustic trail, blending her signals into the canyon's ambient noise. The strategy spoke of experience, of knowing exactly what could hear them.

When a particularly loud echo returned from one of her pings, Ara froze. Her hand shot up in warning, and she pressed herself against the canyon wall. Several minutes passed before she dared another soft tone, testing if whatever had triggered her concern had moved on.

The group continued their careful descent, following Ara's minimalist sound guidance. Each ping revealed another piece of their path, but never enough to draw attention. She was painting their route in quick, careful brushstrokes, leaving as light a trace as possible on the canyon's acoustic canvas.

Butch lagged behind Jin and Ara, watching their silent exchanges. While Jin nodded and gestured in response to unheard messages, Butch caught only fragments, a shifted expression, a tilted head, hands moving in conversation he couldn't join. The gap between them grew wider with each step.

He adjusted the crowbar across his back, its familiar weight the only constant in this alien place. His boots scraped against crystal, sending discordant echoes through the canyon. The sounds came back wrong, twisted by whatever acoustic engineering shaped these walls.

Jin turned back occasionally, checking on him, but those glances felt like pity. The boy could hear what Butch could not, the harmonics, the mental speech, whatever silent language Ara used to guide them. Butch was deaf to it all, cut off from vital information by some quirk of his mind or body.

He remembered command posts in the jungle, radio operators parsing coded messages while he waited for translations. This felt worse. At least then, someone would relay the important parts. Here, he caught only what they remembered to speak aloud.

Ara's head snapped toward some sound or sensation Butch could not detect. She grabbed Jin's arm, pulling him into a shadow. Butch followed on instinct alone, trusting their reaction without understanding its cause. They pressed against cold stone while something passed nearby, something he never saw or heard.

When they moved again, the silence felt heavier. Butch watched Ara's graceful movements, her precise steps guided by information he could not access. She was reading this place like a map written in sound while he stumbled through blind.

The oxygen-rich air filled his lungs, but isolation pressed against his chest. He was an outsider here, more than just human, cut off from whatever wavelength connected the others. Each step reminded him how alone he truly was.

***

A screech pierced the canyon walls, high-pitched and alien. Ara's body tensed, her fingers splayed against the crystalline surface. Her eyes tracked upward, scanning the jagged rim far above them. The sound died away, but her posture remained rigid, alert.

Jin followed her gaze. Through the twisted shadows of the canyon, a dark shape moved across the gap of sky, too quick to identify, gone before he could focus on it. The air grew thick with tension.

Ara pressed forward, her movements more urgent now. The canyon walls squeezed inward, forcing them to walk single file through passages barely wider than Butch's shoulders. Crystal formations caught what little light filtered down, casting fractured reflections that played tricks with depth and distance.

Butch's skin prickled. Static electricity seemed to build in the narrowing space, raising the hair on his arms. Each step brought them deeper into the suffocating passage where shadows bent wrong, stretching and contracting against the laws of nature. What should have been simple darkness took on impossible geometries.

The crowbar across his back felt heavier, as if responding to some unseen pressure. Ahead, Jin and Ara navigated the tight corners with practiced ease, but Butch's broader frame forced him to turn sideways at points, rough crystal scraping against his clothes.

The distorted shadows made everything uncertain. A formation that looked meters away might prove inches from his face, while distant shapes loomed suddenly close. The canyon played with perspective like a funhouse mirror. There was nothing amusing about these illusions.

Butch's boot caught on something metallic. He crouched down, fingers brushing cold metal beneath the crystal dust. With a firm tug, he pulled free an ornate helmet, its left side caved in, the metal warped and torn. Dried blood had turned black against the iridescent surface, forming abstract patterns where it had run down the decorative scrollwork.

Jin moved closer, studying the intricate designs etched into the metal. The craftsmanship was unlike anything he had seen, delicate swirls that seemed to shift and flow even in the dim light. The damage stood in stark contrast to its beauty, violence carved into art.

Ara's expression remained unreadable as she glanced at the helmet. Her fingers traced the air above it, never quite touching the surface. The crystal formations around them hummed at a frequency Jin could barely perceive, but she offered no explanation. Her silence felt deliberate, heavy with unspoken history.

The helmet had wedged itself into a broken ledge, as if thrown there with tremendous force. Impact marks scarred the surrounding crystal, telling a story of desperate violence. Whatever happened here had been brutal and final.

Butch turned the helmet over in his hands. The inside bore markings similar to the ones they had seen on the stone blocks earlier. Time and exposure had failed to completely erase them, though their meaning remained a mystery.

When he looked up to ask Ara about the markings, she had already moved ahead, her back turned to the grim discovery. The set of her shoulders made it clear some stories were not ready to be told.

Butch's eyes traced the gouges in the crystal wall. Deep scratches marked desperate handholds, spaced at human intervals.

Blood had dried in the deeper grooves, dark against the translucent surface. His calloused fingers found the marks. Someone had tried to climb up, their nails leaving desperate trails in the mineral face.

The spacing matched a human reach. Each gouge told of panic, of someone trying to escape whatever had pursued them. The pattern ended abruptly fifteen feet up, where impact marks scarred the wall.

"Stay close to the wall," Butch said, keeping his voice low. His shoulders pressed against the cool crystal as they edged past the site.

The air hit his lungs wrong, too pure and too rich. Each breath felt like gulping pure oxygen, making his head swim. Nature was not meant to be this clean. It stripped away the familiar scents of decay and growth that marked living forests. This sterile atmosphere set off every survival instinct he had developed.

Jin stumbled slightly, adjusting to the strange air density. "It's like breathing mountain air, but more intense."

"Too intense," Butch muttered. His chest tightened with each breath, like his body rejected the unnatural purity. The oxygen saturation made his movements feel lighter, almost disconnected. That lightness came with a cost. Every sound seemed sharper, every shadow deeper.

Ara moved ahead with practiced ease, her movements suggesting long familiarity with these conditions. She navigated the narrow ledge without hesitation, finding purchase where the humans struggled. Her adaptation to this environment only highlighted how alien it was to them.

The crystal walls rose around them like frozen waves, their surfaces reflecting and refracting what little light filtered down. The effect created false depths, making distance impossible to judge accurately. Butch kept one hand on the solid wall, trusting touch over sight in this deceptive terrain.

***

A flash of movement caught Butch's eye, something dark against the crystal sky above. Before he could shout a warning, the creature dropped onto a narrow ledge behind them, its leathery wings spreading wide for balance. The Iron-Wing's body was gaunt, all sinew and bone beneath tattered membrane. Scars crossed its chest where something had tried and failed to kill it.

Its head tilted, throat working. A series of clicks emerged, an unnatural mimicry of Ara's harmonic ping. The sound bounced wrong off the crystal walls, a crude approximation of her precise tones.

Ara's face transformed. Her usual controlled expression shattered into something ancient and furious. A low growl rose from her chest, resonating with the crystal around them. Her body tensed, recognition and rage radiating from her rigid posture.

"Do not move," she projected into their minds, her mental voice sharp with warning. Her fingers spread, ready to cast harmonics.

The Iron-Wing's yellow eyes fixed on them, intelligent and calculating. Its wings trembled with barely contained violence as it took a step forward, talons scraping against crystal. Another series of clicks emerged, this time closer to Ara's warning tone, learning, adapting, mocking.

A second screech pierced the air as another Iron-Wing crashed into the crystal wall above them, sending shards raining down. The impact's echo multiplied through the canyon, making it impossible to tell if more were coming.

Butch shoved Jin against the wall as talons raked the space where they had stood. The ledge crumbled beneath their feet, barely wide enough for two to stand shoulder-to-shoulder.

Ara's hand shot up, harmonics rippling, but the sound scattered off the crystal faces, dispersing before reaching its target. The confined space twisted her resonance into useless fragments.

"Down!" Butch yanked Jin aside as an Iron-Wing dove past, wings scraping stone.

Ara's spear flashed out, catching the creature's membrane. Dark blood splattered the crystal. The Iron-Wing wheeled back, clicking in rage.

The second one dropped onto their ledge, cutting off retreat. Its clicks merged with its partner's, creating a disorienting chorus that bounced between walls.

Ara spun her spear in a defensive arc, forced to rely on steel instead of song. The blade sang through air as she parried razor-sharp talons.

Butch did not hesitate. He lunged at the nearest Iron-Wing, crowbar swinging in a brutal arc. The creature's clicks turned to shrieks as steel met bone. No resonance, no harmony, just the raw force of survival driving his strikes.

The ledge groaned beneath their feet as four bodies grappled in the narrow space. Crystal shards skittered into the void below. Somewhere behind him, Jin pressed against the wall, trapped between fighters as echoes of battle filled the canyon.

The second Iron-Wing lunged past Ara, its talons extended toward Jin. He scrambled backward along the narrow ledge until his heel hit empty air. Crystal fragments crumbled beneath his feet as he pressed against the wall, nowhere left to run.

The creature's clicks turned triumphant. Its wings spread wide, blocking any escape. Yellow eyes locked onto Jin as it coiled to strike.

Ara spun, spear flashing, but the first Iron-Wing blocked her path, forcing her to parry a flurry of slashing claws. She could not reach Jin in time.

Her throat constricted as she gathered harmonics. At this range, this close to Jin, the resonance could harm him too. There was no choice.

The burst exploded from her chest, raw, concentrated sound that hit the Iron-Wing like a physical blow. This close, barely three feet away, the harmonics could not disperse through the crystal canyon.

The creature's triumphant clicks turned to shrieks of pain. It veered sideways, wings spasming as the sound attacked its sensitive membranes.

Jin slumped against the wall, head spinning as the resonance wave passed through him. His vision blurred, equilibrium shot. The creature's strike missed him by inches.

Butch seized the moment. He hurled himself off the ledge, crowbar raised. His body slammed into the disoriented Iron-Wing mid-flight. Both figures disappeared into the void between crystal walls, leaving only the echo of alien shrieks and the clang of steel on bone.

***

The group huddled in a narrow crevice, hidden between towering crystal faces. Jin's chest heaved as he slid down the rough wall, legs shaking from the aftermath of Ara's harmonics. His head still spun, equilibrium thrown by the concentrated sound blast.

Butch massaged his ears, face tight with tension. Blood trickled from a gash on his forearm where he had caught himself on a crystal edge during his climb back up. The crowbar lay beside him, its metal surface scratched and stained darker than before.

"That was close." His voice came out rough, barely above a whisper. His hands would not stop moving, checking gear, touching the crystal shard in his pocket, rubbing his temples. Pure adrenaline kept the tremors at bay.

Ara stood perfectly still, her breathing imperceptible despite the recent fight. Her spear rested against the wall, but her fingers stayed curled as if still gripping it. She scanned the canyon above them, head tilted to catch any echo of pursuit.

Only after ensuring they were not followed did she turn to Jin. Her eyes held something heavy, not quite guilt but a weight of knowledge. She reached toward his temple where the harmonics had hit hardest, then pulled back without touching. Her mental presence brushed against his consciousness, gentle now, assessing the damage her defensive blast had caused.

The look she gave him carried volumes of unspoken meaning. She knew exactly what her resonance could do to human minds. She had chosen to use it anyway, gambling his safety against certain death. Her expression said she would make the same choice again if needed, but the cost of that decision lived in her eyes.

The wind's howl echoed through the crystal canyon, warping and twisting until it sounded like distant voices. Butch pressed his back against the cold stone, crowbar resting across his knees. His fingers traced the rough edge of the crystal shard in his pocket, its vibrations feeling wrong against his skin, like touching a live wire underwater.

Jin huddled deeper into his jacket, still pale from the harmonic blast. The air tasted too clean in his lungs, each breath sharp enough to cut. Above them, the canyon walls stretched toward an alien sky, their faces smooth and angular like the inside of a geode. The crystals caught what little light filtered down, throwing back warped reflections of their small group.

Ara remained motionless, head cocked slightly. Her stillness was not human, more like a sensor array waiting for input. The wind tugged at her clothes, but she did not seem to feel it. Her eyes tracked something in the distance that neither man could see.

The walls around them felt alive, as if the entire canyon were one massive organism. Every surface seemed to pulse with stored energy, waiting to transmit any sound that might betray their presence. Their breathing came shallow and measured, each exhale a potential signal to whatever hunted above.

They had half the canyon left to cross. The path ahead twisted through narrow passages where the crystal faces pressed close enough to touch both shoulders at once. Places where sound could trap them, where harmonics could shatter their bones before they had room to run.

The wind died for a moment, leaving them in perfect silence. Then it returned with a different note, higher and keener, like metal being drawn across glass. None of them moved. None of them spoke. They just listened to the canyon's song, each lost in private fears of what waited in the depths ahead.

Ara moved ahead with fluid grace, each step precise and measured. Her harmonics came in quick pulses now, sharp pings that mapped the crystal faces without drawing attention. The sound barely carried past her lips, more vibration than noise.

Butch kept his eyes on the canyon rim, scanning for movement against the pale sky. The crowbar hung loose in his grip, ready to swing. His shoulders ached from the earlier fight, but adrenaline kept the pain distant. The crystal shard in his pocket hummed against his leg, its frequency changing with each of Ara's navigational tones.

Jin gripped the glass spear with white knuckles, its smooth surface slick with sweat. He positioned himself between his companions, trying to match Ara's careful footwork while staying within arm's reach of Butch. The weapon felt wrong in his hands, too light and too perfect. Its edge caught the filtered light and scattered it in ways that hurt his eyes.

They moved as one unit through the narrowing passage. Ara's harmonics guided them around blind corners and past unstable crystal formations. Her movements grew more rigid with each step, tension visible in the set of her shoulders. The canyon's acoustics had changed, sound bounced differently here, creating dead zones where even her precise pings returned nothing but silence.

Butch noticed her unease and adjusted his grip on the crowbar. Something about this section of canyon felt wrong. The walls pressed closer, forcing them to walk single file. The crystal faces had shifted from smooth planes to jagged edges that caught at their clothes. Above them, the rim had narrowed to a thin strip of sky barely wider than his outstretched hand.

Jin's breathing came faster as the passage constricted. The spear scraped against crystal with each step, sending tiny shivers through his arms. Ara's navigational tones grew shorter, more clipped. Her usual fluid movement had become almost mechanical, each foot placed with exaggerated care.

The air changed texture, thicker now, with an electric charge that made their skin prickle. Ara's next tone died in her throat, cut off mid-pulse. She raised one hand in warning, freezing mid-stride.

CHAPTER 7

The group picked their way forward, each step calculated against the strange pull of gravity. Crystal formations jutted at odd angles, forcing them to duck and weave through gaps barely wide enough for shoulders. Their feet landed lighter than they should, the reduced gravity turning normal strides into floating movements that threatened to pitch them forward.

Butch's eyes swept the jagged rim above, tracking shadows that might mean pursuit. His crowbar stayed low and ready, though the narrow passage left little room to swing. Each time his boot slipped on the glassy surface, muscle memory fought against the world's alien physics. A lifetime of knowing exactly how his body should move meant nothing here.

Jin's progress slowed to careful shuffling. The glass spear forced him to angle sideways through tighter spots, its perfect edge threatening to catch against the walls. His knuckles had gone white around the shaft, less from fear now than the constant effort of maintaining balance.

Ara moved like water through the confined space, her body flowing around obstacles in practiced patterns. She never presented a clear target to any angle above, always keeping some form of cover between herself and open sky. Her path seemed random but revealed itself as deliberate, each position offering multiple escape routes, each pause placing solid crystal at her back.

The passage kinked sharply left, then right, forcing them to edge through sideways. Crystalline formations crackled underfoot, the sound amplified by the canyon's acoustics. Butch fought the urge to rush forward, knowing speed would only lead to mistakes. Instead, he matched Ara's methodical pace, keeping his center of gravity low despite the persistent feeling of being too light.

Jin's foot caught a loose crystal edge, sending shards tinkling into the depths below. His body pitched sideways, arms windmilling against the strange gravity that made every movement both too fast and too slow.

Butch's hand shot out, fingers locking around Jin's forearm in an iron grip. The motion came without thought, pure reflex born from years of grabbing falling things in his warehouse job. His other hand braced against the crystal wall, muscles tensing to counter Jin's weight.

Ara spun in place, her movements liquid-smooth despite the confined space. Her eyes had registered the danger before Jin's foot even slipped. A soft, steady hum rose from her throat, not quite music, not quite sound. The note hung in the air like mist, filling the space between crystal formations.

Jin's panicked breathing steadied. His body straightened as if invisible hands had reached out to right him. The sound wrapped around him, defining the edges of space, making solid what had seemed uncertain moments before. His feet found purchase on the ledge as naturally as stepping onto familiar ground.

Butch kept his grip firm until Jin nodded he was steady. The hum barely registered in his ears, more vibration than sound, like bass felt through a wall. But he watched Jin's response with quiet attention, noting how the boy's movements grew more certain, more grounded.

***

The group wedged themselves into a natural shelf carved into the crystal wall, barely deep enough to qualify as an alcove. Ancient erosion had smoothed its edges, creating a temporary haven from the exposed ledge.

Butch's weathered hands moved with practiced efficiency, checking Jin's side where the earlier sonic blast had caught him. His fingers probed gently through the fabric, testing for hidden injuries. No words passed between them, just the slight pressure of examination and Jin's controlled breathing when Butch found tender spots.

Ara knelt at the alcove's edge, one hand pressed flat against the crystal surface. Her head tilted at an angle that made her seem more alien than ever, as if listening to something. The canyon's depths stretched below her, a maze of refracted light and shadow that disappeared into darkness.

Jin's gaze wandered from the void to study Ara's silhouette. He found himself captivated by the exotic contours of her face, particularly the elegant slope of her forehead and pronounced brow ridge. The scattered illumination played across her skin in an ethereal dance that reminded him of ancient hominid reconstructions from his university anthropology textbooks, though he felt only wonder, not fear, at her otherworldly appearance. There was something mesmerizing in her stillness, like watching a statue breathe. The harmonics she had used to save him still echoed in his mind, not quite memory, not quite sound.

The four of them, three bodies and the heavy silence, shared the cramped space like survivors in a lifeboat. Every exhale seemed to bounce off the crystal walls, amplified by the canyon's natural acoustics. They breathed shallow, instinctively quiet, as if the very air might betray their position to whatever hunted above.

Dust motes danced in the strange light, carrying tiny rainbow refractions. They swirled in invisible currents, marking air patterns too subtle to feel. Butch tracked their movement with the same intensity he had once watched jungle canopies for signs of movement. Jin watched Ara. Ara watched the depths. And the silence watched them all.

The crystalline fragments clinked softly as Ara adjusted her pack, the sound amplified by the canyon's acoustics. Jin's eyes caught the briefest flash, geometric shapes that could not be natural, each shard wrapped in what looked like silk but moved like liquid metal. The fragments pulsed with a faint inner light, similar to the portal that had brought them here.

Ara's head snapped around, her alien features sharp and severe. The movement was too quick, too precise, like a predator sensing threat. Jin dropped his gaze to the crystal floor, but not before noting how her hand had shifted to cover the pack's opening.

Butch leaned against the wall, arms crossed. His eyes narrowed as they moved between Jin and Ara, reading the sudden tension. His weathered features revealed nothing, but his fingers tightened slightly on his forearm, a subtle tell Jin had learned to recognize.

The silence stretched, broken only by the whisper of cloth against crystal as Ara pulled her pack closer. The shards' glow dimmed, as if responding to her touch. She repositioned herself, angling her body to block Jin's view while maintaining her watch on the canyon below.

***

Butch and Ara crept forward along the crystal ledge, leaving Jin to rest against the alcove wall. Their footsteps made no sound. Ara moved like flowing water, while Butch placed each step with the careful precision of an old soldier. The canyon's strange acoustics twisted the light around them, creating false shadows that danced across the crystalline surfaces.

Ara stopped at a bend in the passage. Her throat vibrated with a sound too low to hear, more sensation than noise. The pulse rippled through the air, touching the crystal walls with invisible fingers. Her eyes half-closed, reading the echoes like Butch once read terrain maps.

Butch felt nothing. The hum that made the crystals resonate passed through him without effect. He watched Ara's face, noting how her features settled into that unnaturally still mask she wore when concentrating. Whatever she sensed remained hidden from him, locked behind that wall of alien perception.

Behind them, Jin straightened. His hand pressed against the crystal wall as if steadying himself, head tilted in that same listening pose Ara held. The echo of her harmonic pulse had reached him, not as sound, but as something deeper. Like remembering a song without hearing it. His eyes met Ara's for a moment, sharing something Butch could not grasp.

Ara's expression remained carefully neutral, but her fingers tightened on her spear. She held herself too still, too controlled. Whatever message she had sent, intentional or not, had revealed something she had not meant to share.

Jin shifted against the crystal wall, watching Ara's unwavering vigilance. The question had burned in his mind since their first night. "Why don't you sleep?"

Ara's fingers traced patterns in the air, her movements precise and deliberate. The crystal walls caught fragments of her reflection, multiplying her image across their faceted surface. "There are things that wait in stillness." Her voice carried that distinct Hollow resonance, more vibration than words, each syllable layered with harmonic undertones.

Butch raised an eyebrow but kept his peace, cleaning his crowbar with methodical strokes. His eyes tracked Ara's movements as she paced the narrow ledge, noting how she maintained constant awareness of their positions. She never fully turned her back to either of them, always keeping them in her peripheral vision with the fluid grace of a practiced guardian.

The crystal shard in Butch's pocket hummed faintly, responding to the frequencies in Ara's voice. Jin felt the echo of her words settle into his bones, carrying weight beyond their surface meaning. The canyon's strange acoustics caught her harmonics, spreading them like ripples through the air.

***

The group rounded another bend in the crystal passage when Butch's foot struck something that clattered across the ground. Not crystal, but bone. Small, delicate bones bleached white by time.

Jin crouched down, his hand hovering over the remains. The bones weren't scattered randomly. They formed perfect spirals across the ground, each curve precise and measured. Dozens of goblin-sized skeletons had been dismantled, their pieces arranged in mathematical patterns that stretched across the ledge.

Ara's breathing changed. Her usual fluid grace locked up, muscles rigid as she stared at the bone spirals. The harmonics in her throat cut off mid-pulse, leaving an unnatural silence.

"Some kind of ritual?" Jin traced the air above one spiral, not daring to touch. "Like their burial customs?"

Ara's head snapped side to side, a sharp gesture that carried none of her usual measured control. "Not theirs." Her voice came out flat, stripped of its musical undertones. "This pattern belongs to something older. Much older."

The crystal walls caught her words, bouncing them back distorted and strange. Butch shifted his grip on the crowbar, eyes scanning the shadows above. The bone spirals seemed to move in the corner of his vision, though when he looked directly at them, they remained still.

Jin pulled back from the remains, wiping his hands on his jeans, though he hadn't touched anything. The perfect mathematical precision of the spirals made his skin crawl. No primitive goblins had arranged these. Each curve, each spacing between bones spoke of cold calculation and ancient purpose.

Ara knelt beside the bone spirals, her long fingers hovering over the crystal surface. The walls here had a different quality, darker, with veins of purple that caught what little light filtered down. She pressed her palm flat against the stone, eyes half-closed.

A hum built in her throat, not her usual quick pulses for navigation, but something deeper. The notes descended one by one, each tone hanging in the air longer than it should. Jin's teeth began to ache, a sensation like biting tinfoil spreading through his jaw. The crystal beneath Ara's hand took on a subtle glow that followed the path of her song.

Butch watched, but felt nothing. No vibration, no resonance, not even the usual pressure change that came with Ara's harmonics. The crystal walls remained dark and silent to him, yet Jin had backed away, hands pressed to his temples.

Ara's song faded. Her eyes opened, but her hand remained against the stone. "This land remembers," she whispered. The words seemed to sink into the crystal rather than echo back.

CHAPTER 8

Butch pushed aside a curtain of hanging moss, revealing a jagged split in the canyon wall. Blue-green light pulsed from within, cast by patches of fungus that swelled and deflated like sleeping lungs. The air that drifted out carried the sharp bite of mineral water and something older, the musty breath of deep places.

Ara froze at the threshold. Her usual fluid grace locked up, shoulders rigid beneath her worn leather armor. The harmonics that normally hummed in her throat fell silent.

Jin stepped closer to peer inside. The fungal glow painted his face in sickly shades as he traced the rough-hewn edges of the opening with his eyes. "Natural formation?"

"No." Ara's voice came out flat, stripped of its musical undertones. Her hand drifted to the crystal fragments in her pack, fingers curling around the fabric as if seeking reassurance. "This was cut. Long ago."

The walls of the rift bore subtle marks, too regular to be natural, too weathered to be recent. Whatever had carved this passage had done so with purpose, the angles precise despite centuries of erosion.

Butch ran his palm along one of the grooves. The stone felt wrong under his calloused fingers, not the glassy smoothness of the crystal canyon, but something more organic, almost flesh-like in its texture. He pulled his hand back, wiping it against his pants.

As they cleared the last bend in the canyon, Butch felt it shift. The weird tug and pull that had haunted every step began to fade. His boots landed solid now, not that half-floating stumble they'd been fighting. He rolled his shoulders, testing the weight in them. Better. Steady.

He took a breath, deep and measured. The air wasn't thick in his lungs anymore. Still rich, but not buzzing through his veins like high-altitude oxygen. Jin let out a sharp exhale beside him.

"Feels normal again," Butch muttered. "Or... close enough."

The fungus continued its slow breathing, each pulse of light revealing deeper shadows within. Water dripped somewhere in the darkness, the drops falling with mechanical precision. The sound echoed back wrong, suggesting spaces larger than should exist within the canyon wall.

Ara remained motionless, staring into the gloom as if reading something in its depths. The usual subtle movements of her face, the micro-expressions that accompanied her telepathic communication, had gone still as stone. Only her eyes moved, tracking something the others couldn't see.

Jin opened his mouth to speak, but Ara raised her hand for silence. She cocked her head, listening to frequencies beyond human perception. The fungal light cast strange shadows across her alien features.

A low tone emerged from Ara's throat, not her usual crystalline harmonics, but something deeper, older. The sound rippled through the air like ink in water, carrying undertones that made the fungal patches pulse in sympathy. Her eyes half-closed, face tilted upward as the vibration built in her chest.

Butch shifted his weight, the crowbar hanging loose in his grip. He'd seen that expression before, not on Ara's alien features, but on the faces of old women in villages in the Philippine mountains when they entered *Dambana*, sacred sanctuaries where the boundary between the physical realm and supernatural dimensions grew thin. The same distant reverence, the same connection to something vast and unknowable.

Her throat worked as the tone modulated, threading through octaves that shouldn't exist. The sound didn't echo like normal noise; instead, it seemed to sink into the stone itself, absorbed by the flesh-like walls.

Butch watched her closely, noting how her fingers splayed against her thighs, how her spine straightened by degrees. The usual fluid grace of her movements had transformed into something more formal, ritualistic. Even her breathing changed, becoming shallow and controlled.

The crystal fragments in her pack glowed in response to her song, casting purple shadows across her sharp features. Her silver hair caught the light, creating a halo effect that made her seem both more and less human.

Butch recognized ceremony when he saw it. Not the polished pageantry of modern religion, but something rawer, the kind of bone-deep knowing that came from generations of passed-down wisdom. He remained perfectly still, unwilling to break whatever moment was unfolding.

Jin shifted his weight, the crystal dust crunching beneath his feet. "Is this it? Deep Fold?"

Ara's silver hair caught the bioluminescent light as she shook her head. The movement carried an ancient gravity, each strand catching and reflecting the pulsing glow. "This is where it begins." Her voice held depths beyond the words, layers of harmonic memory that made the fungal patches flutter in response.

Jin's hand tightened on his glass spear, knuckles white against the translucent surface. The passage loomed before them, its flesh-like walls drinking in the light. He hesitated at the threshold, feeling the weight of countless years pressing down from the stone above.

Butch didn't wait. He adjusted his grip on the crowbar and stepped into the opening, his movements carrying the steady purpose of a man who'd faced darkness before. The blue-green light caught the edges of his silhouette, throwing strange shadows across the organic curves of the walls.

Ara followed, her steps precise and measured. The crystal fragments in her pack hummed softly, resonating with something deep within the passage. Their purple glow mixed with the fungal light, creating shifting patterns that danced across the stone.

Jin took a deep breath of the mineral-laden air and stepped after them. The walls seemed to close in slightly, the texture of the stone changing subtly with each step deeper into the ancient cut. Their footsteps echoed back wrong, suggesting vast spaces hidden beyond the narrow confines of the passage.

***

The passage widened into a cavern where bioluminescent patterns traced the walls like frozen lightning. Waves of soft blue-green light rippled through the growths, creating an otherworldly aurora against the stone. The phosphorescent patches pulsed with their own rhythm, not the mechanical precision of the fungus outside, but something more organic, almost alive.

As Ara moved through the space, certain clusters brightened in response to her presence. The light followed her path like curious children, creating a trail of intensified glow that lingered briefly before fading back to its natural state. Her usual melodic hums fell silent. Instead, she tilted her head, silver hair catching the shifting light as she focused on sounds beyond human perception.

Jin reached out towards a particularly bright cluster, fingers hovering just above the surface. When he made contact, the growth immediately dimmed, retreating from his touch like a sea anemone.

The darkness spread outward in a circle, leaving a temporary void in the living light show.

Butch kept his hands firmly on his crowbar, maintaining a deliberate distance from the walls. His eyes tracked the moving patterns, searching for anything that might hide within the shifting glow. Years of survival had taught him that beauty often masked danger, especially in unfamiliar territory. He stepped carefully, keeping to the center of the passage where the stone remained bare.

The air grew thicker here, heavy with mineral scents and something else, an organic musk that reminded Jin of overripe fruit. Each breath carried complex layers of age and decay, suggesting depths far beyond their immediate surroundings.

Ara's fingertips traced geometric paths across the crystalline surface, following invisible lines that only she perceived. Her movements flowed with practiced grace, each gesture precise and purposeful. The wall responded to her touch with subtle luminescence, purple light bleeding through ancient veins of mineral.

Jin caught fragments of melody rising from the contact points, delicate notes that hung in the air like morning mist. The sound formed patterns just beyond comprehension, suggesting meanings that dissolved when examined too closely. His breath synchronized with the subtle harmonics, his body responding to frequencies that bypassed conscious thought.

Butch shifted his weight, adjusting his grip on the crowbar. Where Jin heard music, he detected only the faintest vibrations, ghost notes at the edge of perception. The disparity left him feeling isolated, cut off from whatever silent conversation passed between his companions. His jaw tightened as he watched Ara's increasingly tense movements.

The elf's usual fluid grace gave way to sharp, angular gestures. Her silver hair caught the bioluminescent light as she pressed harder against the wall, searching with growing urgency. The subtle glow beneath her fingers pulsed erratically now, matching her agitation. Her shoulders drew tight, her spine rigid with focus or fear.

The silence from their guide grew heavier with each passing moment. Where before she had freely shared observations and warnings, now she withdrew into herself. Her fingers continued their desperate dance across the stone, but her expression had closed like a door against unwanted visitors.

Jin opened his mouth to ask what troubled her but caught himself. Something in Ara's rigid posture warned against breaking her concentration. Whatever she read in these ancient walls commanded her complete attention, and bred a tension that filled the chamber like smoke.

***

The air grew viscous, pressing against their skin like invisible honey. Jin's chest tightened with each breath, though the oxygen remained pure and plentiful. Something else saturated the atmosphere, an invisible weight that spoke of countless years and forgotten memories.

His lungs worked harder against the resistance. Not a physical barrier, but the accumulated pressure of time itself. It felt like walking through the halls of an ancient temple, where the very air held the whispers of countless prayers.

Butch's hand never strayed far from the crowbar at his belt. His weathered fingers brushed the metal occasionally, drawing comfort from its solid presence. The weapon had already proven its worth against flesh and bone, but what good was steel against the weight of history itself?

Ara paused mid-step, her silver hair catching the bioluminescent light. Her throat vibrated with a single, pure note that cut through the heavy air like a blade. The sound carried purpose, not communication, a key fitting into an invisible lock.

The path ahead, which had twisted and branched in confusing angles, suddenly seemed to straighten. Not through any physical change, but as if Ara's harmonic had adjusted their perception of the space. What was maze-like moments before now revealed its true course with crystalline clarity.

Jin blinked, trying to understand how the same tunnel could appear so different. The note faded, but its effect remained. Like a compass finding true north, their route forward had been calibrated by that brief musical touch.

The group halted before a section of wall that did not quite match its surroundings. Beneath centuries of fungal growth and mineral deposits, precise tool marks caught the dim light. The arch rose twelve feet high, its curves too perfect for nature's hand.

Butch ran his palm across the stone. "Man-made. Or whatever passes for man here."

Pulses of blue-green light rippled through the fungus wherever his fingers disturbed it. The glow spread outward in geometric patterns, transforming the arch into a living circuit board of bioluminescence.

Ara stepped forward, her movements precise and reverent. Her throat vibrated with a complex series of tones, not music exactly, but something older. The sound made the crystals in her pack gleam purple through the fabric.

Hidden glyphs emerged on the arch's surface, each one trembling in resonance with her voice. Triple flames. Spiraling paths. Faces without mouths that seemed to watch with hollow eyes. The symbols did not just appear — they awakened, as if Ara's harmonics had roused them from sleep.

She pressed her palm against the central glyph. The stone felt warm beneath her fingers, almost alive. No physical change marked the arch's opening, no grinding stone or shifting rocks. Instead, the barrier dissolved emotionally, like a wall of grief crumbling under acceptance.

Jin stumbled, overwhelmed by the sudden shift in reality's texture. The arch remained solid stone, yet something fundamental had changed. A doorway now existed where solid rock had been — not in space, but in meaning.

"Butch?" Jin's voice was thin, uncertain.

Butch steadied him with a firm grip. Jin could only stare at the impossible opening, trying to process how stone could remain stone while simultaneously becoming an entrance. His mind struggled to contain two contradictory truths: the arch was sealed, and the arch was open. Both facts existed simultaneously, like a quantum state that refused to collapse into a single reality.

***

The trio crossed the threshold, each step carrying them deeper into the impossible passage. The stone walls thrummed with a faint pulse, like a sleeping giant's heartbeat. Crystalline veins traced geometric patterns overhead, their purple glow casting strange shadows across ancient surfaces.

Ara stopped, her silver hair reflecting the ambient light. She pressed her palm flat against the tunnel wall, fingers splayed across the living crystal. A single note emerged from her throat, not loud, but pure and final. The sound rippled outward through stone and air, through flesh and bone.

Jin gasped as the resonance passed through him. Not painful, but profound, like being recognized by something vast and ancient. The sensation lingered in his chest, a phantom fingerprint pressed into his very being.

Butch watched Jin's reaction with sharp eyes, his own body registering nothing of the harmonic wave. His hand tightened on the crowbar, muscles tensing at his companion's visible discomfort.

'Now they know we're coming,' Ara said, her voice carrying both warning and resignation. She pulled her hand away from the wall, leaving no mark where she had touched, yet something fundamental had shifted in the air around them.

The crystalline passage sealed itself with a whisper of violet light, geometric patterns realigning into seamless stone. Jin's fingers traced the wall where the entrance had been moments before, finding only cold, ancient rock beneath his touch. The finality of their situation settled over him like a physical weight.

Butch moved forward without hesitation, his crowbar catching purple reflections as he advanced deeper into the tunnel. His footsteps echoed with purpose, each one carrying him further from the sealed threshold and whatever lay behind it.

Ara's usual fluid grace faltered. Her chest rose and fell in quick, shallow bursts, though she made no sound. The silver markings along her neck pulsed erratically, matching her uneven breathing. When Jin glanced her way, she turned sharply, avoiding his gaze.

'The resonance barrier,' she said, her mental voice tighter than usual. 'It remembers those who cross. To return would require...' She trailed off, her fingers curling into fists at her sides.

Jin lingered at the sealed entrance, his palm still pressed against the stone. Something about the barrier's energy called to him, not exactly a sound, but a feeling that hummed in his bones. The same sensation he had felt when Ara's harmonics had first touched his mind.

'Move,' Butch called back, his voice carrying an edge of urgency. 'Whatever's behind us isn't worth studying.'

The passage stretched ahead, crystal veins threading through rock like frozen lightning. Their new path offered only one direction – deeper into the mountain's ancient heart. Jin's hand fell away from the wall as he turned to follow the others, leaving the sealed threshold and its mysteries behind.

CHAPTER 9

The tunnel widened, its crystalline walls falling away to reveal a cathedral-like expanse that stretched beyond sight. Ancient stone columns rose from darkness into shadow, their surfaces wrapped in spiraling vines that pulsed with pale blue light. The air hung thick with age and moisture.

Phosphorescent fungi clung to the columns in patches of electric green and soft purple, their glow reflecting off pools of black water that dotted the chamber floor. The sound of trickling water echoed from somewhere in the vast space, its source hidden in the gloom.

Butch swept his crowbar in a slow arc, testing the nearest patch of bioluminescent growth. The fungus dimmed at his approach, then brightened once he passed - like a living thing shrinking from touch.

Jin's boots splashed through a shallow puddle, sending ripples across the mirror-dark surface. The water felt wrong against his skin - too thick, too alive. He pulled back quickly, wiping his shoe against drier ground.

Ara moved between the towering columns with careful steps, her silver markings casting additional light in the darkness. Her fingers traced patterns in the air as she walked, mapping unseen currents. The vines nearest her trembled and reached toward her passing form, their glow intensifying briefly before fading back to baseline luminescence.

The chamber's ceiling vanished into darkness overhead, but occasional glimpses of crystal formations caught the bioluminescent light, suggesting impossible heights. More water sounds echoed from multiple directions now - dripping, flowing, splashing - creating a discordant symphony that made orientation difficult.

Massive tree roots, thick as bridge cables, burst through the stone floor in places. They twisted up the columns like serpents frozen in mid-strike, their bark black and glossy in the ethereal light. Smaller tendrils branched off into delicate networks that spread across the chamber floor, forming natural pathways between the deeper pools of standing water.

The air itself seemed to glow faintly, filled with drifting motes of bioluminescence that swirled in their wake. Each breath drew in the ancient atmosphere, heavy with the scent of damp stone and something older - something that spoke of depths and darkness and time beyond measure.

Jin turned in slow circles, mouth slightly open as he took in the impossible vastness of the chamber. The dancing lights reflected in his eyes as he traced the path of massive roots up into darkness. His fingers reached out unconsciously toward the nearest patch of glowing fungi, drawn to its ethereal beauty.

"It's like something from a dream," he whispered, his voice carrying strange harmonics in the massive space.

Butch planted his feet wider apart, crowbar held low but ready. His eyes never lingered in one spot, scanning methodically between columns and across the network of pools. The trickling water sounds made it harder to pinpoint potential threats, and the shifting shadows played tricks with depth perception. His grip tightened on the crowbar as a distant splash echoed through the chamber.

Ara remained motionless at the entrance, her silver markings pulsing faintly in rhythm with the bioluminescent vines. Her usual fluid grace had hardened into stone-like stillness. Only her eyes moved, tracking something invisible in the air - patterns or frequencies beyond human perception. The delicate muscles in her throat worked silently, as if tasting the ancient atmosphere for hidden meanings.

When Jin stepped toward her with a question forming on his lips, she raised one hand in a sharp gesture for silence. Her expression remained carefully blank, but tension radiated from her rigid posture. The nearby vines dimmed slightly, drawing away from her presence rather than reaching toward it as before.

A subtle vibration threaded through the chamber, building from somewhere deep beneath their feet. The sound layered itself in complex harmonics - not quite musical, not quite mechanical. It resonated through the crystalline walls and pulsed in the bioluminescent growth, creating patterns of light that rippled outward like waves on water.

Jin's shoulders tensed as the frequencies hit him. His teeth ached with it, bones humming in sympathy with tones that seemed to bypass his ears entirely. He pressed his palms against his temples, trying to steady himself against the overwhelming sensation.

Butch glanced at Jin's distress with concern, but his expression remained neutral. The harmonics registered only as a faint background noise to him, like distant machinery or the drone of cicadas on a summer night. He adjusted his grip on the crowbar, more focused on watching the shadows between columns than the sound itself.

Ara's entire bearing shifted as the frequencies washed over her. Her rigid posture melted into fluid grace, silver markings brightening as she aligned herself with the chamber's song. She drew in a deep breath, letting the layered tones flow through her body like water. Her throat worked silently, matching and mapping each component of the complex harmony.

The group moved forward together, passing between two massive columns wrapped in pulsing vines. The harmonics grew stronger, more defined, as they crossed some invisible threshold. The air changed texture, becoming thicker and charged with potential. They had entered what could only be the Grove - though it bore little resemblance to any earthly forest.

Bioluminescent patterns shifted and flowed across every surface, responding to their presence. The massive roots beneath their feet trembled with subsonic frequencies. Even the pools of black water rippled in perfect synchronization with the chamber's song.

Jin stumbled slightly as another wave of harmonics washed over him. Butch steadied him with one hand, while Ara moved ahead with newfound purpose, her steps falling into rhythm with the Grove's pulsing energy.

The harmonics shifted, wrapping around Ara like a living thing. Her silver markings blazed brighter, pulsing in perfect synchronization with the chamber's song. The sound accepted her, welcomed her, as if recognizing something familiar in her resonance.

Jin pressed his hands against his ears, but the pressure only intensified. The frequencies bypassed his skull entirely, vibrating through his bones and core. His vision blurred at the edges as the chamber's deep song overwhelmed his senses. Each step forward felt like wading through invisible currents of sound.

Butch moved steadily beside him, seemingly untouched by the overwhelming harmonics. Where Jin struggled against waves of sound, Butch walked through empty air. The crowbar in his hand remained steady, his movements precise and controlled in the face of frequencies that threatened to shake Jin apart.

The chamber's song built to impossible depths - layers upon layers of tone that existed below the threshold of human hearing. Yet they felt it in their blood, in their marrow, in the spaces between thoughts. It was like standing in the heart of a bell that rang at the frequency of the world itself.

Ara's throat worked silently as she aligned herself with the sound, becoming part of its complex pattern. Her movements grew more fluid, more certain, as if the chamber's acceptance had transformed her from visitor to native. The bioluminescent vines reached for her now, recognizing her as their own.

Jin stumbled forward, caught between Butch's steady presence and Ara's transformed grace. The harmonics pressed against his mind like a physical weight. He could feel the sound reshaping his understanding of space and time, forcing his consciousness to expand beyond normal human limits.

The chamber sang its ancient song, and they walked deeper into frequencies too vast to comprehend.

***

Movement flickered through the upper reaches of the chamber. Dark figures shifted through patches of fungal light - tall, graceful shapes with skin tones ranging from copper to deep mahogany. They wore fitted leather armor adorned with intricate geometric patterns, the surfaces catching and reflecting the bioluminescent glow. Glass-tipped spears glinted in their hands, alongside strange crystalline devices that pulsed with inner light.

Their features mirrored Ara's - the same curved, shell-like ears and silver-grey eyes adapted for the dim underground. But where

Ara's markings glowed with controlled power, theirs remained dark. They moved with precise, practiced grace through the hanging vines and crystal formations, their footsteps completely silent on the ledges above.

Some crouched at the edges of stone outcroppings, spears held ready. Others traced patterns in the air with polished tools that caught and redirected the chamber's ambient harmonics. Their leather armor flexed soundlessly with each movement, the protective plates arranged to allow maximum mobility while guarding vital areas.

Ara lifted her hand in a fluid gesture, her throat vibrating with a deep, resonant chord. The sound rippled through the chamber like a physical presence. In response, the figures melted backward into shadow, their forms dissolving into the darkness between patches of fungal light. Within moments, the upper reaches appeared empty once more, though Jin could feel unseen eyes tracking their movement through the Grove.

Ara moved forward with deliberate steps, her silver markings pulsing in rhythm with the chamber's song. Jin and Butch followed close behind, their boots barely making sound on the damp stone floor. The path narrowed between two crystalline formations that curved like ribs around them.

A figure emerged from behind a curtain of phosphorescent vines. Young for an elf, with unblemished brown skin and fresh leather armor that hadn't seen combat. His grey eyes widened at the sight of Jin and Butch, fingers tightening on his glass-tipped spear.

The young elf's throat vibrated with a questioning harmonic - not aggressive, but firm. The sound carried undertones of protocol and duty, rising at the end like a musical question mark. His free hand traced a geometric pattern in the air, a formal gesture that matched his tone.

Ara drew herself up, her markings flaring brighter. Her response cut through the chamber's ambient song - a single, sharp note that made the crystals around them resonate. Authority rang in that tone, backed by something deeper that made the young guard take an involuntary step backward.

The elf's posture shifted. His eyes darted to Ara's glowing markings, recognition and unease crossing his features. He lowered his spear slightly but remained in their path, caught between respect for a Hollow and distrust of the strangers she guided.

His gaze never left Jin and Butch as he pressed himself against the wall, making space but not truly yielding. The message was clear - Ara's status granted her passage, but her human companions were another matter entirely.

***

The chamber walls curved like the inside of a giant nautilus shell, their surfaces smooth and organic. Patches of bioluminescent fungi cast a soft blue-green glow that barely reached the corners.

Unlike the resonant main caverns, this space swallowed sound; each footstep and whisper died quickly, absorbed by the living stone.

Jin sat cross-legged on a woven mat, running his fingers over the wall's surface. Tiny vibrations hummed beneath his touch, a constant subtle tremor like a sleeping giant's breath. The stone felt neither warm nor cool, but somewhere in between, as if it maintained its own careful temperature.

'Can't hear it properly,' Butch muttered, pressing his palm flat against the curved wall. His weathered face showed concentration as he tried to sense what Jin felt so clearly. 'Just feels like regular rock to me.'

Jin closed his eyes, letting the subharmonics wash through him. 'It's like... music without sound. Like feeling bass through your chest at a concert, but gentler.' He paused, searching for words. 'The whole place feels alive.'

Butch grunted and settled onto his own mat, keeping his crowbar within arm's reach. The chamber was sparse but carefully arranged - sleeping mats, clay water vessels, and strange crystalline lamps that responded to touch. Everything curved and organic, as if grown rather than built.

'Wonder what Ara's telling them about us,' Jin said quietly. The words fell flat in the dampened air.

'Nothing good, probably.' Butch stretched his shoulders, wincing at old aches. 'Did you see how those guards looked at us? Like we were something that crawled out of the deep.'

The walls continued their subtle song, a rhythm just below hearing. Occasional echoes of distant harmonics filtered through - elvish voices perhaps, or the Grove itself breathing. The chamber felt both welcoming and alien, like being cradled in the palm of something ancient and only half-understood.

'They really look like elves,' Jin whispered, his voice barely carrying in the sound-dampening chamber. 'I mean, except for the pointed ears not being there.'

Butch ran his hand through his greying hair. 'Maybe wood elves, ya? Not like those white-skin elves from the movies.' His Filipino accent thickened as he kept his voice low. 'These ones got the brown skin like back home.'

Jin studied the organic curves of their temporary quarters while Butch paced the perimeter, checking each possible exit. The constant pressure and soft bioluminescence made Butch's movements more deliberate, more cautious.

'Those brow ridges though,' Butch continued, tapping his own forehead. 'And that sloping forehead - reminds me of those caveman stuffs from the Discovery Channel.'

'Hominids,' Jin corrected. 'Our human ancestors.'

Butch shrugged, clearly uncomfortable with the chamber's alien architecture. 'Sure, I guess. Never went to college.' He positioned himself where he could watch both entrances, the crowbar resting across his knees. The subtle vibrations through the walls made his shoulders tense.

The constant thrum of harmonics pressed against them like a physical weight. Butch shifted his position again, unable to find comfort in the strange space. His eyes darted between the curved passages, mapping escape routes through muscle memory born of old survival instincts.

Ara's silhouette filled the chamber entrance, her form motionless against the bioluminescent glow. Silver markings traced paths across her skin, dimmer now in the sound-dampening space. She remained at the threshold, neither entering nor retreating, her presence heavy with unspoken weight.

Jin looked up from his spot on the floor. 'Hey.' The word fell flat in the dead air.

Butch kept his eyes fixed on the far wall, his scarred hands steady on the crowbar. His pocket flashed purple - quick, sharp, like a camera flash in the dark. The light died as fast as it appeared.

Ara's head snapped toward the burst, her movements precise and controlled. Her fingers brushed against her hip, tracing the outline of something hidden beneath her garments. The gesture looked almost unconscious, protective.

Neither spoke. The chamber's subtle vibrations continued their endless song, felt more than heard through the living stone.

Jin rose from his mat, stepping carefully across the chamber's curved floor toward Ara. The harmonics grew stronger as he approached, like bass notes rising through his bones. Butch followed, his movements measured and alert despite the chamber's disorienting resonance.

Within arm's reach of Ara, Jin felt the familiar mental connection snap into place. The sensation still unsettled him - like thoughts becoming liquid, flowing between minds without words.

Are we safe? Jin projected the question through their shared consciousness.

Ara's silver markings pulsed once, dim in the bioluminescent light. *For now.*

Butch nudged Jin's shoulder, his weathered face tight with concern. 'Ask her what they want from us.'

Jin transmitted Butch's question through their mental link. The harmonics shifted, deepening like a cello's lowest note.

Ara's response came with crystal clarity: *Not what. Who.*

The words hung in the dampened air as the chamber's walls continued their subtle vibration, swallowing all other sound.

CHAPTER 10

A deep note thrummed through the Grove's living walls, pure and resonant. The sound carried no urgency, yet the entire chamber stirred with purpose. Throughout the curved passages, elves rose from their resting places in fluid, synchronized motion - as natural as leaves turning towards sunlight.

Jin's skin prickled. The tone settled into his bones, drawing forth emotions that weren't quite his own - a collective peace, a shared rhythm of life. His breath synced unconsciously with the Grove's pulse.

Butch shifted uncomfortably on his mat. Something pressed against his sternum, not quite sound but a physical weight. He rubbed his chest, trying to ease the strange sensation. The crowbar remained steady in his other hand.

Ara stood motionless in the chamber's entrance, her silver markings catching the bioluminescent light. Her eyes closed, body perfectly still as she merged with the Grove's morning signal. No muscle twitched, no breath disturbed her communion with the living structure.

Through the curved passages, brown-skinned figures moved with practiced grace. Their steps fell in perfect time, neither rushed nor delayed. Each elf responded to the harmonic as if to their own heartbeat, flowing through the organic architecture like blood through veins.

The tone held steady, neither rising nor falling. Jin felt tears form without sadness, his body responding to frequencies his mind could not fully grasp. The sensation was not unpleasant - like being gently lifted by an ocean wave.

Butch watched the synchronized movement with a veteran's wariness. His fingers tightened around the crowbar's familiar weight as the pressure in his chest continued, just shy of discomfort. The elves paid him no attention, caught in their morning ritual.

The Grove's signal filled every space, every curve, every chamber - not sound alone, but life itself expressing its endless cycle through pure harmonic resonance.

The harmonics built in cascading layers, each new tone weaving through the chamber like threads of light. Dozens of brown-skinned elves stood in concentric circles, their voices rising and falling in patterns too precise for human throats. The sound carried meaning beyond music - joy and sorrow merged into pure expression.

Jin leaned forward, transfixed. The resonance pulled at something deep within him, drawing forth emotions he could not name. Tears traced silent paths down his cheeks as the harmonics touched memories of Mina, of his father, of moments lost and found. His hands trembled with each new layer of sound.

Butch pressed his back against the curved wall, eyes scanning the chamber's organic architecture. He counted three passages leading out, each curved just enough to obscure its destination. The crowbar lay across his lap, ready. While the elves swayed with their song, he mapped escape routes and defensive positions. The pressure in his chest remained, but he refused to let it distract him.

Ara took position between her charges and the gathering, her silver markings pulsing softly with each harmonic wave. She made no move to stop Jin from watching, nor to pull Butch from his vigilance. Her stance spoke volumes - this moment belonged to her people alone. Though Jin could feel it and Butch could sense it, they remained outside its true meaning, separated by more than mere distance.

The elves' song continued to build, their bodies moving in perfect synchronization. Some raised crystalline shards that caught the bioluminescent light, scattering it in geometric patterns across the chamber walls. Others pressed their palms to the living stone, sending vibrations through the Grove's very structure.

***

The harmonics faded, leaving only echoes rippling through the Grove's living walls. Ara turned to face Jin and Butch, her silver markings still pulsing with residual energy. Her throat worked, struggling with unfamiliar movements.

'Sound-song... life-blood of people.' Her voice came rough, halting. The words emerged like scattered pieces of a puzzle she was learning to assemble. 'Grove... remembers all. Through deep-time.'

Jin leaned forward, fascinated by this first attempt at human speech. Butch's grip on the crowbar loosened slightly.

'Words... from your thoughts. I learn.' Ara pressed her fingers to her temple, then gestured to Jin. 'When you speak, I... catch meanings. Like catching light in water.'

She moved her hands in flowing patterns, matching the rhythm of her broken speech. 'Morning-song is... sharing. All connected in Grove. Hollow ones guide the... flow.' Her silver markings flickered as she searched for proper terms. 'Not just music. Is... for balance.'

Jin nodded slowly, pieces clicking into place. 'That's why I could feel it so strongly?'

'Yes-no.' Ara's brow furrowed. 'You have... echo. Old resonance.' She turned to Butch. 'You... different. Silent inside. Like stone that won't... ring.'

Butch raised an eyebrow. 'That why their yelling attacks don't work on me?'

'Dead-spots in song.' Ara tapped her chest, mirroring where Butch had felt the pressure. 'Some frequencies... cannot touch.'

Her words grew more confident as she pulled them from Jin and Butch's surface thoughts, though her syntax remained alien. 'Grove is... living memory. My people guard the... harmonics. Keep balance.' She gestured to the retreating elves. 'They fear humans because... because...'

She paused, struggling to translate concepts that had no direct equivalent in English. 'Echo of Lost Flame brings... discord. Changes the song.'

Ara's markings pulsed as she studied Butch. 'You are... not burning. You are water on flame.' Her hands traced patterns in the air. 'Others fear discord, but you...' She pressed her palm against her chest. 'You make quiet in storm.'

Jin's eyes widened. 'You mean he cancels out harmful frequencies?'

'Like stone in river.' Ara's fingers curled into fists, then spread wide. 'Not break wave. Make wave... go around.' She touched the crystal fragments in her pack. 'Others sing to hurt. You...' She shook her head, frustrated by the limitations of speech. 'You make safe space.'

Butch's weathered face remained neutral, crowbar balanced across his knees. 'Not sure if that's good or bad, coming from you folks.'

'Good-not good. Is...' Ara's throat worked. 'Is needed. Grove knows.' She gestured to the living walls. 'Songs grow strong, need quiet places too.'

Jin leaned forward. 'That's amazing. You're getting better at this - at speaking.'

'Words still... wrong shape.' Ara's silver markings flickered. 'But meaning flows better when...' She touched her temple, then pointed to Jin. 'When mind-bridges stay open.'

Butch shifted his weight. 'Still don't know if you're saying I help or hurt your songs.'

'Both-neither.' Ara's expression softened. 'Like night needed for day. Silence needed for song.' She moved closer, her movements deliberate. 'You are... balance point.'

Butch rubbed his temples, trying to parse Ara's halting words. His own struggles with English bubbled up - years of hesitation, of keeping sentences short to avoid mistakes. A dry chuckle escaped his lips.

'Look at me, trying to understand her English when mine still gives me nose bleed.' He shook his head. 'Maybe we need three translators, not just one.'

Jin shifted closer to them both, trying not to laugh. 'I think she's saying that sometimes you need one dangerous thing to stop another. Like how silence can break sound, or...' He paused, searching for the right comparison. 'Like using fire to fight fire.'

'Oh.' The strain left Butch's body. 'Like when they start planned fires to shield against runaway infernos in the jungle?'

'Yes.' Ara's voice carried new confidence with the simple word. She hummed softly, her markings pulsing as she absorbed their exchange. 'Danger... stops danger. Quiet... stops loud.'

Her hands moved in careful patterns as she matched concepts to sounds, her body swaying slightly with each new word she captured from their thoughts. The air around her rippled with subtle harmonics as she aligned her understanding with their speech.

'Balance,' she said, the word emerging clear and precise. She touched her chest, then pointed to Butch. 'You... balance.'

***

Two elders emerged from a crystalline archway, their copper-brown skin marked with age, their movements precise and measured. Unlike the younger guards, they wore intricate glass beads woven through their hair and carried staffs tipped with purple-veined crystal.

Their harmonics cut through the chamber, not speech but pure resonant tones that made the walls shimmer. The sound carried weight, authority, and barely concealed disdain.

Ara's silver markings flared as she straightened, her posture shifting from guide to something more official. She responded with a single pure note that seemed to bend the air itself. The elders' expressions remained frozen, but they inclined their heads slightly, the bare minimum of acknowledgment given to one of her station.

More tones followed, each one making Jin's bones ache. The elders' harmonics grew sharper, their questions clear even without words. Ara's responses came shorter, terser, her markings pulsing with visible strain.

The exchange ended abruptly. The elders turned away without gesture or sound, vanishing back through the arch as if the humans did not exist.

Jin watched Ara's shoulders drop slightly once they had gone. "That seemed... tense."

Butch kept his eyes on the archway, crowbar resting across his knees. His weathered face revealed nothing, but his fingers tightened imperceptibly around the metal.

Ara moved closer to Butch, her silver markings casting soft light across his lined face. She placed a hand near, but not touching, his white-knuckled grip on the crowbar.

"Safe here." Her voice carried the careful cadence of newly learned words. "No need for iron-stick."

Butch's eyes flickered between her and the crystalline archway where the elders had vanished. His fingers flexed around the crowbar's worn grip, muscle memory from hours of combat refusing to let go.

"You sure about that?" His voice stayed low, measured. "Those two didn't seem too happy to see us."

Ara's markings pulsed once, steady and calm. "Elders... but Grove is mine too." She touched her chest, where the silver patterns ran deepest. "My voice has weight here. Authority."

Butch studied her face, reading the quiet confidence there. His grip on the crowbar loosened fraction by fraction, decades of survival instinct warring with trust. Finally, he gave a short nod and hooked the weapon through his belt loop.

"Your house, your rules." He settled back against the wall, though his hand never strayed far from the crowbar's handle. "But I'm keeping it close."

Ara's markings brightened slightly, approval perhaps, or simple acknowledgment of his caution. She inclined her head in a gesture that mirrored the elders', but where theirs had held dismissal, hers carried respect.

Butch shifted his weight against the curved wall, eyes still tracking the archway where the elders had disappeared. "What did they want?"

Ara's silver markings dimmed as she processed his words, searching for human language to bridge the gap. "Grove... not accept yet." Her fingers traced patterns in the air, matching the rhythm of her broken speech. "Not time for your kind here."

"They don't want us here," Jin translated, feeling the lingering echo of the elders' dismissive harmonics in his chest.

"Yes." Ara nodded, her markings pulsing with each carefully chosen word. "Not want you. Not break Grove." She gestured to the living walls around them, to the delicate balance of sound and light that seemed to flow through every surface.

Butch's hand drifted back to his crowbar. "Then maybe we shouldn't..."

"No." Ara moved between them and the archway, her stance protective rather than threatening. "You stay. I stay." Her markings brightened with certainty. "My voice keeps safe. My authority."

She pressed her palm against the wall, sending a ripple of silver light through the organic surface. "Grove remembers. Grove changes slow. But you stay safe with me."

Jin leaned forward, his voice tight with urgency. "My sister— will they help us find her?"

Ara's markings flickered, a brief dimming that spoke volumes. She pressed her fingers against the living wall, drawing strength from its pulse.

"Working. Much resistance." Her words came slower now, each one chosen with care. "Elders fear change. Fear what humans bring."

"But we have to..." Jin's voice cracked. "She's all I have left."

Ara turned to face him fully, her silver patterns brightening with conviction. "I promised. Will use all authority as Hollow." She straightened, and for a moment, her presence filled the chamber. "My voice carries weight. Will make them listen."

"Hollow?" Jin's brow furrowed. "What does that mean? What are you?"

Ara's markings pulsed once, then settled into a steady glow. She moved away from the question, her attention shifting to the archway where soft footsteps approached.

"First, eat." She gestured as a young elf entered, carrying a wooden platter laden with unfamiliar fruits and what looked like bread. "Body needs strength."

The elf set down the platter without meeting their eyes, then retreated with practiced grace. The food gave off subtle aromas-sweet, earthy scents that made Jin's stomach growl despite his worry.

"But..." Jin started to press about the Hollow question.

"Eat." Ara's tone carried no argument. "Talk after. Promise."

***

Jin and Butch stared at the platter before them. The spread looked familiar, too familiar after days of foraging through the alien forest. More berries, fruits, and fungus dotted the wooden surface, though these had been properly prepared. Steam rose from carefully carved mushroom caps, and the fruits had been sectioned with precise cuts.

Butch picked up a purple-veined mushroom, studying its cooked surface. "Your people don't eat meat?"

"No." Ara gestured to a massive fungal growth that stretched up the chamber wall, its cap wider than Butch's arm span. "These give more strength. Better healing."

Jin sampled a steamed berry cluster. The cooking had transformed the bitter wild taste into something rich and complex. "It's good. Different from raw."

147

Butch chewed thoughtfully on the mushroom. His eyes narrowed at Ara's careful phrasing. "You said 'your people.' Are there others who do eat meat?"

Ara's markings flickered, caught in the slip. She touched the wall, drawing a steadying breath. "Yes. Other tribes exist." Her fingers traced the grain of the living surface. "Not all elves same. Not all follow Grove ways."

"How many..." Butch started to ask.

But Ara had already moved toward the archway, her markings dimming. The question hung unanswered in the humid air.

***

Jin studied the elves moving through the Grove's passages. Their ages seemed to fall into clear groups, not unlike humans. Children darted between the bioluminescent vines, their laughter a cascade of musical notes. Young adults, close to Jin's age, carried crystalline tools with practiced grace. The older ones, weathered like Butch, moved with measured steps and authority. And the elders, their skin lined with time, commanded space with mere presence.

Ara fell somewhere between, perhaps in her thirties by human standards, though Jin knew such comparisons might mean nothing here.

The social divide grew more apparent each day. When Ara approached with Jin and Butch, the older adults and elders would shift away, their harmonics becoming clipped and formal. But the younger ones gravitated closer, especially the children. They would peek around corners, mimicking human words they had learned from Ara.

"Hello!" a young elf called out, the word careful and precise. Others joined in, their pronunciation improving with each attempt.

The younger adults showed similar curiosity, though more reserved. They exchanged complex tones with Ara while stealing glances at the humans.

Butch watched an elder turn sharply away from their approach. "They don't like us much, do they? The older ones?"

Ara's silver markings rippled. Instead of words, she released a meandering harmonic unlike anything they had heard before. The sound drifted without structure or resolution, neither statement nor question, just uncertainty given voice.

The young elves nearby tilted their heads at the unusual tone, while several adults shot disapproving looks in their direction.

Jin and Butch wandered through the Grove's winding paths, their steps measured and careful. Every so often, tall elves in ornate leather armor would appear, their glass spears catching the bioluminescent light. With firm harmonics and stern gestures, they redirected the humans away from certain passages.

"Another dead end," Butch muttered as they turned back from a crystal-lined corridor.

They found themselves in what appeared to be a marketplace, rows of carved alcoves filled with goods. Woven fabrics in earth tones hung beside containers of dried fungi. Crystalline tools caught and reflected the blue-green light from above. Elves moved between the stalls, exchanging items through an intricate system of gestures and harmonics.

"Look at this." Butch paused at a display of fresh produce, fruits and vegetables unlike anything they had seen before. His eyes softened. "Reminds me of the *palengke* back home, before the big supermarkets came. Same feeling, everyone knowing everyone, trading what they grew or made themselves."

Jin watched an elderly elf carefully wrap purple-veined mushrooms in broad leaves, handing them to a younger one. The exchange was accompanied by a gentle harmonic that seemed to carry both gratitude and blessing.

"Even the way they arrange things." Butch gestured to the neat rows of goods. "My mother used to say you could tell a good market by how they displayed their wares."

A group of elven children darted past, carrying small baskets of glowing fungi. Their laughter rang out in perfect musical notes. Several older elves shot disapproving looks at the humans, pulling their goods closer as they passed.

"Some things don't change," Butch said quietly. "Every small town has its welcome and its walls."

The evening fire cast dancing shadows across the curved chamber walls. Butch sat cross-legged near the flames. Ara settled beside him, her silver markings catching the firelight.

"Fire moves like water," she said, the words halting but clear, each syllable carefully formed as she explored the unfamiliar sounds. "But hot. Loud inside." Her silver markings pulsed faintly as she struggled to translate concepts that, in her native harmonics, would have carried layers of meaning about destruction, renewal, and primal force.

Butch's mouth twitched. "Loud?"

"Yes. Crack-pop sounds," she said, her silver-traced fingers weaving through the air as if conducting an invisible orchestra. Her movements mirrored each lick and dance of the flames, studying their chaotic rhythm. "Different from Grove-song. Not smooth like wind through branches. More... sudden. Like breaking twigs, but alive." Her markings pulsed faintly as she tried to capture the alien concept in words.

A log shifted, sending sparks upward. Ara watched them rise and fade, her head tilted in curiosity. She began to hum, not the formal harmonics of the morning ritual, but something simpler, almost primitive. The sound wove through the fire's natural rhythm.

Butch rubbed his arms against the evening chill. "You are learning our words pretty quick."

"Words come from thoughts. Your thoughts..." She tapped her temple. "Like echoes. I catch them."

She continued her gentle humming, never taking her eyes off the flames. Unlike the other elves who retired to their chambers, Ara remained alert and present, studying every flicker and shadow as if cataloging them for future reference. Her markings pulsed softly in time with the fire's rhythm, casting faint blue traces across her brown skin. The melody she wove was simpler than the formal harmonics of her people, yet it carried an ancient quality, as if she were reaching back through time to something more primal, more raw than the practiced songs of the Grove.

CHAPTER 11

Ara moved through a narrow offshoot of the main Grove passages, her silver markings providing just enough light to navigate. The walls pressed closer here, their surface rougher and less maintained than the polished chambers they had left behind. Thick roots broke through the stone at odd angles, forcing them to duck and weave.

Butch followed second, his crowbar occasionally scraping against the wall when the path twisted unexpectedly. The ceiling dropped lower, forcing him to hunch his shoulders. His breaths came out measured and controlled, each step placed with careful precision despite the awkward space.

Jin brought up the rear, one hand trailing along the damp stone for balance. The harmonics felt different here, muffled and distorted, as if the very rock rejected the Grove's songs. The few patches of bioluminescent fungi cast sickly shadows rather than the vital glow they had shown in the main chambers.

Ara maintained her pace without looking back, her movements precise and purposeful. No harmonics escaped her, no attempts at the broken English she had been practicing. Her markings pulsed with an irregular rhythm that matched neither her steps nor the distant Grove-song.

The path kinked sharply left, then right, descending at an uncomfortable angle. Water trickled somewhere in the darkness, its pattern strange and arrhythmic. Loose gravel shifted under their feet, forcing them to brace against both walls for stability.

Butch opened his mouth to speak, but Ara raised her hand in a sharp gesture—the universal signal for silence. Her markings dimmed to barely a glimmer, leaving them in near-total darkness.

The darkness pressed against them as they waited, frozen in the narrow passage. After several long moments, Ara's markings slowly brightened again, casting weak purple light across the rough stone walls.

Jin shifted his weight, pebbles crunching beneath his feet. "Why are we down here?"

Ara's markings flickered, a brief pattern of light that Jin had begun to recognize as hesitation. "Council needs trail integrity confirmed."

Her voice carried the careful, measured tone of someone selecting each word with precision. The halting English felt more pronounced than usual, as if she were using the language barrier to maintain distance from the truth.

Butch's grip tightened on his crowbar. He had spent enough years reading between lines to recognize evasion when he heard it.

"Trail integrity?" Jin pressed, picking up on the same tension.

Ara touched the wall, tracing a geometric pattern that did not match the natural rock formation. "Yes. Must check... paths remain true." Her markings pulsed once, sharp and bright, before settling back to their dim glow.

The space between her words held more weight than the explanation itself. Her usual fluid movements had become rigid and mechanical, each gesture too precise, too controlled. Even without the ability to sense harmonics like Jin, Butch could read the discomfort in her posture.

Jin opened his mouth to ask another question, but Ara had already turned away, moving deeper into the passage. Her steps were quick now, almost urgent, as if physical distance might end the conversation.

The passage widened slightly, revealing scored marks in the stone walls. Not the elegant geometric patterns of the Grove, but cruder cuts—deep gouges that formed distinct symbols. A spiral here, a triple flame there, faces without mouths staring out from the rock.

Jin traced one with his finger, feeling the depth of the cut. "These aren't like the Grove marks."

Ara's markings flickered, her steps faltering for just a moment. She touched a spiral symbol, her fingers following its curve with practiced familiarity. But she said nothing, moving past it with deliberate speed.

Another set of marks appeared, these more weathered and partially hidden beneath mineral deposits. Jin recognized the triple flame pattern they had seen before. "Ara, what are these?"

Her shoulders tensed. The silver lines across her skin pulsed with an uneven rhythm. Still, she pressed forward.

"Ara." Jin's voice carried more force this time.

She stopped, her hand resting on a particularly deep-cut spiral. Her markings dimmed to almost nothing before brightening again. When she spoke, her words came slow and careful.

"Older walk here." She touched the spiral again. "One... not come back." Her fingers traced the pattern's center. "I go where they... vanish."

The weight of unsaid things hung in her halting phrases. She turned away from the symbol, her usual grace replaced by rigid movement, as if carrying some invisible burden.

***

Jin stepped closer to Ara, his voice softening. "Did you know them? The one who vanished?"

Ara's markings dulled to a deep purple, almost black. She pressed her palm flat against the spiral carving, her shoulders dropping. The harmonics around her shifted, no longer the bright, precise tones of her usual speech, but something deeper, heavier.

The sound reminded Jin of distant thunder or waves breaking against stone.

She spoke then, but not in English. The words flowed like water over rocks, each syllable layered with multiple tones that seemed to exist simultaneously. The phrase carried weight beyond its sound, resonating in Jin's chest with an almost physical presence.

"What does that mean?" Jin tried to mimic the first part of her phrase.

Ara turned to him, her markings brightening slightly. She repeated the words slower, breaking down each complex tone. Jin attempted to follow, but his throat couldn't produce the overlapping frequencies. The sounds came out flat, single-noted where they should have been layered.

She touched his shoulder, shaking her head. Her expression held no judgment, only a kind of gentle understanding. She demonstrated again, and Jin realized what he was hearing wasn't just multiple tones; it was multiple tones occurring in the same space, at the same moment. His human vocal cords simply weren't designed to create such sounds.

He tried once more, managing to hit two of the tones in sequence rather than simultaneously. Ara's markings pulsed with what might have been appreciation for his effort, but the attempt only highlighted how far human speech fell short of their harmonic language. Even an opera singer with perfect pitch couldn't replicate what seemed to be a biological feature of elven speech.

Butch kept his distance, letting Jin and Ara work through their language lesson. His fingers brushed the shard through his pocket fabric—a quick, subtle touch. The crystal's pulse matched his heartbeat for a moment, then faded.

The passage walls felt wrong. Not the living stone of the Grove, but something older. Dead, maybe, but not quiet. His crowbar hung loose in his grip, ready. The spirals carved into the rock reminded him of snail shells back home, but twisted wrong, like someone had taken the natural pattern and bent it into shapes that shouldn't exist.

Ara's head turned sharply toward him. Her silver markings shifted to deep blue as she produced a questioning tone, not quite music, not quite speech. The sound brushed past him like wind through empty rooms.

Butch met her gaze and gave a single, measured nod. No words were needed. He had seen that look before, in other fights, other places—the look that said, *I know you know something's wrong.* The look that asked, *Are you ready?*

The crystal in his pocket went still. Butch didn't reach for it again. Some things were better left unspoken, especially when your gut said run but your feet had to keep moving forward.

***

A discordant wave rippled through the passage, not the pure harmonics of the Grove, but something jagged and wrong. Jin stumbled, his hand flying to his temple as the sound scraped across his nerves like broken glass.

Ara's markings flashed crimson. Her entire body went rigid, head tilted as if listening to something far away. The usual fluid grace of her movements locked into stark angles.

Butch's grip tightened on his crowbar. He didn't hear the tone, but he felt its echo—a pressure in his chest like the moment before an explosion.

"Not Grove tone." Ara's voice came out flat, stripped of its musical qualities. "Wrong echo."

She pressed her palm against the wall, sending out a careful ping of sound. The response that came back made her jerk her hand away as if burned. Her markings pulsed erratically, cycling through colors Jin hadn't seen before—deep reds and sickly yellows.

Jin tried to replicate what he had felt, to understand the wrongness of it. "It wasn't layered like your speech. It was…" He searched for words. "Sharp. Like something breaking."

Butch kept his eyes on the darkness ahead. The crystal in his pocket had gone cold, not just quiet, but actively empty. Whatever that sound was, it had silenced even the fragment's usual hum.

Ara moved closer to them, positioning herself slightly ahead. Her usual harmonics shifted into something more controlled, contained. When she spoke again, her voice carried none of its previous warmth. "This place remembers old songs. Not all songs should wake."

The dissonant tone didn't return, but its absence felt heavy, like the pressure before a storm when even birds go quiet. The spiral carvings on the walls seemed darker, their patterns more pronounced in the dim light.

Ara's harmonics changed, becoming precise and measured, each note carefully contained like a soldier checking their ammunition. The sound wasn't her usual flowing melody, but sharp packets of tone that hit the walls in controlled bursts. Her silver markings dimmed to a low pulse, barely visible in the darkness.

The passage absorbed her song without response. Usually, the Grove's walls sang back, resonating with their own harmonics. This silence felt deliberate, as if something was actively choosing not to answer.

Butch caught the shift in her stance, the way her feet planted wider, how her shoulders squared. He had seen that posture before, in another life, when point men spotted trouble ahead. Without explanation or ceremony, Ara moved to position herself between Jin and whatever lay in the darkness beyond.

Her fingers splayed against the wall, sending out another pattern, shorter this time, almost like Morse code. Still nothing. The spiral carvings remained dark, refusing to light up as they had before.

Jin opened his mouth to ask a question, but Ara raised her hand sharply, a universal signal for silence. Her usual fluid grace had transformed into something harder, more tactical. Each movement now seemed calculated and precise.

Butch recognized that kind of silence, not empty, but full of intent. He adjusted his grip on the crowbar, keeping it low and ready. The crystal in his pocket remained cold and quiet.

***

Later, they found refuge in a small alcove carved into the passage wall. Ancient glyphs decorated the space, their edges worn smooth by time. Jin slumped against the cool stone, exhausted from the lingering effects of the discordant wave.

Ara's silver markings had settled back to their usual soft glow, but her eyes fixed on Butch's pocket with unusual intensity. She gestured toward it, her movements sharp and precise.

Butch's hand instinctively tightened around the crowbar. The crystal shard had grown warm again, its familiar weight pressing against his leg. He studied Ara's face, the way her markings pulsed with each breath, how her fingers curled in an unmistakable *give it here* motion.

After a long moment, he reached into his pocket. The fragment caught what little light filtered through the passage, its edges gleaming dull purple. As he held it out, it pulsed once, faintly, like a dying heartbeat.

Ara didn't take it. Instead, she produced a low, careful hum, not her usual complex harmonics, but a single pure note. The crystal responded immediately, its glow intensifying until purple light spilled between Butch's fingers.

Her eyes widened. She leaned closer, examining the shard without touching it. Her lips moved, forming a word that seemed to catch in her throat, something ancient and heavy with meaning. The sound wasn't English, wasn't even her harmonic speech. It came out rough and guttural, like stone grinding against stone.

Ara's markings flickered as she struggled to form the words. Her usual grace faltered, replaced by halting speech and tense gestures.

"This... not Grove. Not elf-make." She pointed at the crystal in Butch's hand. "You... carry... deep old."

Jin shifted closer, wincing as he moved. "Is it dangerous?"

"Only if listen. Only if..." Ara's fingers traced patterns in the air. "Only if... sing back."

Butch's grip tightened around the shard. "What is it?"

Ara shook her head, then pressed her forehead against Jin's. Images flowed between them—stone towers rising from distant plains, their surfaces etched with spiral patterns. Elven scouts discovering similar crystals buried in ancient chambers. Each shard singing with its own unique frequency, yet none matching the harmonics of the Grove.

Jin translated as the memories continued. "She says her people have found others like it. Some even far beyond the Grove, outside their territories. Inside stone towers. But they never knew what they were."

Ara's markings dimmed as she pulled back from Jin. Her fingers traced the air, mapping invisible frequencies. The crystal in Butch's hand continued its faint pulse, like a beacon calling into the dark.

"First finding, they sleep." She shaped the words with care, each syllable precise. "No song. No light." Her hand swept toward the passage walls. "Not like Grove stone. Not like..." She touched her own chest, where the markings spiraled across her skin.

Jin leaned forward. "What changed?"

"We try many sounds. Many songs." Ara's brow furrowed. "Then, accident. Young one drop crystal. Hit floor wrong way." She mimicked the motion of something falling. "Make sound we never hear before. Crystal wake up."

Butch studied the shard. "Wake up how?"

"Light first. Then..." Ara's markings flashed with frustration as she searched for the right words. "Sound wrong. Not Grove harmony. Not elf song." She pressed her palm against the nearest wall. "Grove stone, we understand. We speak, it answers. These crystals..." She gestured at the fragment. "They speak different language. Alien sounds."

Her fingers curled inward. "We try learn their song. Try copy their voice." Her expression hardened. "But wrong inside. Like trying catch smoke with hands. Always slip away."

Jin watched the purple light play across the alcove's ceiling. "But they still react to something?"

"Yes. Some tones make them..." Ara's hands moved in complex patterns. "Make them remember. But remember what? Not elf memory. Not Grove memory." She shook her head. "Something older. Something that walk here before Grove grew roots. Or maybe not memory at all, something else."

The crystal's pulse quickened for a moment, then settled back into its steady rhythm. Ara watched it with wary eyes, her markings reflecting its glow.

Butch squinted at the crystal shard, turning it over in his calloused hands. The purple light cast strange shadows across his weathered face.

"Ay nako, these old eyes." He held the fragment closer, then farther away. "Jin, come here. Maybe your young eyes see better than mine."

Jin shifted closer, careful not to aggravate his injuries. The crystal's glow painted his features in ethereal shades as he leaned in to examine it.

"Hard to tell in this light." Jin tilted his head, angling the shard toward what little illumination filtered through the passage. "But wait..." His fingers traced the crystal's surface. "There's something. Like... patterns? Or maybe they're just cracks running deep inside."

Butch grunted, rubbing his eyes. "Getting old sucks. Used to have eagle eyes, now everything blur-blur."

Butch rolled the crystal between his calloused fingers, its deep purple glow casting strange, shifting shadows across the weathered planes of his face. He traced one of the hairline fractures with his thumb, mesmerized by how the light seemed to pulse beneath his touch. "What about the other ones you found? What did your people do with them?" His voice was quiet but intent, the question carrying weight beyond simple curiosity.

Ara's markings pulsed and shifted to a deeper shade of violet, her bioluminescent patterns reflecting her unease with the subject. "Council keeps them. In vaults, deep below." Her slender fingers traced intricate geometric patterns in the air, each movement deliberate and weighted with meaning. "Say too dangerous. Say better locked away than risk wrong song." There was something in her tone, a hesitation perhaps, that suggested she didn't entirely agree with the Council's decision, though she kept that doubt carefully masked behind her measured words.

"Then why haven't they tried taking this one?" Butch's grip tightened around the shard. "Could've grabbed it while I slept."

Ara's markings flickered with amusement, a slight curve touching her lips. "They afraid trying." She gestured at Butch's pocket, where the crystal usually rested. "You scare them."

CHAPTER 12

The first rays of dawn painted the Grove's crystalline walls in amber and rose. Two figures descended the sloping passage with practiced grace, their movements fluid and synchronized like dancers following an unheard rhythm. The lead scout's armor, fashioned from layered bark and volcanic glass, caught the morning light. His spear, tipped with the same glass, hummed faintly with each step.

He carried a resonance tool at his belt, a curved device that looked almost like a musical instrument crossed with a compass. His brown skin marked him as one of the Sun Elves, distinct from Ara's paler complexion. Every movement spoke of efficiency, each step placed with deliberate care that made no sound against the crystal floor.

His companion matched his pace, both of them scanning their surroundings with the heightened awareness of veteran trackers. When they reached the bottom of the slope, the lead scout acknowledged Ara with a pure, clean tone, a single note that carried layers of meaning. The sound held respect for her station as a Hollow but maintained professional distance.

His grey eyes, adapted for low-light scouting, swept over Butch and Jin. Though his gaze lingered on the humans for a moment, taking in their alien features and strange clothing, he offered no greeting or reaction. His face remained impassive, revealing nothing of his thoughts about these outsiders in their midst.

The lead scout produced a series of overlapping tones that rippled through the air, short, precise bursts that made the crystal walls shimmer with faint patterns. His companion joined in, adding deeper harmonics that wove through the first set of sounds. Their voices created a dense tapestry of information, efficient and coded.

Jin felt the frequencies vibrate in his chest, catching fragments of meaning that slipped away before he could grasp them. He glanced at Ara, hoping for translation, but her silver markings had shifted to a muted grey. She stood perfectly still, absorbing the sonic report without offering explanation.

Butch kept his eyes on the scouts' hands, noting how they gestured in small, controlled movements. The way they positioned their feet told him more than their alien song. They were marking exit routes and establishing defensive positions. He had seen similar behavior in jungle patrols, though never accompanied by this strange music.

Ara's responses came in clipped, single tones, acknowledgments rather than conversation. Her usual flowing harmonics had become stark and functional. When the lead scout indicated a particular direction with his spear, her markings flickered briefly before settling back to grey.

The scouts' report concluded with a rising harmonic that made the crystals pulse once before fading. They departed as smoothly as they had arrived, leaving Jin looking between Ara and Butch with questions plain on his face. Ara remained focused on the passage ahead, her shortened responses suggesting she had no intention of sharing what she had learned.

The lead scout's resonance cut through the morning air, three sharp, overlapping tones that rang against the crystal walls. The sound carried purpose and urgency, marking the start of their patrol hunt. His harmonic command bounced through the passage, each echo adding layers of tactical information.

Ara's response came slower, flatter, acknowledging the order while maintaining distance. Her silver markings shifted to a deep blue as she adjusted her stance, checking the glass spear at her side. The scout's grey eyes narrowed slightly at her muted reply, but he made no comment.

Jin opened his mouth, questions already forming. "What did he—"

Ara's hand touched his arm, gentle but firm. Her newly learned English came carefully, each word chosen with precision. "Listen now. Words... after."

Butch gripped his crowbar tighter, muscles tensing as he recognized the pre-mission tension in the air. He had been here before, though never with alien elves giving the orders. "Just like old times," he muttered, his Filipino accent thick with irony. "Always passenger, never driver."

The scout produced another series of tones, shorter this time, coordinates and timing wrapped in harmonic code. His companion moved into position, glass-tipped spear ready. The morning light caught their armor, making the volcanic glass shimmer like frozen water.

Jin tried to parse the overlapping frequencies, catching fragments of meaning that slipped away before he could grasp them. The scout's resonance felt different from Ara's, harder and more militant, lacking her fluid grace. Each note carried weight and expectation, demanding immediate compliance.

***

The patrol moved in careful formation through the crystalline passage. The Sun Elf scout took point, his steps precise and measured as he navigated the uneven terrain. Every few meters, he released controlled bursts of sound, short, sharp harmonics that mapped their path forward.

Ara followed three paces behind, her silver markings dimmed to match the ambient light. When the scout's tones wavered or scattered against complex crystal formations, she added her own resonance, subtle adjustments that refined his sonic mapping. Her movements mirrored his efficiency but carried a different quality, more fluid than rigid.

Butch and Jin brought up the rear, maintaining the distance Ara had specified with hand signals. The crowbar stayed ready in Butch's grip as his eyes tracked between the walls and their guides. Jin focused on matching the patrol's careful footwork, trying to minimize the sound of his boots against the crystal floor.

The scout's harmonic bursts created brief patterns of light in the crystalline walls, geometric echoes that faded quickly but left clear directional markers. Ara's corrections appeared as softer ripples, smoothing the harsh edges of his tones into more stable frequencies. Their combined resonance built a temporary map in sound and light, guiding the group through the complex network of passages.

Each time the scout signaled a direction change, Ara reinforced the command with a purer tone that seemed to stabilize the crystal's response. The interplay between their harmonics revealed a practiced efficiency, his military precision balanced by her deeper understanding of the Grove's resonance patterns.

Butch studied the patrol's movements, his veteran instincts picking up patterns beneath the surface. The scouts didn't just signal, they moved in sync, their steps falling into subtle rhythms that conveyed meaning without sound. A slight pause in stride meant danger ahead. Two quick steps followed by a longer one indicated a safe path.

The crowbar felt steady in his grip as he matched their cadence, recognizing how the elves' bodies telegraphed information through timing rather than gesture. When the lead scout slowed his pace, the others adjusted instantly, not from watching but from feeling the shift in rhythm.

Ara's movements added another layer to this silent language. Her silver markings pulsed in counterpoint to the patrol's steps, creating a complex tempo that reminded Butch of drumbeats he had heard in mountain villages back home. The way she positioned herself between formations spoke volumes, each placement precisely timed to maintain the group's collective rhythm.

The crystal walls caught their synchronized movements, reflecting brief patterns of light that seemed to dance with their steps. Butch noticed how the scouts read these reflections without looking directly at them, their bodies responding to changes in the light's rhythm as naturally as breathing.

This wasn't just walking; it was a coordinated dance where every beat carried meaning. Butch's muscles tensed and relaxed in response, his body unconsciously adapting to their rhythm. Even Jin had fallen into step, though the younger man probably hadn't realized it yet.

A subtle shift in the patrol's tempo drew Butch's attention forward. The lead scout had altered his stride pattern, three short steps now instead of two. Without a word or gesture, the entire group adjusted to the new rhythm. Message received and acknowledged, all through the timing of their steps.

The patrol halted at a junction where three passages merged. Dark stains marred the crystal floor, old blood mixed with the oily residue goblins left behind. A resonance marker lay shattered, its fragments scattered across scorched patches of phosphorescent moss.

The lead scout knelt to examine the tracks. His fingers traced the gouges where clawed feet had scraped against crystal, reading their age and direction through touch. Rising smoothly, he produced a complex tone that split and echoed down each passage, a sound that suggested multiple viable routes through the maze ahead.

Ara's markings flickered as she stepped forward. Her answering resonance cut through his lingering harmonics with surgical precision. The sound carried weight and certainty, dismissing two paths outright while emphasizing the dangers of his preferred route.

The scout's posture stiffened. Though his face remained impassive, his next tone emerged cold and formal, a challenge wrapped in protocol. The crystal walls amplified his harmonics, transforming them into rigid geometric patterns of light that emphasized his tactical assessment.

Ara responded with equal formality. Her counter-tone wove through his fading resonance, creating interference patterns that highlighted flaws in his logic without directly contradicting his authority. Her markings pulsed in strict rhythm, matching the emotionless precision of their sonic debate.

Neither raised their voice. Neither gestured or shifted stance. Their disagreement played out entirely through layered harmonics that grew increasingly complex and austere. Each new tone built upon the last, adding evidence and argument while maintaining rigid adherence to Grove protocol.

The other scout watched silently, his own markings dimmed to near invisibility. This was a clash between rank and role, his superior's tactical command against a Hollow's deeper understanding of resonance patterns. Protocol demanded he remain neutral until their tones reached consensus.

*****

While the elves debated through their harmonics, Butch crouched near the junction, running weathered fingers across the crystalline grooves. His eyes followed subtle variations in the scattered moss, reading signs the others had overlooked. Without interrupting the sonic exchange, he shifted position and traced a third path, a narrow passage half-hidden behind crystalline outcrops.

The trail looked cleaner, lacking the obvious scrapes and gouges that marked the other routes. He pointed silently, letting his observation speak for itself.

Ara's markings flickered as she turned to study his choice. Her resonance fell quiet as she examined the hidden passage. After a moment, she gave a single, definitive nod.

The lead scout, whose harmonics had grown increasingly rigid during the debate, paused mid-tone. His stance suggested reluctance, but his tactical training recognized the value of Butch's find. The cleaner path meant fewer enemies had used it, reducing the risk of ambush or detection.

Jin watched the exchange with surprise. He had never seen Ara defer so quickly, especially to someone who could not perceive the Grove's harmonics. Her usual pattern was to analyze, debate, then reach careful consensus. This immediate acceptance of Butch's judgment broke that pattern completely.

When Jin caught her eye, silently asking for explanation, Ara's markings dimmed. She offered no clarification, maintaining the formal posture that matched the scout's professional restraint. Whatever insight had led her to trust Butch's assessment, she kept it to herself.

The lead scout produced a short, crisp tone, acknowledgment rather than agreement. He gestured for the group to proceed, allowing Butch to take point alongside him. The debate ended as formally as it had begun, with protocol preserved despite the unexpected shift in tactical approach.

***

The group paused at a wider section of the passage where phosphorescent fungi cast blue-green light across the crystal walls. The lead scout, a lean, brown-skinned elf with careful movements, drew Ara aside with a subtle gesture.

His harmonics came soft but precise, layered tones that spoke of protocol and tradition. The sound bounced off the crystalline surfaces, creating overlapping echoes that Jin could feel in his bones, though he couldn't grasp their meaning.

Ara's response emerged deeper, almost subsonic. Her markings shifted to muted copper as she answered, her usual fluid grace becoming rigid and contained. The exchange lasted mere seconds, but the weight of it lingered in the air.

When she rejoined Jin and Butch, her shoulders carried new tension. The silver lines across her skin had dulled to ash.

"He say I..." She struggled with the human words. "...forget place. Forget duty." Her voice came clipped and formal, stripped of its usual warmth.

The lead scout turned to face Jin and Butch, his glass-tipped spear held at rest. His harmonics flowed like water over stone, precise, measured tones that spoke of authority and formal introduction. The sound carried layers of meaning that made Jin's chest vibrate, while Butch stood unaffected.

Ara's markings shifted to pale silver as she translated. "He is Ahko. Scout Leader for Deep Fold Grove."

"Echo?" Jin tested the name, the 'r' rolling awkwardly off his tongue.

"Iko," Butch echoed, equally clumsy with the pronunciation.

The scout's expression remained neutral, but he repeated his name with deliberate clarity. "Ah-ko." Each syllable rang pure and distinct in the crystal-lined passage.

"Ahko," Jin and Butch said in unison, almost finally matching the proper cadence.

The scout's shoulders relaxed a fraction as he gave a slight shrug of acceptance.

"He says close enough," Ara translated, her markings brightening briefly with something like amusement.

Jin picked at the unfamiliar fungi and berries from his wooden bowl. The texture felt strange against his tongue, somewhere between mushroom and fruit, with an earthy sweetness that didn't quite match anything he knew.

Ara stood at the canyon's edge, her silver markings pulsing slowly as she scanned the darkness beyond. She hadn't touched food since they'd stopped. Her stillness made her look more statue than person, except for the occasional shift of her markings' glow against the crystal walls.

Across the makeshift camp, Ahko and his scouts huddled in their own circle, sharing a meal of similar vegetation. Their harmonics came soft and controlled, practical sounds for practical matters.

They kept their distance, maintaining clear separation between themselves and the humans.

Jin's thoughts drifted as he chewed. He pictured Mina's face the last time he saw her—eyes wide with terror as the creatures dragged her through the portal. The memory twisted his stomach into knots. Then came his father's final moments, swinging that golf club like a man possessed, fighting to reach her until the swarm of creatures overwhelmed him. Jin remembered the sickening crunch as his father's titanium driver connected with skull after skull, buying precious seconds with each desperate swing.

A firm hand squeezed his shoulder. Jin looked up to find Butch watching him with quiet understanding. The older man didn't speak, didn't need to. His presence alone anchored Jin back to the present moment.

Jin set his bowl aside, the strange fungiberry forgotten, as he studied Ara's rigid posture. Her markings cast shifting patterns against the crystal walls, betraying tension beneath her controlled exterior.

"Do you regret bringing us?" The question came quiet but direct.

Ara turned from her vigil, her silver markings dimming to a soft glow. She met Jin's gaze with deliberate focus, each word carefully shaped by unfamiliar vocal cords.

"I do not... regret." The pause stretched as she searched for precise terms. "I... choose. Hollow... not servant."

Though her speech came halting and slow, the intent behind each word carried unmistakable weight. Her markings pulsed with quiet determination, underlining her careful declaration.

From his position against the wall, Butch observed the exchange in silence. His weathered features revealed nothing, but his grip on the crowbar loosened slightly as he listened to Ara's measured response.

CHAPTER 13

Ahko's hand shot up, fingers spread in a rigid fan. His posture shifted from fluid motion to carved stone, head cocked at an angle that spoke of practiced awareness.

Ara's markings dulled to near black as she produced a low, rolling tone that made the crystal walls shiver. The sound confirmed whatever Ahko had detected, though it carried an edge of question beneath its certainty.

Jin strained his ears but caught nothing beyond the subtle whisper of their own breathing and the distant drip of water on stone. The passage seemed empty, lifeless, yet the elves' sudden alertness raised the hair on his neck.

Butch's movements became measured and deliberate. His eyes tracked upward along the crystalline formations that stretched into shadow above them. Something nagged at his senses, not quite sound, not fully instinct, but a soldier's intuition that refused to be ignored. His fingers tightened around the crowbar as he eased his weight onto the balls of his feet.

The group's pace slowed to a careful crawl. Each step landed with practiced silence as they pressed closer to the passage walls.

Ahko's hand remained raised, his fingers now curling in subtle patterns that the other scouts read with practiced ease.

Ara positioned herself between Jin and the unseen threat, her markings now completely dark except for the faintest silver outline. She moved like liquid shadow, each motion precise and controlled as she guided Jin toward a deeper patch of darkness along the wall.

The crystal-lined passage held its breath around them, waiting.

A piercing shriek shattered the crystalline silence. The Iron-Wing's cry bounced off the walls in a discordant echo that set Jin's teeth on edge. Above them, shadow became flesh as the creature dropped from its perch, wings snapping open with the brittle sound of breaking bone.

Ahko barked a series of sharp tones, but the warning came too late. The Iron-Wing's talons closed around one of the scouts, lifting him clear off the ground. The scout's spear flashed in the dim light as he twisted in the creature's grip, driving the glass tip deep into its chest.

The Iron-Wing's shriek turned wet and gurgling. Its wings seized, muscles spasming as it released the scout. Both plummeted. The scout hit the ground hard, rolling across the crystal floor with a sickening crunch. The Iron-Wing crashed beside him, its body convulsing as dark blood pooled beneath its bulk.

Chaos erupted through the narrow passage. The remaining scouts spread out in defensive formation, spears raised as their harmonics bounced off the walls in sharp, urgent patterns. The injured scout lay crumpled but moving, his breath coming in ragged gasps as he clutched his side.

Ahko's throat vibrated with layered tones, his command splitting into multiple frequencies that ricocheted off the crystal walls. The sound fractured, multiplied, and became a storm of competing harmonics that filled the passage with chaos. His scouts froze, unable to parse meaning from the acoustic mess that surrounded them.

Ara's markings flashed urgent silver as she attempted to cut through the noise. Her counter-signal, meant to stabilize and redirect the scattered sound, hit the walls and shattered into more echoes. The crystalline surfaces seemed to drink in each tone, twisting it before spitting it back distorted and wrong.

The injured scout tried to rise, his own pain-sounds adding to the acoustic tangle. Each groan bounced and warped until it became impossible to tell where the original noise had started. The passage itself seemed to be screaming, every surface throwing back its own version of their voices.

Butch watched the elves' growing confusion as they lost their primary means of coordination. Their usual fluid grace turned choppy and uncertain. Even Ahko's confident posture wavered as his attempts at control dissolved into the crystal-born cacophony.

Jin pressed his hands against his ears, but it did little good. The sounds seemed to bypass his flesh entirely, vibrating through his bones and skull. He could feel Ara's frustrated attempts to establish order, each pure note she produced immediately swallowed by the acoustic storm.

The passage had become a maze of sound, every command lost in translation, every signal corrupted by the endless reflections of crystal on crystal. What should have been precise communication had transformed into auditory quicksand, dragging them deeper into confusion with each attempted correction.

The acoustic chaos drove them apart like leaves scattered by wind. Crystalline formations split their path into jagged channels, forcing the group to separate as they sought stable ground. The scouts dove for cover, their usual coordinated movements now desperate and disjointed.

Jin's foot caught on an uneven crystal edge. He pitched forward, arms windmilling as the ground rushed up to meet him. Before he could hit the stone, Butch's hand clamped around his bicep. With a grunt, Butch hauled Jin behind a jutting crystal formation, pressing them both against its cool surface.

"Stay down," Butch muttered, his voice barely audible above the warped echoes filling the passage. His eyes tracked movement in the shadows above while keeping Jin pinned against their makeshift shelter.

Jin's chest heaved as he tried to catch his breath. The crystal at his back vibrated with discordant frequencies, each wave of sound making his teeth ache. Through gaps in the formation, he caught glimpses of the others—Ara's silver markings flashing like distant lightning, Ahko's rigid form trying to maintain some semblance of control, the scattered scouts attempting to regroup despite the acoustic interference.

Butch kept one hand firmly on Jin's shoulder, ensuring he stayed in cover as another wave of corrupted harmonics washed over them. The crowbar in Butch's other hand remained steady, ready.

A dark shape plunged through the chaos, its wingspan blocking what little light filtered through the crystals. The Iron-Wing's talons scraped against stone as it dove toward their position, sending sparks across the passage floor.

Butch's hand shot out, shoving Jin flat against the ground. The creature's wing edge caught Butch's shoulder, but he rolled with the impact. As the Iron-Wing banked for another pass, Butch tracked its movement through the storm of corrupted harmonics.

The beast wheeled tight in the confined space, wings folded close as it streaked past their crystal shelter. Butch timed his strike, letting the creature commit to its dive before stepping into its path. The crowbar's hook end swung in a precise arc, catching the Iron-Wing's shoulder muscle with a wet crack.

Butch planted his feet and yanked downward. The lighter gravity amplified his strength, turning the pull into a savage slam. The Iron-Wing hit the crystal floor with bone-crushing force, its shriek cut short by impact. Dark blood sprayed across the stone as the crowbar's hook tore through muscle and sinew.

The Iron-Wing's body twitched, its wings scraping against crystal as it struggled to right itself. Blood pooled beneath its broken form, yet still it fought, talons scrabbling for purchase on the slick stone.

Butch reversed his grip on the crowbar. His movements carried the fluid grace of muscle memory—not the clean efficiency of military training, but something rawer, learned in desperate fights where survival meant being more savage than the enemy.

The curved end of the crowbar caught the creature's jaw, forcing its head back against the crystal floor. Butch's weight followed the strike, pinning the thrashing body with his knee. The Iron-Wing's eye fixed on him—not with animal fear, but with cold intelligence that made his grip tighten.

The crowbar rose and fell. Bone cracked. Tissue split. Dark blood painted the crystal in abstract patterns. Butch's strikes carried mechanical precision, each impact calculated to inflict maximum damage. The creature's struggles weakened, then ceased altogether as its skull gave way beneath the relentless assault.

When Butch finally stepped back, his breath came in controlled bursts. Blood dripped from the crowbar's hook, marking his path as he retreated from the ruined corpse. His face remained impassive, but his knuckles showed white against the crowbar's dark metal.

The second Iron-Wing's talons raked empty air as Butch dropped and rolled, the lighter gravity lending his movements an unnatural fluidity. Blood from the first kill made the floor treacherous, but Butch used the slick surface to his advantage, sliding into a defensive crouch.

His crowbar left red streaks across the crystal as he adjusted his grip. The tool's familiar weight centered him, grounding his focus as the Iron-Wing banked for another pass. Butch's muscles coiled, ready. Each breath came measured and even, his heart settling into the steady rhythm of combat.

The Iron-Wing's wings scraped against crystal formations as it wheeled in the narrow space. Its movements carried predatory grace, but Butch recognized the calculated patience in its circling. This one had watched its companion die. It would not make the same mistakes.

Butch planted his feet, crowbar held low and close. Blood dripped from the hook end, marking time with soft plinks against stone. His eyes never left the creature above, tracking each subtle shift of wing and tail. The Iron-Wing's intelligence made it dangerous, but intelligence meant it could feel fear. Fear meant it could hesitate.

The creature's head snapped toward him, its yellow eyes reflecting pinpoints of bioluminescent light. Recognition passed between them, predator to predator, killer to killer. Butch's fingers tightened around the crowbar's shaft as he prepared to meet its attack.

Ara's markings pulsed brilliant silver as she faced the Iron-Wing on the narrow ledge. Her throat vibrated with layered harmonics, but the sound dispersed through the open chamber, losing potency as it spread. The creature's head tilted, studying her with predatory calculation.

The Iron-Wing's talons scraped crystal as it edged closer. Ara's usual defensive range would not work here; the space was too vast, stealing power from her resonance. Her markings shifted to deep crimson as she took a measured step forward.

Another step. The creature's wings mantled, creating currents of stale air. Ara's fingers tightened around her glass blade as she closed the final distance. At arm's length, the Iron-Wing's yellow eyes locked onto hers. Its muscles bunched, preparing to strike.

Ara's tone changed, not the broad harmonics she typically employed, but something concentrated and sharp. The sound hit the Iron-Wing like a physical blow at this range. Its wings seized, body going rigid as the focused resonance overwhelmed its senses.

Without hesitation, Ara drove her blade up under the creature's jaw. The glass edge parted flesh and bone with surgical precision. Dark blood spilled across the crystalline ledge as the Iron-Wing's body convulsed, then went still.

Ahko moved with practiced grace along the crystal ledge, his spear held low as he circled behind the second Iron-Wing. His boots found purchase on the slick surface, each step calculated and silent. The creature's attention remained fixed on Butch, giving Ahko the opening he needed.

The Iron-Wing's tail whipped around without warning, catching Ahko mid-stride. The impact sent him sprawling across the crystal floor, his spear clattering away into shadow. He rolled with the fall, but his shoulder struck a jagged formation with a dull crack.

Butch did not hesitate. He launched forward, crowbar abandoned as he slammed into the Iron-Wing's back. His arms locked around the creature's torso, using their combined momentum to drive it away from Ahko. The beast's wings thrashed, razor edges slicing through Butch's sleeve as they crashed against the passage wall.

Dark blood made Butch's grip treacherous as he fought to maintain his hold. The Iron-Wing's muscles twisted beneath his fingers, its spine contorting at an impossible angle as it tried to reach him with its talons. Butch pressed harder, keeping the creature pinned against the crystal surface despite its frenzied struggles.

Ara struck like liquid shadow, her glass blade finding the gap between the Iron-Wing's shoulder blades. The weapon sank deep, parting flesh and bone with terrible precision. The creature's body went rigid, then limp, its wings dropping like broken sails.

Butch released his hold, letting the carcass slump to the floor. His chest heaved as he stepped back, blood dripping from his torn sleeves. Across the passage, Ahko pulled himself upright, favoring his injured shoulder.

Their eyes met in the dim light. No words passed between them, only sharp nods of acknowledgment, the sound of ragged breathing, and the soft plink of blood on crystal.

***

Ara knelt beside the fallen scouts, her markings casting a soft silver glow across their still forms. Her fingers traced the brutal gashes where Iron-Wing talons had torn through armor and flesh. The bodies lay twisted among shattered crystal shards, their glass-tipped spears broken beside them.

Blood pooled beneath one scout's head where it had struck the wall. The other lay face down, his chest cavity crushed. Neither had stood a chance in the confined space, their harmonics scattered uselessly against the chamber's acoustics.

Butch wiped his crowbar clean on a torn piece of sleeve before sliding it through his belt. Dark stains marked his arms where the Iron-Wing's wings had sliced through fabric. His movements remained steady despite the fresh cuts, each action deliberate and controlled.

The third scout was nowhere to be seen. No blood trail marked his passage, no broken crystals indicated a struggle. He had simply vanished during the chaos of battle, leaving only silence in his wake.

Ahko stood at attention, his injured shoulder held stiff. His throat vibrated with a pure, sustained note—a soldier's farewell to fallen comrades. The tone carried respect and loss in equal measure, echoing softly through the crystal passage before fading into darkness.

The sound touched something ancient in the air, a recognition of sacrifice that needed no translation. Ara's markings pulsed once in response, acknowledging the depth of what had been lost.

Jin knelt beside the fallen scout, his hands trembling as they hovered over the broken glass blade still clutched in death-rigid fingers. The scout's face bore no expression of fear or pain—only the quiet acceptance of a warrior who knew the risks. Blood had dried along the scout's neck in delicate patterns, like dark rivers carved through copper earth.

Butch's weathered hand settled on Jin's shoulder, warm and solid. The weight anchored Jin to the present, keeping him from drowning in memories of another body—his father's final stand with a golf club against impossible odds.

"Not your fault." Butch's voice carried the gravel of experience, of too many similar moments lived through.

Jin's fingers brushed the scout's armor, tracing the intricate weave of bark and crystal. "He was protecting us. They all were."

"Yeah." Butch's grip tightened slightly, nodding his head in understanding.

The crystal walls caught their whispers, carrying them in fractured echoes before swallowing them whole. Jin's shoulders shook under Butch's hand, but no tears fell. The time for crying had passed somewhere between his sister's abduction and now.

Ahko examined the gash across his fellow scout's shoulder, producing low harmonic tones that made the wound edges pulse. The injured elf grimaced but held still, letting the sound work through damaged tissue.

Ara turned to Butch, her silver markings dimming as she noticed dark stains spreading across his sleeve. She reached for his arm, but he pulled back.

"Is fine." Butch started to rise.

Ara's hand shot out, gripping his wrist with surprising strength. "No move. Will... fester."

The word hit Butch like a physical blow. His mind flashed to images he had buried deep—wounds gone wrong in humid jungles, flesh turning black beneath hasty bandages. He pushed the memories down, forcing his breathing steady.

Ara pulled a small clay pot from her pack, the contents gleaming with bioluminescent specks. The ointment felt cool against Butch's torn skin as she spread it with practiced fingers. From another pouch, she retrieved what looked like dried moss patches tinged with purple.

The fungal bandage adhered instantly to his arm, conforming to the wound's shape. Ara leaned close, her throat vibrating with a focused tone. The patch responded, trembling against Butch's skin.

Warmth spread throughout, then settled into a gentle pulsing that matched his heartbeat.

"Falls when skin joins." Ara tapped the edge of the patch. "Good medicine. Deep Fold make."

Butch flexed his fingers, testing the bandage's give. The pain had already dulled. He nodded his thanks, and Ara's markings flickered briefly in acknowledgment before she moved to check on the others.

Ahko's harmonic tone cut through the chamber, low and urgent. The sound carried complex layers of meaning that made nearby crystals vibrate with sympathetic resonance. His glass spear traced a pattern in the air, pointing back the way they had come.

Ara's markings shifted to a muted gray as she listened. She nodded once, her own harmonics joining his in agreement. The combined tones painted a clear picture of collapse and danger.

She turned to Jin and Butch, her features tight with concentration as she formed the unfamiliar words. "No back. No..." Her fingers brushed the crystal walls, searching for the right concept. "No roof safe."

The passage groaned above them, emphasizing her point. Tiny shards of crystal rained down, glinting in the bioluminescent light.

"We go..." Ara's markings pulsed as she struggled with the translation. "Bone-path."

Butch exhaled heavily, shoulders dropping. His weathered features showed no surprise, just weary acceptance. He gave a single nod, adjusting his grip on the bloodied crowbar.

Jin looked between them, noting how Ahko's posture had stiffened at the mention of the bone-path. Whatever route lay ahead, it clearly wasn't meant for casual travel.

The crystal walls seemed to lean inward, their once-pristine surfaces now scarred and cracked from the Iron-Wing battle. The familiar harmonics of the Grove felt distant here, replaced by discordant echoes that set Jin's teeth on edge.

They turned the final bend in the fractured passage, and the mountain opened into a hollowed dome of stone. No crystal, no resonance just age and silence.

On the far wall, half-swallowed by shadow and time, stretched a mural.

Jin stepped forward, heart thudding. The light from his torch caught pigment faint, cracked, but unmistakable.

Stick figures. Two distinct groups. One with circles within circles for heads sound, memory, resonance. The other bore simple flames where their faces should be.

They stood together, side by side, facing a line of towering beings broad-shouldered, long-tailed, and reptilian-headed, drawn in jagged black strokes.

Butch squinted at it. "I don't get it."

Ara didn't answer at first. Her eyes stayed fixed on the figure with the circle head.

"We don't speak of this," she said quietly. "But the stone remembers."

Jin stared a moment longer, the shapes settling in his mind.

"I think I get it," he said softly. "But I think my college professor might want to take a look."

CHAPTER 14

They left the chamber in silence.

The mural stayed with Jin — those rippling heads, the fire-marked faces, and the towering shapes that loomed above them. He didn't know what it meant, not really. But it felt old. Important. Like something meant to be remembered, even if no one spoke of it.

Butch kept his thoughts to himself, eyes forward, jaw tight. Ara said nothing. Her markings had dimmed.

The bone-path earned its name. Massive ribs curved overhead like ancient archways, their surfaces worn smooth by time and the elements. Each bone segment dwarfed anything Jin had seen in natural history museums, twice the size of the blue whale skeleton he had once marveled at during a school trip.

Jin's fingers traced the weathered surface of what might have been a vertebra, large enough to serve as a shelter. "These can't be real. Nothing's ever been this big."

Butch kept his eyes moving, tracking shadows between the towering remains. His crowbar seemed small against the scale of their surroundings. It wasn't that he had never cared much for museums or prehistoric creatures — he just never had a chance to see any. But here, now, even he felt humbled by the sheer magnitude of what lay before them.

Ara touched one of the massive bones, producing a soft tone that made the structure resonate. The sound traveled through the skeletal maze, revealing paths and spaces beyond their sight. Her markings shifted through shades of blue as she interpreted the echoes.

Ahko moved with practiced efficiency, using his spear to point out secure paths through the bone field. His harmonics carried warnings about unstable areas where ancient remains had partially collapsed.

They passed what appeared to be a skull, its eye sockets large enough for Jin to stand in. The bone structure didn't match any creature he recognized — too many jaw hinges and strange ridges where horns or other features might have attached.

"What were these?" Jin whispered, though he wasn't sure Ara knew the English words to explain.

Ara's markings pulsed as she considered his question. She placed her hand on the massive skull, closed her eyes, and listened to something only she could hear. After a moment, she simply shook her head. Some knowledge, it seemed, was lost even to the Grove's memory.

Butch reached into his pocket, fingers brushing past the crystal shard to find his phone. The black screen reflected nothing but his own tired face. He pressed the power button. No response. With a quiet sigh, he slipped it back into his pocket.

Ara's markings flickered with curiosity as she watched the motion. Her head tilted slightly.

"Phone," Butch said before she could ask, tapping his pocket. "Not working now."

Jin pulled out his own device, its screen equally lifeless. "Been checking mine too. Nothing since we came through." He turned it over in his hands, examining the case for damage. "Maybe the portal fried them? All that energy..."

Ara stepped closer, her attention fixed on Jin's phone. Her fingers traced the air above its surface, sensing for harmonics that weren't there.

"It's for communication," Jin explained, holding it up. "Like... we use it to talk to people far away."

Ara's markings brightened with understanding. She produced a series of sharp, clear tones that carried through the bone maze, bouncing off ancient surfaces before fading into the distance. "Like whistle-song," she said, her English careful and measured. "For scouts."

"Yeah, but much further," Jin said, confused. "Across whole cities. Around the world."

Ara's markings pulsed as she processed the concept. She touched her own throat, then gestured to the phones. The implications of such technology seemed to intrigue her.

Butch watched their exchange silently, his mind on other concerns. Those phones had been their last connection to home — to emergency services, to maps, to any hope of outside help. Now they were just dead weight in their pockets, useless as stones. He slipped his phone back into his pocket. At the very least, it should be under warranty. If they got back.

The group emerged from the bone-path onto a narrow ridge where harsh sunlight bore down on exposed rock. Jin squinted against the glare, his eyes still adjusted to the dim passages they had left behind. The light felt wrong — too sharp, too direct, like standing under a magnifying glass.

Then, without warning, the temperature plummeted. Jin's breath clouded in front of his face as cold air rushed across the ridge. The shift happened so fast his skin prickled with goosebumps.

"Weather's broken here." Butch rubbed his arms, his crowbar tucked close. The metal had gone from burning hot to freezing cold against his palm in seconds. "Like someone playing with a thermostat."

Ara's markings flickered in response to each temperature swing. She produced low tones that seemed to measure the changes, her face concerned at whatever data she gathered.

Another blast of heat washed over them. Sweat beaded on Jin's forehead, only to freeze moments later when the cold returned. The cycle continued, transforming the ridge into an environmental gauntlet.

"Back home, we wait five minutes if we don't like the weather," Butch said, managing a tight smile despite his discomfort. "Here? Maybe five seconds."

Ahko's harmonics carried notes of warning. He gestured to crystalline formations along the ridge that showed signs of stress from the rapid temperature changes — hairline fractures spreading with each thermal shock.

Jin's legs burned with exhaustion as he stumbled on the uneven ridge. The wild temperature swings made every step a challenge — one moment his muscles seized from cold, the next they felt like melting wax. He slipped on a patch of frost, catching himself against the crystalline wall just as it turned scorching hot.

"Careful," Butch called back, his voice tight with concern.

Ahead, Ara and Ahko moved with practiced grace despite the conditions. Their bodies seemed to flow around the thermal disturbances as if dancing to some unheard rhythm. Jin tried to match their pace but fell further behind.

His breath came in ragged gasps. The thin air and shifting temperatures made each inhalation feel like swallowing glass. Sweat froze on his skin before it could drip.

Ahko turned back, his expression unreadable as he watched Jin struggle. The scout's harmonics carried notes that might have been impatience or criticism — Jin couldn't tell anymore. His head throbbed too much to focus on the subtle meanings.

"I need..." Jin started to say, but pride made him swallow the words. They had already lost time treating injuries and burying scouts. He couldn't be the reason for another delay.

Ara's markings pulsed with concern as she observed Jin's fatigue. She stepped toward him, but Ahko's sharp tone stopped her. The two elves exchanged rapid harmonics that set the crystal walls humming.

Butch positioned himself between Jin and the arguing elves. His crowbar tapped a quiet rhythm against his leg — a habit Jin had noticed emerged whenever tension rose in the group.

"We rest," Butch said firmly, though his voice carried an edge that suggested he expected resistance.

Ahko's response came as a burst of discordant notes. The scout's grip tightened on his spear.

***

As dusk crept across the fractured landscape, pale lights materialized in the cooling air. They drifted like dandelion seeds caught in an invisible current, each one pulsing with its own gentle rhythm.

Jin raised his hand, tracking the closest wisp. "Look at that."

Butch's fingers closed around his crowbar. The lights reminded him of lures—beautiful things that drew prey closer.

Ara's hand shot out, stopping both of them. Her markings dimmed to barely visible silver threads against her skin. "No touch. No sound. They..." She searched for the right words, her face tightening with concentration. "They watch echo."

The wisps bobbed and weaved through the air, neither approaching nor retreating. Their glow intensified whenever Ara or Ahko produced even the faintest harmonic tone. Like moths drawn to sound instead of flame, they clustered around areas where resonance lingered in the crystal walls.

One floated near Jin's face. Up close, its light revealed complex patterns swirling within—geometric shapes that shifted and reformed in endless combinations. The wisp responded to his breath, dancing away from the small disturbance in the air.

Butch lowered his crowbar but kept his grip firm. The lights didn't seem hostile, but experience had taught him that beauty often hid danger in this realm. Still, he noticed how they avoided direct contact, maintaining a careful distance from all solid matter.

Ahko stood perfectly still, watching the wisps with ancient understanding in his eyes. His usual commanding presence softened as the lights swirled around him, drawn to the residual harmonics that clung to his crystal-tipped spear.

The wisps continued their silent observation, their glow casting strange shadows across the ridge. They drifted toward every whispered word or shuffled step, transforming sound into intricate dances of light.

The crystal shard in Butch's pocket pulsed with a faint purple glow, its rhythm out of sync with the drifting lights. The wisps changed direction, drawn to this new resonance like curious fireflies. Their patterns shifted from geometric precision to chaotic swirls as they clustered around him.

Butch's hand tightened on his crowbar. The lights pressed closer, their glow intensifying until his face was bathed in their ethereal radiance. The shard's pulse quickened, matching their frequency.

Ara's throat vibrated with a deep, steady tone—not her usual harmonics, but something older and heavier. The sound rippled through the air like stones dropping into still water. The wisps dimmed instantly, their intricate patterns dissolving into simple points of light. One by one, they faded from view until only darkness remained.

She turned to Butch, her silver markings barely visible in the gloom. Her gaze fixed on his pocket where the shard lay hidden, lingering longer than comfortable. Questions burned behind her eyes, but her lips remained sealed. The silence between them felt deliberate, weighted with unspoken knowledge.

Ahko watched this exchange from his position by the ridge wall. His fingers traced patterns on his spear's crystal tip as his eyes narrowed, darting between Ara and Butch. The scout's posture remained rigid, his expression hardening with each passing moment. Suspicion radiated from him like heat from sunbaked stone.

***

The group picked their way across a vast expanse of broken crystal, each shard catching the dim light like frozen lightning. Spires jutted from the ground at impossible angles, their once-perfect geometries now reduced to jagged ruins. The fragments crunched beneath their boots, each step releasing tiny harmonics that died in the thick air.

Ara paused beside a fallen column, her markings pulsing with muted blues. "Here was song-field." Her fingers traced the crystalline surface. "Many voices. Many echoes."

She knelt and grabbed a nearby stick, sweeping away layers of grey ash to create a smooth patch of ground. With precise movements, she sketched lines and shapes—a crude map taking form in the dust. Her markings flickered as she worked, reflecting deep concentration.

Jin circled one of the larger crystal fragments, drawn to markings etched into its base. Spirals wound their way across the stone beneath the crystal, identical to the patterns they had encountered in the underground passages. His fingers hovered over the carvings, not quite touching.

"Ara," he called softly. "These symbols..."

She looked up from her map drawing, her markings shifting to a darker shade when she saw what he had found. The stick dropped from her fingers.

"Old fight," she said, her voice heavy with ancient memory. "No winner." Her hands moved in subtle gestures as she spoke, unconsciously forming shapes that mimicked the spirals.

Butch moved away from the others, scanning the ground methodically. His eyes caught a glint of purple beneath a fallen crystal spire. Kneeling, he brushed away debris to reveal another shard, this one wedged deep in dark stone. Unlike the piece that hummed in his pocket, this fragment lay inert, a dull, lifeless thing despite its perfect geometric form.

He reached for it, but Ara's hand shot out, gripping his wrist. Her markings had shifted to a deep indigo, almost black.

"Dead echo. Leave sleep." Her words came out clipped, urgent. When Butch met her gaze, he saw something close to fear in her eyes. She released his wrist and stepped back, her fingers moving in quick, defensive patterns.

Butch withdrew his hand, nodding once. Whatever power these crystals held, he trusted Ara's warning. He had seen enough in his life to know when something was better left untouched.

Jin drifted closer, drawn to the embedded shard. He crouched beside the stone, studying how the crystal's facets caught what little light filtered through the ruins. His expression turned distant, lost in thought. Even as Butch and Ara moved on, continuing their path through the crystal field, Jin lingered. His eyes remained fixed on the dead shard, as if trying to decode some message in its geometric patterns.

"Jin." Butch's voice cut through his trance. "We need to move."

Jin stood slowly, but his gaze kept drifting back to the embedded crystal. Each backward glance lasted longer than the last until the shard disappeared behind a wall of broken stone.

***

The wind screamed across the crystal wastes, driving ash and fragments before it. Butch spotted the dark opening first, a natural shallow cave carved beneath an ancient basalt ridge. The black stone rose like a wave frozen in time, its surface scarred by whatever catastrophe had shattered the crystal field.

"Here." He gestured to the others, already moving toward the shelter.

Ahko entered first, sending precise harmonic pings into the darkness to map the space. His tones returned clean—no threats, no hidden passages, just solid rock and blessed stillness. The scout's shoulders relaxed a fraction as he moved deeper.

Jin stumbled in after him, exhaustion evident in every line of his body. He slid down against the smooth basalt wall, letting his head fall back against the cool stone. The wind howled overhead, but inside the hollow its fury became distant, muted.

Ara paused at the entrance, her markings cycling through shades of green and blue as she performed her own sound check of the space. The patterns of light played across the basalt walls, creating ghostly shadows that danced and faded.

"Safe echo," she confirmed, joining the others. "Wind stays out."

The shallow cave curved inward like a half-moon, just deep enough to shelter them from the elements while maintaining a clear view of the crystal field beyond. The basalt walls absorbed sound rather than reflecting it like the crystals outside, creating a pocket of near silence that felt almost sacred after their long trek through the ruins.

Butch positioned himself near the entrance, crowbar within easy reach. The weapon's metal surface bore fresh scratches from their earlier encounter with the Iron-Wings. He watched ash swirl past the opening, but the wind's fingers could not reach inside their shelter.

Jin huddled closer to the cave wall, wrapping his arms around his knees. The memory of those pale lights still burned behind his eyelids—their geometric dance, the way they had clustered around Butch's crystal.

"What were those things?" His voice cracked from thirst and exhaustion. "Those lights back there."

Ara's markings shifted to a deep indigo as she traced patterns in the settled ash with her fingertip. "Memory. Old, but not gone."

"Memory of what?" Jin leaned forward, watching her fingers move through the grey powder.

She paused, silver eyes distant. Her markings pulsed once, bright then dim. "Echo stays. In crystal, in bone, in air. Sometimes... becomes light."

Ahko produced a sharp harmonic note that made Jin's teeth ache. Ara responded with a softer tone, their exchange brief but tense. The scout's expression remained unreadable as he resumed his watch position.

"You mean they're actually memories? Like, floating around out there?" Jin glanced toward the hollow's entrance where ash continued to spiral past.

Ara nodded slowly. "Your kind would say... ghost? No. Not spirit. Just... echo. Sound never dies here. Light never fades. Only changes shape."

Butch's hand drifted to his pocket where the crystal shard lay hidden. "That why they came at me?"

"Crystal remembers old songs." Ara's markings flickered with uncertainty. "Remembers... more than should."

Butch settled at the edge, legs dangling over a light drop. The crystal shard pressed against his palm, cold despite his body heat. Below, the ruined valley stretched like a wound, its crystalline bones catching what little light filtered through the ash-filled sky.

Ara lowered herself beside him, her movements fluid and silent. Her markings had dimmed to barely visible silver threads across her skin. She did not speak or move, just shared the silence as ash drifted past them in lazy spirals.

The wind died down, leaving only the subtle pulse of the shard against Butch's calloused hand. Each throb felt like a word just beyond understanding, a whisper in a language he had never learned but somehow recognized. The sensation crept up his arm, into his chest, settling somewhere behind his sternum.

Ara hummed—a single, pure note that rippled through the air. The sound should have made him flinch, should have triggered that instinctive resistance he had shown to all their harmonics. But Butch did not move. The note passed through him like water through sand, leaving only the crystal's steady pulse.

"Starting to hear more than I want to," he muttered, eyes fixed on the distant horizon where crystal spires jutted like broken teeth.

***

The group gathered their minimal belongings, preparing to venture back into the crystal wastes. Jin stretched his stiff muscles while Butch checked his crowbar's grip, worn smooth from constant use.

Ara and Ahko froze mid-motion. Their heads snapped up in perfect synchronization, ears lifting as they oriented toward something beyond human perception. Ara's markings shifted from silver to a deep purple, while Ahko's fingers tightened around his glass-tipped spear.

The two elves tilted their heads at identical angles, like predators catching a distant scent. Neither moved, their bodies held in perfect stillness as they listened to frequencies far beyond mortal range.

Jin glanced at Butch, who shrugged and kept his crowbar ready. Whatever the elves detected remained hidden from human senses. No sound reached their ears, and no movement caught their eyes across the crystal-strewn landscape.

Ara's markings pulsed with increasing urgency, though she maintained her rigid posture. Ahko shifted his weight to a defensive stance, yet neither elf made a sound. Their focused concentration transformed them into living statues, every muscle tensed as they processed whatever distant signal had captured their attention.

The crystal shard in Butch's pocket remained cold and silent, offering no insight into what commanded such intense focus from their elven guides.

After several tense moments, Ara's markings faded back to their usual silvery hue. Her posture relaxed, though a new tension lined her face. Ahko lowered his spear tip to the ground, his earlier defensive stance melting away.

Both elves produced identical pure tones, short, crisp notes that hung in the air for a heartbeat before dissipating into the crystal-laden wind.

"What was that about?" Butch kept his grip firm on the crowbar, scanning the horizon for threats that never materialized.

Jin stepped closer to Ara, trying to read her expression. "Did something happen?"

"Council calls." Ara's words came slow and measured, each syllable carefully formed. "They want us return to Grove."

Ahko's face remained impassive as he watched the exchange, his spear now planted firmly in the ashen ground. His eyes never left the humans, studying their reactions with the careful attention of a seasoned scout.

"Wait, what council? How did they even reach us out here?" Jin looked between the two elves, confusion evident in his furrowed brow.

"You hear something now?" Butch asked, his weathered features skeptical.

"Message comes through echo stone of stone and air." Ara touched the crystal formations beside them. "Just those born with these." She gestured to her large seashell-shaped ears. "Council wants speak with us."

Jin frowned, glancing at the distant horizon where the Grove lay hidden beyond sight. "That signal came all the way from there?"

Ara shook her head, silver markings shifting as she considered how to explain. "Direct harmonic cannot reach so far." She pressed her palm against a crystal formation. "We send tone-echo-tone, like…" She paused, searching for the right words. "Like shouting in canyon, but sound travels through crystal and air humans cannot hear."

Ahko produced a series of overlapping tones that resonated through the nearby formations, demonstrating the principle. The harmonics rippled outward, creating subtle patterns in the crystalline structures before fading away.

"Relay towers," Ara continued, sketching lines in the ash with her finger. "Each catches echo, sends to next, until reaches forward scout." She pointed to several spots on her crude map, indicating the network of transmission points. "Ancient system, from before my time."

Ahko nodded, adding his own harmonic note that seemed to confirm her explanation. His expression remained neutral, but his posture suggested pride in the sophisticated communication network.

"Council knows where we are," Ara said, glancing at Ahko. "He sends position updates through relay." She gestured to her fellow elf. "Tells them which path we take, what dangers we find."

Jin looked between the two elves, understanding dawning on his face as he realized they had never truly been beyond the Council's reach.

Ahko pivoted sharply, his glass-tipped spear sweeping an arc through the ashen air as he oriented himself. Without a word or backward glance, he set off at a brisk pace along a new heading that cut diagonally to their previous path. His movements carried the fluid certainty of one who knew exactly where he needed to go.

Ara fell into step behind him, her usual measured grace replaced by a soldier's disciplined march. Her silver markings pulsed with a steady rhythm that matched their footfalls across the crystal-strewn ground. The casual observer might have mistaken her for Ahko's shadow, so perfect was her mirroring of his path and pace.

Jin shot Butch a questioning look but received only a slight head shake in response. The Filipino's weathered features had settled into the calm mask he wore when reading dangerous situations. His grip adjusted on the crowbar as he took position behind Ara, leaving enough space to swing if needed.

The quartet moved through the wasteland with mechanical precision. Ahko chose paths that avoided the larger crystal formations, leading them through spaces where the ground felt more stable beneath their feet. Each step kicked up small clouds of grey ash that clung to their clothes and skin.

Jin brought up the rear, trying to match the others' careful footwork. The sudden shift in their group's dynamic felt like a physical weight pressing against his chest. Gone was the cautious but collaborative atmosphere of their previous travel, replaced by something that felt more like a military escort.

The crystal shard in Butch's pocket remained cold and silent as they walked, offering no insight into the Council's summons that had transformed their mission so completely. Only the sound of boots crunching through ash and the occasional whisper of wind through crystal formations broke the tense silence.

The group moved in tight formation through the crystal wastes. Ahko led with unwavering focus, each step precise and measured. Ara matched his pace exactly, her silver markings dulled to a muted grey that reflected their somber mood. Butch kept his crowbar ready while maintaining a steady distance behind the elves. Jin brought up the rear, trying to process the sudden shift in their dynamic.

No one spoke. The only sounds were boots crunching through ash and the whisper of wind across crystal formations. Even the usual harmonic communications between Ara and Ahko had ceased, replaced by an alertness that seemed to draw energy from the very air.

The landscape began to transform subtly as they progressed. Patches of luminescent fungi appeared more frequently along their path, their blue-green glow intensifying with each cluster they passed. The crystal formations grew shorter but more numerous, creating a maze-like pattern that Ahko navigated with practiced ease.

Tendrils of phosphorescent light crept along the ground, weaving between rocks and crystal shards. The pale illumination cast strange shadows that danced across their faces. Above them, strings of bioluminescent growth draped from crystalline outcrops like living curtains, their light pulsing with gentle rhythm.

The air grew thicker, carrying the complex scents of organic decay and mineral-rich moisture. Fungal colonies spread across the walls in geometric patterns, their glow responding to the group's presence with subtle fluctuations in brightness. The harsh edges of the wasteland softened under layers of living light.

Jin noticed how the fungal illumination seemed to follow their movement, creating a corridor of gentle radiance that guided their way. The effect transformed the previously stark landscape into something almost beautiful, despite the tension that still gripped their small party.

As the familiar bioluminescent curtains of the Grove's outer threshold came into view, Ara held up her hand, bringing the group to a halt. Her silver markings pulsed with cautionary patterns.

"Step careful. They listen before they speak." Her words came out in measured tones, each syllable precisely formed.

Jin recognized the entrance passage where they had first arrived, but something felt different. The harmonic resonance that had once filled the air now held a sharper edge, like music played slightly out of tune. The walls themselves seemed to vibrate with heightened awareness.

Butch adjusted his grip on the crowbar, noting how the fungal lights dimmed slightly at their approach instead of brightening as they had before. His pocket remained cold where the crystal shard rested, offering no insight into the changed atmosphere.

Ahko produced a series of pure tones that echoed through the crystalline structures. The sound carried authority and formal protocol, unlike his usual tactical signals. He waited, head tilted, as the harmonics rippled outward through the Grove's outer chambers.

The response came as a complex wave of overlapping frequencies that made Jin's teeth ache. Ara's markings flickered rapidly as she processed the message, while Ahko's posture stiffened further. The Grove's answer clearly carried more meaning than simple acknowledgment.

Butch noticed how both elves positioned themselves slightly differently than during their first visit—Ara closer to the humans, Ahko maintaining precise distance between them and the entrance. Their careful positioning spoke volumes about the changed situation, even if the humans could not hear the actual conversation taking place through harmonic frequencies.

The crystal formations lining the threshold pulsed with deep purple light, their patterns more rigid and geometric than the organic flows they had displayed previously. The Grove itself seemed to hold its breath, waiting.

CHAPTER 15

A layered harmonic call rippled through the crystal passages, its overlapping tones carrying unmistakable authority. Ara's markings shifted from muted grey to brilliant silver as she processed the summons. Without hesitation, she gestured for Butch and Jin to follow.

"The Council calls. You come with me." Her words carried the same weight as the harmonics that had summoned her.

Ahko stepped forward, his stance rigid with protocol. "Hollow, these are not our kind. The Inner Sanctum—"

Ara cut him off with a single pure note that made nearby crystals resonate. Her markings pulsed with authority as she faced him. "They walk with me."

The scout commander's fingers tightened on his spear, but he could not challenge a Hollow's direct command. He fell back, jaw clenched, as Ara led her companions toward the heart of the Grove.

The passage narrowed as they descended, its walls closer and more organic than the outer chambers. Each step produced echoes that felt wrong—too sharp, too lasting. The sound of Jin's boots against stone repeated unnaturally, bouncing back with harmonics that should not exist. Even Butch's measured breathing seemed to catch and multiply in the air.

Jin opened his mouth to speak, but Ara raised her hand for silence. The passage itself rejected sound, turning every noise into discordant waves that pressed against their ears. Only Ara's movements produced clean tones, her steps blending perfectly with the Grove's natural resonance.

They walked in enforced quiet, surrounded by walls that transformed their smallest sounds into warnings. The crystal formations grew denser, their purple light more concentrated. Bioluminescent fungi retreated from their path instead of reaching toward them as before.

Butch kept his crowbar close, noting how even the metal's slight tap against his leg created uncomfortable reverberations. The crystal shard in his pocket remained cold and still, as if hiding from the Grove's attention.

Dozens of elven faces lined the curved walls of the Inner Sanctum, their copper-brown skin catching the purple light of embedded crystals. Not a single young face appeared among them; these were the elders and adults of the Grove, their grey eyes sharp with centuries of wisdom and prejudice.

Jin fought the urge to shrink under their collective gaze. The elders' stillness felt predatory, like cats watching prey. Only the rise and fall of their chests betrayed life as harmonics filled the chamber—deep, resonant tones that made Jin's bones ache.

Butch stood straight-backed beside him, crowbar hanging loose but ready at his side. The veteran's face remained neutral, but his knuckles whitened around the metal as the harmonics grew stronger.

The Council members wore simple robes adorned with spiral patterns that seemed to shift in the crystal light. Their silence spoke volumes—no greetings, no acknowledgment beyond those penetrating stares that tracked every human movement.

"They see you. They decide now." Ara's voice carried forced calm, but tension threaded through each word. Her markings pulsed with muted urgency as she positioned herself slightly ahead of Jin and Butch, a subtle shield between her charges and her people.

The harmonics swelled, multiple tones weaving together into something that pressed against Jin's chest like a physical weight. Still, the elders made no other movement, their faces masks of stone as they observed the outsiders who had breached their sacred space.

*****

The Council's harmonics shifted, directing focused tones toward Ara. Her markings rippled as she absorbed their resonant questions, translating selectively for Jin and Butch.

"They ask what you are. Why you came. What fire brought you through the tear."

Butch's grip tightened on his crowbar. The ceremony felt wrong, too formal, too controlled. He kept his response direct and grounded.

"I'm here because they took people. Jin needs help finding his sister. That's all I know, that's all I can say."

Ara's voice carried his words into pure harmonics, the sound echoing through the chamber. She turned to Jin, her markings pulsing with encouragement.

Jin stepped forward, his voice shaking. "We're humans, from Earth. Another place, another world. There was a portal, an opening. A violet tear that brought creatures to our home." His hands clenched as memories flooded back. "They took my sister, Mina. They took so many others. She's all I have left after they killed my father."

His voice cracked. Tears welled in his eyes as the image of his father fighting them burned in his mind. Ara's markings flared brilliant silver as she pressed her forehead to Jin's temple. She channeled his raw grief and desperation, projecting the emotional echo toward the Council — his sister's terrified face, his father's sacrifice, the violet portal swallowing lives whole.

"Please," Jin pleaded, the word breaking. "Help me find her. Help us find all of them. The goblins took them."

At the translation of *goblins*, a ripple of recognition passed through the chamber. Those who hadn't received Ara's projection whispered their own word for the creatures, the sound harsh and guttural. Fear and ancient anger flickered across copper-brown faces as the elders exchanged knowing looks.

"They're in danger," Jin continued, tears flowing freely now. "Every moment we wait... please. Please help us find them."

***

Jin slumped against the crystal wall outside the Council chamber, his shoulders shaking. The harmonics still hummed through the stone, but the words remained indecipherable. His hands trembled as he pressed them against his face.

"What if... what if they refuse?" Jin's voice cracked. "What if they keep us here? Every minute we waste, Mina could be..."

"Hey." Butch's voice cut through Jin's spiral, his Filipino accent thick and sharp. He gripped Jin's shoulder with calloused fingers. "Look at me."

Jin raised his head, meeting Butch's steady gaze.

"Even if they don't help us, we go." Butch's words carried the weight of absolute certainty. "We find your sister. We find our people. With or without them."

"But how..."

"And they cannot stop us." Butch's accent grew heavier, each word deliberate and dangerous. His grip tightened on Jin's shoulder. "Just let them try."

The crystal walls seemed to absorb the threat, carrying its echo through the ancient stone. Jin stared at Butch, seeing something older, harder a man who had faced impossible odds before and refused to yield.

"You understand me?" Butch's voice remained low, but iron ran through it. "We don't need their permission. We need information, yes. But after that?" He released Jin's shoulder, straightening to his full height. "After that, they either help or they stay out of our way."

Ara emerged from the shadows of the crystal passage, her silver markings pulsing with a soft violet glow. Her bare feet made no sound against the stone floor as she approached Butch and Jin.

"I will help," she said in careful English, each word precise despite her accent. "Even if my people won't."

Jin started to speak, but Ara tapped her large, seashell-shaped ear with a slender finger.

"Good hearing." Her lips curved into a slight smile. "But do not worry about others listening. Only I understand your words."

***

Hours crawled by, marked only by the subtle shifts in the crystal's phosphorescence and Butch's internal rhythm. The massive doors finally parted with a resonant hum that vibrated through the stone floor.

Ara straightened, her markings shifting from silver to a deep purple. She gestured for Jin and Butch to follow, her movements precise and formal.

The Council chamber stretched upward into darkness, its walls lined with crystalline formations that caught and amplified every sound. Dozens of elders sat in tiered circles, their copper-brown skin and elaborate markings glowing in the dim light. Their glass-tipped staffs rested against ornate chairs carved from living crystal.

Butch's boots echoed against the stone floor as they approached the center. The crowbar at his belt felt heavier with each step. Jin walked beside him, shoulders back despite the tremor in his hands.

The Council's combined harmonics filled the chamber, not with sound, but with presence. The air itself seemed to thicken. Jin swayed slightly, overwhelmed by the resonance. Butch remained steady, the frequencies washing over him without effect.

Ara positioned herself slightly ahead of them, her stance protective rather than submissive. Her markings pulsed in rhythm with the chamber's energy as she faced the assembled elders. The highest tier held three figures whose elaborate markings spiraled across their entire bodies, their eyes reflecting centuries of accumulated knowledge.

Ara lifted her chin, silver markings blazing as she prepared to speak for her human companions before the assembled Council.

Ara's markings flickered erratically as she translated the Council's harmonics, her voice growing tight. "They propose the Test of Echo, a field that reads your..." She paused, searching for words. "Your truth inside. Not strength. Not skill. What you are."

Her markings flared crimson. "This test is sacred. Dangerous. Not for outsiders. Never for—" She broke off, turning to the Council with a sharp tone that made the crystals shiver.

The eldest member's response needed no translation. His gesture was final, absolute.

"No." Butch's voice cut through the harmonics. "Just me. Jin stays."

Jin stepped forward. "Like hell. We do this togeth—"

"Not happening." Butch's hand clamped on Jin's shoulder. "Your sister needs you alive."

Ara's fingers trembled as she conveyed Butch's words through harmonic tones. The Council stirred, their markings rippling with interest.

"Tell them that's my only offer." Butch's grip tightened on his crowbar. "Or else."

Ara hesitated, her markings pulsing deep purple. When she translated, she didn't speak the threat. She didn't need to. Butch's stance, the way he held his weapon, the cold calculation in his eyes, all screamed across the chamber's resonant field.

The Council members' markings flickered in rapid patterns. They recognized the promise of violence in Butch's bearing, the absolute certainty that he would tear through their sacred halls if pushed.

***

The Council's harmonics rippled through the chamber, a swift exchange that lasted mere breaths. Their markings pulsed in synchronized patterns, conveying decisions faster than spoken words could travel.

Ara's shoulders tensed as she absorbed their response. Her silver markings darkened to stormy grey. She stepped forward, her harmonics rising in passionate defense. The sound made the crystal walls sing, carrying the weight of her conviction.

The eldest Council member lifted his staff. The crystal tip flared, cutting off Ara's plea mid-tone. His response came in short, sharp frequencies that brooked no argument.

Ara's markings flickered with suppressed emotion as she turned to Butch and Jin. "They accept your terms." Her voice carried an edge of barely contained frustration. "But they refuse my request to guide you through the test."

The Council's harmonics continued, each elder adding layers of sound that built into an impenetrable wall of denial. Ara's fingers clenched at her sides, her markings cycling through shades of grey and purple as she fought to maintain composure.

She tried once more, her harmonics taking on a formal, almost ritual quality. The sound echoed off the crystal walls, carrying ancient undertones of duty and obligation.

The Council's response was immediate and final. Their combined harmonics crashed through the chamber like a physical force, making Jin stumble back. Even Butch felt it this time, not as sound, but as pressure against his skin.

Ara's markings went completely dark. She bowed her head, defeat evident in every line of her body.

***

The elders led Butch to a circular chamber where a shallow pool of grey ash spread across the floor. Crystalline formations jutted through the surface like broken glass, their edges catching what little light filtered down from above.

Butch removed his shoes and rolled up his pants. The ash felt cool between his toes as he stepped into the pool. It shifted and swirled around his feet, responding to his presence with subtle movements that seemed almost alive.

Nothing happened.

The crystals remained dark. The ash continued its lazy dance around his ankles. The chamber held its breath, waiting.

Ara's markings pulsed with rapid, anxious patterns. Her hands clenched at her sides as she watched, every muscle taut with tension. The elders exchanged quick harmonics, their tones carrying notes of confusion and impatience.

Jin's heart hammered in his chest. He took an involuntary step forward, stopped only by Ara's outstretched arm. His eyes darted between Butch's stoic face and the dead crystals, searching for any sign of change. The longer the silence stretched, the tighter his throat became.

"What's wrong?" Jin whispered, his voice barely a breath. "Why isn't anything happening?"

But Ara didn't answer. She stood frozen, her markings cycling through shades of grey as she held her breath, watching the ash swirl around Butch's feet with an intensity that bordered on fear.

The ash beneath Butch's feet flickered with a faint purple glow. The crystal shard in his pocket pulsed in response, its warmth spreading through the fabric of his clothes. Ancient symbols carved into the chamber walls ignited one by one, creating a circle of violet light that cast strange shadows across the gathered faces.

Butch stood unmoved at the center of the pool while chaos erupted around him. The Council members staggered as if struck, their markings flaring wildly. Jin dropped to his knees, hands pressed against his temples. Ara's silver patterns strobed erratically as she braced herself against the wall.

A high-pitched whine filled the chamber, building to impossible frequencies. One of the eldest Council members collapsed, his staff clattering against the stone floor. Others rushed to help him, their movements jerky and uncoordinated as they fought against the sound.

The crystals mounted atop their ceremonial staffs began to vibrate. Cracks appeared in their surfaces, spreading like lightning across glass. One by one, they shattered with sharp reports that punctuated the rising harmonic assault. Crystalline shards rained down, scattering across the ash-covered floor.

Through it all, Butch remained still. The sound passed through him like water through a sieve, leaving no impression. The ash continued its lazy dance around his feet, now glowing with steady purple light. His expression stayed neutral, almost bored, as he watched the Council members struggle to maintain their composure amid the acoustic storm.

"Butch?" Jin called out, his voice strained against the piercing frequencies.

But Butch didn't respond. He simply stood in the pool of illuminated ash, the shard in his pocket pulsing in time with the symbols that burned ever brighter on the ancient walls.

***

The Council chamber erupted into chaos as the elders argued through discordant harmonics. Their markings flashed with competing colors, some bright silver with reverence, others dark crimson with fury. The crystal shards from their shattered staffs still littered the floor, crunching beneath their feet as they paced and gestured.

One elder pressed his forehead against the wall, producing deep resonant tones that made the chamber vibrate. "The ash responded. The walls awakened. He carries the old frequencies within him."

"He destroyed our focusing crystals with his mere presence," another shot back, her markings pulsing angry red. "His very nature disrupts the Grove's harmonics. He is discord given form."

The debate split the Council into factions. Those who saw Butch as fulfillment of ancient prophecies pointed to how the Test's ash had danced around him, how the forgotten symbols had ignited at his touch. Others viewed him as a threat, arguing that anything capable of shattering Grove crystals could not be trusted.

Ara stood apart from the arguing elders, her silver markings dimmed to a troubled grey. She watched Butch through narrowed eyes as he leaned against the far wall, seemingly unaffected by the harmonic chaos swirling around him.

Something about his presence felt fundamentally wrong, like a reflection in troubled water. His immunity to their harmonics could mean many things. The old stories spoke of both saviors and destroyers who walked untouched by sound.

But Ara had seen him fight. She had witnessed his protective instincts and his calculated mercy. The Test had revealed his power, yes, but not his purpose. Her markings shifted through uncertain patterns as she weighed the evidence against legend.

The Council's argument grew more heated, their harmonics clashing in painful waves. Some called for Butch's immediate expulsion from the Grove. Others demanded he be taken deeper, to the ancient chambers where the first crystals were found.

The harmonics reached a fever pitch, overlapping tones threatening to crack the very walls. An elder with copper-brown skin stepped forward, his markings blazing silver as he gestured at Butch.

"The ash remembers what we forgot. No human has triggered such resonance since the Time of Burning."

Another elder pressed both hands against a crystal formation. "The patterns match the ancient records. When the towers fell, when the first portals opened—"

"Enough." Ara's voice cut through their harmonics like a blade. Her markings pulsed with calm, steady light as she moved to stand between Butch and the Council. "You see what you expect to see. You hear what you fear to hear."

The chamber fell silent. Even the walls seemed to hold their breath.

"He is not fire," Ara said, her tone carrying the weight of certainty. "He is mirror. What you fear, he shows."

The elders exchanged troubled glances as her words settled into the silence. One of them touched a broken crystal staff, producing a weak harmonic that Butch absorbed without effect.

"Look how the ash moved for him," Ara continued. "Not with destruction, with recognition. The walls didn't crack. They awakened. They remembered."

Jin watched from the doorway as Ara's markings shifted to a deep blue, matching the ancient symbols that still glowed on the walls, the color of truth-speaking and memories unveiled.

"Your crystals shattered because they held frequencies that should have died ages ago. He didn't break them. He revealed what was already broken."

Jin moved to stand beside Butch, his shoulder brushing the older man's arm in quiet solidarity. The Council's harmonics had settled into an uneasy silence, broken only by the soft crunch of crystal shards under shifting feet.

"What did you feel in there?" Jin asked, keeping his voice low. "When the ash started glowing?"

Butch shrugged, his expression carefully neutral. "Nothing. Just ash under my feet."

"But the symbols, the purple light—"

"Maybe that's normal." Butch's hand drifted to his pocket, then deliberately moved away. "Maybe they're just seeing what they want to see."

The elders watched their exchange with intense focus, their markings rippling in response to each word. Butch met their stares with calm indifference.

"Look," Butch addressed the Council through Ara, his voice steady. "I don't know what your test proved. But we came here for one reason — to find the people taken from our world. You can help us, or you can let us go find them ourselves."

Ara translated, her harmonics carrying the weight of his words. The Council stirred, their markings flickering between colors as they processed his response.

"The test results mean something to you," Butch continued. "Fine. Use that however you want. But we're not leaving without finding those hostages."

***

The group emerged from the Grove's inner chambers into the phosphorescent-lit tunnels when rapid footsteps echoed through the crystal walls. A young elf scout sprinted toward them, his markings pulsing with urgent rhythms. He skidded to a halt before Ara, pressing his forehead against a crystal formation to transmit his message.

Ara's markings flashed crimson. Her fingers traced patterns in the air as she absorbed the harmonic report, each gesture growing sharper and more precise. The scout's own markings dimmed to a dull amber as he completed his transmission.

Jin stepped closer, reading the tension in Ara's shoulders. "What is it?"

"Distant site," Ara said, her newly learned English clipped and careful. "Scouts see... movement. Many bodies. Goblins."

Butch's hand tightened around his crowbar. "How far?"

But Ara didn't answer. Her gaze fixed on Butch with an intensity that made the air feel heavy. Her markings shifted through colors Jin had never seen before deep violet bleeding into something darker, almost black. When she finally spoke, her voice caught on the words as though they burned her throat.

"You..." She touched her throat, struggling with the human sounds. "You must lead."

The scout watched their exchange with evident confusion, his own harmonics creating subtle ripples in the tunnel's atmosphere. Ara's markings pulsed once, twice, before settling into a steady silver glow.

"Or burn," she finished, the words falling like stones into silence.

CHAPTER 16

The journey to Fracture Vale stretched across three grueling days. Butch's muscles ached from climbing through twisted crystal formations, while Jin struggled with the alien atmosphere that felt too pure, too sharp in his lungs. Ara and the scout led them through paths that seemed to defy gravity, where shadows bent wrong and distance warped like heat mirages.

The Vale revealed itself gradually, a massive canyon system split by violent geological forces. Ancient ruins dotted its cliffsides, half-buried in crystalline growths. Purple veins of mineral deposits pulsed through the rock walls like frozen lightning.

"Goblins claim this ground," Ara explained, her voice carrying unusual weight. "Many tribes gather here. Make nest in old vaults, broken places."

The scout produced harmonics that made nearby crystals resonate. Ara translated the tactical report: over two hundred goblins moving through the lower passages, more than any recent gathering. They had taken the women through these canyons.

Butch studied the terrain through narrowed eyes. Broken pillars and fallen arches suggested this place once held significance beyond its current residents. The ruins bore sophisticated architectural elements that the crude goblin camps could not have produced.

"The Vale remembers," Ara said, noting his attention to the ruins. "Before goblins, before Grove, others built here." She traced her fingers along a partially buried glyph. "Now goblins rule deep paths. Use old tunnels, old machines they find. Make territory none challenge."

The scout's harmonics shifted to warning tones. Ara nodded grimly. "Vale dangerous. Tectonic instability. Ground shifts without pattern. Paths appear, disappear. Goblins know safe ways through chaos."

The scouting party moved like shadows through the Vale's twisting passages. Ahko took point, his lean frame barely visible against the crystal-studded walls. Behind him, Ara's silver markings provided the only real illumination, pulsing with subdued light that matched her careful steps.

Butch's shoulders burned under the weight of extra supplies—medical packs, climbing gear, emergency rations. The crowbar hung at his belt, its familiar weight a comfort against the alien landscape. The lighter gravity helped, but hours of vertical climbing had taken their toll.

Jin kept his eyes on the deeper shadows where the purple crystal light could not reach. Every scrape of loose rock made him flinch, remembering the Iron-Wings' attack. The seven elite scouts Ahko had chosen moved in perfect coordination, their glass-tipped spears catching purple reflections as they maintained defensive positions around the group.

Ahko raised his fist. The formation froze. His fingers moved in precise patterns—signals the scouts understood instantly. Two broke off to secure the high ground while three others checked a narrow pass ahead. The remaining pair maintained rear guard, their harmonics reduced to barely perceptible vibrations.

Ara stood beside Ahko, her usual grace replaced by combat-ready tension. Her markings dimmed further as she matched Ahko's tactical silence. When she did move, it was with the same military precision as the other scouts, evidence of training that went beyond her role as a Hollow.

The group advanced through the Vale's throat, where crystal formations created natural choke points. Ancient rubble forced them to climb single file over fallen columns. Scorch marks and deep claw gouges in the stone spoke of recent goblin activity. The scouts' eyes tracked every shadow, every possible ambush point, while maintaining perfect silence.

Jin's whisper barely carried over the sound of shifting crystal. "Shouldn't there be more of us for this?"

Butch kept his eyes on the terrain ahead while adjusting the crowbar at his belt. "This ain't the fight. This is just to look, see what we dealing with."

A soft harmonic tone emanated from Ahko's direction—not quite agreement, but acknowledgment of Butch's tactical assessment. The scout commander's fingers traced quick signals to his team, directing their movements through the narrowing passage.

Ara's silver markings pulsed once as she turned to Jin. "Warpath comes later. Today, we watch."

Her words carried the weight of experience, suggesting she had done this before, slipping through enemy territory with minimal forces, gathering intelligence rather than engaging. The eight elite scouts moved like shadows among the crystal formations, their glass-tipped spears catching purple reflections as they maintained perfect spacing.

Jin noticed how the scouts positioned themselves—never bunching up, always maintaining clear lines of fire, covering each other's blind spots with practiced efficiency. This was not a war party; it was a reconnaissance team, chosen for stealth and speed rather than raw combat power.

The Vale's twisted geography worked in their favor, providing countless places to observe from while staying hidden. Natural crystal formations offered cover, while the irregular terrain created acoustic dead zones where even goblin patrols would not hear them pass.

The group paused at a crystal-studded ledge overlooking a narrow ravine. Scattered below lay the remains of a goblin camp— fire pits still warm, bones picked clean and discarded without ceremony. But something about the scene made Butch's combat instincts flare.

The bones showed precise cuts, cleaner than goblin weapons could manage. Deep grooves in the crystal walls formed perfect geometric patterns, too sophisticated for the crude tools found abandoned nearby.

Jin knelt to examine a shattered spear shaft. "Different from the ones we fought before."

Ara's markings shifted to a muted gray as she traced the strange marks in the crystal. Her fingers followed the geometric grooves, testing their depth and angle. The familiar certainty in her movements faltered.

"Something else walked here. Not goblin. Not ours." Her voice carried an edge of genuine confusion.

Ahko produced a questioning harmonic, but Ara shook her head. The scout commander examined the precise cuts in the bone pile, his experienced eyes finding details that did not match known patterns.

The scouts spread out in defensive positions, their glass-tipped spears ready. Even their harmonics felt uncertain, probing the strange geometric scars for answers that refused to come.

***

Steam rose from a narrow fissure in the crystalline rock, carrying an unnatural warmth that felt more mechanical than volcanic. The group settled against the weathered stone face, their muscles aching from hours of vertical climbing through the Vale's treacherous paths.

Butch dragged his sleeve across his forehead, the fabric coming away dark with sweat. The heat pressed against them like a physical force, different from Earth's natural thermal vents. His crowbar felt hot where it touched the ground.

Jin slumped against the crystal wall, his vision swimming as waves of artificial warmth washed over him. The lighter gravity of this realm usually helped with fatigue, but something about this heat drained his strength faster than normal exertion.

Ara pressed her palm flat against the rock surface, her silver markings shifting through shades of amber and copper. Her fingers traced patterns in the condensation that formed around the vent, testing the rhythm of the heat pulses. The steam carried vibrations that made her markings flicker in response.

The scouts maintained their defensive positions despite the oppressive temperature, their glass-tipped spears reflecting distorted purple light through the rising vapor. Ahko watched Ara's examination of the vent with professional interest, recognizing something in the way her markings responded to the artificial warmth.

The shard in Butch's pocket pulsed with a faint violet glow, its rhythm matching a subtle vibration that trembled through the crystalline ground beneath their feet. He pressed his hand against the rock wall, feeling the mechanical beat travel up his arm.

Ara dropped to one knee, her palm flat against the heated stone. Her markings shifted from amber to a deep purple as she tilted her head, listening to something beyond human perception. Her fingers spread wider, seeking contact with the surface while her expression hardened into focused concentration.

Ahko's grip tightened on his glass-tipped spear, knuckles whitening as he watched Ara's reaction. The weapon's edge caught purple reflections from her markings, casting strange shadows across his copper-brown features. His jaw clenched, but he remained silent, years of military discipline holding back whatever concerns darkened his eyes.

The steam continued to rise around them, carrying that artificial warmth that felt wrong against their skin. Jin watched the interplay between the elves, noting how the other scouts subtly adjusted their positions in response to Ahko's tension.

Butch pulled the shard from his pocket, its pulsing now strong enough to feel against his palm. The crystal's internal patterns seemed to shift and flow with each beat of the hidden rhythm. His eyes met Ara's, and something passed between them, a shared recognition of whatever force drove both crystal and stone to resonate in perfect synchronization.

The vibration continued its steady pulse, like the heartbeat of some vast machine buried deep within the Vale's twisted geology. Ara's markings flickered in time with each tremor, while Ahko maintained his rigid stance, weapon ready but waiting.

***

The ancient bridge stretched across a deep chasm, its cracked stone surface barely wide enough for two to walk abreast. Crystalline formations jutted from the fog below, their edges sharp enough to impale anything that fell.

Ahko led the way, testing each step with precise taps of his spear. The scouts spread out behind him in practiced formation while Ara kept Jin and Butch in the middle of the group.

A high-pitched tone cut through the air. Ara's markings flashed crimson as she spun toward the source. "Move!"

The bridge shuddered. Cracks spiderwebbed through the stone beneath their feet. The first section collapsed, taking two scouts with it into the mist.

Dark shapes burst from hidden alcoves on both sides of the chasm. Goblins poured out like insects, their scaled bodies moving with predatory grace. Glass-tipped spears clashed against crude bone weapons as the scouts engaged the flanking attackers.

Butch shoved Jin toward the far side while swinging his crowbar in a deadly arc. The weapon connected with a goblin's skull, the crack of bone lost in the chaos of battle.

Ara's harmonics pierced through the din, but the bridge's crystalline structure scattered her sound attacks. The goblins pressed in from both directions, forcing the group to bunch together on the deteriorating span.

More stone crumbled away. Ahko grabbed a scout before she could fall, hauling her back as another section gave way. The remaining bridge surface trembled with each impact of combat.

The goblins fought with coordinated savagery, their attacks focused on splitting the group apart. Yellow eyes gleamed with tactical intelligence as they forced their prey toward the weakening center of the bridge.

Stone groaned beneath their feet. The crystal shard in Butch's pocket pulsed with urgent intensity as goblin claws scraped against rock and elven harmonics ricocheted off crystal formations.

The battle compressed into a desperate struggle for survival, caught between the collapsing bridge and the relentless assault from both sides. Scouts fell. Goblins died. And still more scaled bodies emerged from the mist, climbing up from hidden paths to join the attack.

Butch planted his feet on the crumbling stone, muscles tensed as another goblin lunged. His crowbar caught the creature under its jaw, snapping its head back. The body tumbled into the fog below.

Ahko moved like water, his glass-tipped spear a blur of deadly precision. Two goblins fell before they could reach Jin. The scout commander's harmonics merged with the sounds of combat, creating a defensive wall of sound that kept the smaller attackers off balance.

Jin pressed his back against a broken pillar, gripping his borrowed spear with white knuckles. A goblin slipped through the defense, its claws raking toward Jin's face. The spear point caught it in the throat, driven by instinct and desperation.

Ara's silver markings pulsed with combat rhythm as she fought beside Butch. Her blade flashed, opening a goblin from collar to hip. Another creature leaped for her throat. She caught it midair with a focused harmonic burst that shattered its bones.

The remaining scouts formed a tight circle, their weapons moving in synchronized patterns. Glass tips pierced scaled flesh. Bone clubs shattered against crystal-reinforced armor. Blood splattered across ancient stone.

Three goblins attacked Butch at once. He caught the first with his crowbar, knocked the second back with his elbow, but the third slipped past his guard. Its teeth sank into his forearm. Butch slammed it against the bridge rail until its jaw went slack.

Ahko's spear took the creature through its spine before it could recover. The scout commander nodded once, acknowledging Butch's strength while never breaking his defensive stance.

The bridge trembled again. Ara touched the stone, her markings shifting to deep purple. She barked a warning in harmonic tones that made the scouts pull tighter together.

More goblins emerged from the mist, crawling up crystal formations with insect-like grace. Their yellow eyes tracked movement, coordinating attacks with cruel intelligence. The group held their position, weapons ready as scaled bodies pressed in from both sides.

The shard in Butch's pocket burned cold against his skin. Blood ran down his arm where goblin teeth had torn flesh. He adjusted his grip on the crowbar, muscles coiled for the next wave of attacks.

Ahko's spear wove through the air in precise arcs, each movement calculated and clean. The scout commander coordinated his team through short harmonic bursts, directing their glass-tipped weapons to vulnerable points in the goblins' scaled armor. His elite unit moved as one organism, their attacks flowing together in deadly synchronization.

Ara darted between opponents, her blade a silver flash in the mist. At point-blank range, her harmonics hit with devastating force. A goblin's ribs collapsed under the focused sound. Another's skull cracked from the sonic impact. Her markings pulsed with combat rhythm as she carved through the attackers.

Butch kept Jin close, his crowbar painting brutal strokes through the air. He crushed a goblin's throat with the curved end and ripped another's jaw sideways with the straight edge. Blood and teeth scattered across ancient stone. When three creatures rushed Jin at once, Butch caught them with sweeping strikes that shattered bone and tore flesh. His movements were not elegant like the scouts, just raw power and survival instinct.

A goblin slipped past Butch's guard, claws extended toward Jin's face. Jin's borrowed spear came up on reflex, punching through the creature's chest. Hot blood ran down the shaft onto Jin's hands. The goblin's yellow eyes went dark as it slid off the blade. Jin stared at his shaking hands, at the dark stains on his skin. His breath came in sharp gasps until Butch's grip on his shoulder anchored him back to the moment.

The scouts maintained their circular defense, glass blades catching the dim light as they struck with military precision. Ahko directed each movement through subtle tones that his team interpreted instantly, their attacks coordinated through years of shared combat experience.

***

The remaining goblins fell quickly under coordinated strikes. Glass-tipped spears found vital points, while Butch's crowbar crushed scaled bodies with mechanical efficiency. Ara's harmonics shattered bones and burst organs. The last creature died with Jin's borrowed spear through its throat.

Blood steamed where it hit the heated stone, creating wisps of red mist that mixed with the natural fog. The scouts moved through the carnage, ensuring each fallen goblin was truly dead. Their glass blades ended any lingering life with precise cuts.

Ahko directed his team to defensive positions while checking the bridge's stability. The ancient structure groaned beneath their feet, weakened by combat and the constant heat rising from below.

Butch wiped goblin blood from his crowbar, his breathing steady despite the exertion. The wound on his arm had stopped bleeding, though the bite marks remained angry and deep. Jin cleaned his borrowed spear on a dead goblin's leather wrappings, his hands steadier now.

Ara stepped away from the group, her silver markings shifting through shades of purple as she examined a section of collapsed stone near the bridge's edge. Deep gouges marked the ledge where something massive had recently passed. The stone showed signs of precise cutting rather than natural breaks.

Her fingers traced geometric patterns in the scattered debris. "Vault path... near," she said in careful English, her tone carrying weight beyond the simple words.

Butch moved beside her, drawn by an unseen pull. The shard in his pocket pulsed with increasing strength, its rhythm matching some hidden frequency in the stone. He placed his hand against the rock face, feeling vibrations that seemed to reach into his bones.

The scouts watched with tense focus as their human companion connected with something they could not perceive. Ahko's grip tightened on his spear, but he made no move to interfere.

They entered through the carved opening, Butch leading with his crowbar ready. Ancient mechanisms stirred at their presence, awakening from millennia of sleep. Crystalline formations in the walls began to pulse with dim violet light, creating slow waves that rippled outward from where they stood.

The chamber stretched beyond their vision, its ceiling lost in darkness above. Geometric patterns covered every surface, their edges catching the growing illumination. The air felt thick with age and potential, like a held breath finally released.

Ara's markings flickered rapidly, responding to frequencies beyond human perception. She pressed close to Jin, her movements protective rather than fearful. "Wrong echo," she whispered. "Too deep."

The shard in Butch's pocket burned hot against his leg. Its pulse synchronized with the chamber's awakening lights, each beat drawing answering flares from deeper within the structure. Paths of purple energy traced through floor seams, forming complex circuits that spread into adjoining passages.

Ahko signaled his scouts to defensive positions, their glass-tipped spears reflecting the awakening lights. Their harmonics died in the dense air, swallowed by the chamber's own resonance.

"This place..." Jin touched a wall panel that had begun to hum. "It feels like it's been waiting."

Butch nodded, understanding without words. The crowbar in his hand vibrated sympathetically with the rising energy. Each step deeper into the chamber triggered new responses: panels sliding aside, hidden mechanisms whirring to life, ancient systems reactivating in cascading sequence.

The shard's heat grew nearly unbearable. Butch pulled it from his pocket, and its brilliant purple glow cast sharp shadows across the geometric patterns. The chamber's lights pulsed stronger in response, as if recognizing a lost piece of itself.

Ara moved forward, her silver markings now strobing with urgency. "Not meant to wake," she said, her voice tight with concern. "Old sleep. Deep sleep." She reached for the shard but stopped short, her hand trembling in the growing energy field around it.

The chamber continued its slow awakening, each new system adding to the rising hum of power. What had slumbered here was stirring, drawn inexorably toward consciousness by the shard's presence.

CHAPTER 17

The fissure's edges were too clean, too precise to be natural. Ancient metal plates lined the shaft walls, their surfaces etched with complex patterns now broken and dulled by time. Purple light from the shard in Butch's pocket cast strange shadows as they descended.

A deep hum vibrated through the metal plating, different from the Grove's living harmonics. This sound felt mechanical, alien; a frequency that spoke of cold precision rather than organic resonance. The scouts' glass-tipped spears scraped against the walls, creating discordant echoes that died quickly in the dense air.

Ara's usual fluid movements became hesitant and measured. Her silver markings pulsed dimly, responding to frequencies that made her uncomfortable. Even her footsteps, normally part of the Grove's natural song, fell silent against the metal floor.

Butch led without conscious thought, drawn forward by something instinctive. The crowbar in his hand picked up sympathetic vibrations from the walls, transmitting them into his bones. Each step deeper felt inevitable, as if he were following a path laid out long before his birth.

Jin stayed close behind, watching his friend move with unnatural certainty through the darkness. The borrowed spear felt cold in his hands, its crystalline tip failing to reflect the shard's purple glow.

Ahko's scouts spread out in defensive formation, their training evident even in their growing unease. Their attempts at harmonic communication fell flat, absorbed by the metal surfaces that surrounded them.

The shaft continued downward, its angle becoming steeper. Broken panels revealed glimpses of crystal matrices beneath the plating, their structures more rigid and geometric than anything found in the Grove. The hum grew stronger, its frequency settling into a steady pulse that seemed to pull them deeper into the earth.

The chamber opened before them like a geometric dream made solid. Perfect hexagons lined the walls in impossible symmetry, each panel exactly matched to its neighbors without visible seams. The floor stretched out in concentric circles, their spacing measured with inhuman precision. Above, the ceiling formed a perfect dome that seemed to defy structural logic.

Butch stepped forward, crowbar loose in his grip. His muscles remembered something his mind could not grasp—a sensation of having stood in spaces like this before, though he knew that was impossible. The shard in his pocket hummed against his leg, its frequency matching the chamber's underlying tone.

Ara's markings flickered erratically, her usual grace replaced by sharp, defensive movements. She touched one hexagonal panel and jerked back as if burned. Her harmonic attempts to read the space produced no echo, no response; the chamber swallowed her songs without a trace.

"This isn't right," Jin whispered, his voice carrying an edge of wonder despite his words. "Look at those angles. Nothing in nature forms patterns that perfect." He traced the air along one of the circular floor grooves. "It's like someone took mathematics and turned it into architecture."

The scouts spread out with military precision, but their movements seemed clumsy against the chamber's exacting geometry. Their glass-tipped spears looked primitive compared to the technological perfection surrounding them.

Ahko's attempt at harmonic mapping died against the walls. The chamber refused to respond to elven resonance, maintaining its own steady frequency that felt older than the Grove itself.

***

Heat rippled from the floor in steady waves, each pulse matching the chamber's underlying frequency. The metallic surfaces felt warm to the touch, radiating an energy that seemed to flow through the geometric patterns like blood through veins.

Symbols etched into the hexagonal walls flickered as the group moved past them. These were not the organic spirals of the Grove or the crude markings of goblins; they followed rigid mathematical rules, their angles precise to the smallest degree.

Ara approached one panel where the symbols grew more concentrated. Her silver markings dimmed as she reached out, fingers hovering over the ancient patterns. When she touched the surface, she yanked her hand back as if shocked.

"Not elf. Not made by song," she said, her words clipped and tense. The usual melody in her voice had flattened, replaced by something closer to fear.

Butch stepped forward, crowbar hanging loose at his side. He pressed his palm against the same spot Ara had touched. The wall responded immediately, a soft purple glow spreading from his hand through the geometric network of lines. The light pulsed in harmony with the shard in his pocket, creating overlapping patterns that made the metal feel alive beneath his fingers.

The shard in Butch's pocket throbbed with increasing intensity, its lavender glow seeping through the fabric of his clothes. The chamber's mechanical hum shifted, aligning perfectly with the crystal's pulse until the two rhythms became one continuous frequency.

Light bloomed across the hexagonal surfaces, each geometric line brightening in sequence like circuits coming alive. The mathematical precision of the patterns became more apparent as they filled with energy, revealing layers of complexity that had been invisible moments before.

Jin stumbled backward until his shoulders hit the far wall. "Butch..." His voice cracked as he watched the room transform around them.

Ara's markings flickered erratically as she attempted to communicate with the structure. Her harmonics, usually so effective in the Grove, disappeared into the metal without echo or response. She tried different tones, shifting through octaves and frequencies, but the chamber remained deaf to her songs. Her frustration showed in the tight set of her jaw as each attempt failed.

"Structure ignores Grove-song," she said, her words clipped with tension. "Only answers... that." She pointed at Butch's pocket, where the shard continued its steady pulse.

The light in the room increased another fraction, not harsh but persistent, as if the space itself were waking up after a long sleep. The metal beneath their feet warmed slightly, and the hum deepened to a frequency they could feel in their bones.

Ahko's scouts shifted uneasily, their glass-tipped spears reflecting the purple glow. They clustered closer together, instinctively seeking the comfort of their unit as the alien technology continued its activation sequence around them.

***

A section of the hexagonal wall slid apart with mechanical precision, revealing a dark recess. From within, something emerged, a towering form of segmented metal and crystalline joints, its body partially fused with the chamber floor. The construct stood twice Butch's height, its limbs arranged in angles that defied natural anatomy. Purple light flickered behind compound eyes made of layered crystal, each facet catching and refracting the chamber's glow.

The machine made no sound as it oriented toward them. There was no whir of servos, no scrape of metal on metal, just perfect, unsettling silence.

Butch shifted his weight, crowbar held ready. His muscles tensed with practiced control, body angling to protect Jin while maintaining clear sight of the threat. The construct's alien geometry made it impossible to read its intentions or predict its movement.

Ara's markings pulsed rapid silver as she drew her glass blade. She positioned herself opposite Butch, creating a defensive triangle with Ahko. Her attempt at harmonic communication died in the air, absorbed by the chamber's sound-deadening surfaces.

Ahko raised his spear with fluid grace, signaling his scouts to spread out with quick hand gestures. The elves moved with practiced coordination, glass tips aimed at the construct's joints and crystal eyes. Their usual battle harmonics would be useless here, but their tactical positioning spoke of long experience fighting together.

The construct remained motionless, its crystalline eyes tracking their movements with alien precision. Purple light continued to pulse through its segmented frame, matching the rhythm of the shard in Butch's pocket. The chamber's hum deepened, vibrating through the metal floor beneath their feet.

The construct's head swiveled with mechanical grace, compound eyes sweeping across the group. Each crystal facet caught and held their images, analyzing with inhuman thoroughness. The scouts tensed as its gaze passed over them, fingers white-knuckled on their spears.

When it reached Jin, the eyes lingered longer. Purple light rippled through its frame, intensifying as it processed something about him. Jin's breath caught, but he held his ground.

Then it turned to Butch.

The construct's entire body shifted, realigning itself with geometrical precision. The shard in Butch's pocket flared bright enough to shine through the fabric. Its heat pressed against his skin, not burning but insistent.

A single, pure tone emerged from the construct, not a sound made by throat or string, but something fundamental. It bypassed the chamber's dampening properties, ringing clear and perfect. The note held no words, no meaning they could grasp, yet it carried weight. Purpose. Recognition.

Butch met its gaze without moving. His crowbar remained steady in his grip, neither raising it in threat nor lowering it in submission. He had faced enough danger to know when stillness mattered more than action.

"It senses you," Ara whispered, her markings shifting to deep purple. Her voice carried a mix of awe and unease as she watched the exchange between man and machine.

The construct maintained its focus on Butch, crystal eyes refracting countless versions of his image. The shard's pulse matched the rhythm of light flowing through the machine's segmented body, two pieces of something ancient finding resonance.

***

The construct's crystalline joints flexed with mathematical precision as it stepped sideways, each movement plotted in perfect angles. Behind it, another section of the hexagonal wall split apart, revealing a doorway cut from the same alien metal as the chamber.

Purple light spilled from the opening, casting long shadows across the geometric floor patterns. The construct remained motionless in its new position, compound eyes still fixed on Butch.

"Could be a trap," Jin whispered, his borrowed spear trembling slightly.

Butch shifted his grip on the crowbar but kept walking forward. His steps were measured and deliberate, the careful advance of someone who had learned the hard way when to push and when to wait. The shard in his pocket pulsed stronger with each step closer to the doorway.

The scouts adjusted their positions, maintaining coverage while following Butch's advance. Their glass-tipped spears caught and reflected the purple glow, creating a web of light around the group.

Ara made no move to stop him. Her silver markings had shifted to an unusual shade— not quite purple, not quite gray. When she spoke, her voice carried a tremor Jin had never heard before.

"This is not magic." Her words came slow and careful, as if each one had to be chosen precisely. "System. Arithmomancy, maybe."

The construct's eyes tracked Butch's approach, its frame adjusting with tiny movements to maintain perfect geometric alignment with his position. The chamber's mechanical hum deepened as Butch neared the threshold, resonating with the shard's pulse.

The construct stepped aside with mechanical grace as Butch crossed the threshold. The others followed, their footsteps echoing against metal floors that had not felt weight in ages.

Purple light bloomed along the walls in precise geometric patterns, each section awakening in sequence like a slow cascade of consciousness. The mechanical hum shifted pitch, gaining harmonics that made Ara's markings ripple with unease.

Stale air rushed past them as hidden vents activated. Butch wrinkled his nose at the metallic tang, not fresh air being pulled in but old air being cycled through ancient filters. The smell reminded him of sealed basements and forgotten spaces.

"Air's dead," Butch muttered, tapping his crowbar against a wall panel. "System's just moving it around."

Jin stepped closer to examine the awakening patterns, but Ahko pulled him back with a sharp gesture. The scouts spread out in practiced formation, glass spears ready as more of the chamber stirred to life.

Rectangular sections of the floor lit up beneath their feet, tracking their movements with perfect precision. Each step triggered new responses: panels sliding, lights shifting, unseen mechanisms whirring to life after eons of silence.

The construct remained in the doorway, its crystalline eyes fixed on their group as the chamber continued its methodical awakening. Its frame adjusted in tiny increments, maintaining exact angles with each new light pattern that emerged.

Ara touched a wall, then quickly withdrew her hand. "No song-memory here. Only numbers and paths." Her voice carried both wonder and discomfort as she watched the geometric networks spread across the ceiling.

The shard in Butch's pocket pulsed stronger now, matching the rhythm of the chamber's awakening. Purple light spilled from his jacket in sync with each new pattern that emerged around them.

Jin ran his fingers along the geometric patterns, the cold metal surface reminding him of the server racks in his college IT department. The precise arrangement of panels and light paths followed a logic he almost recognized, like computer architecture seen through an alien lens.

Professor Martinez would have lost his mind seeing this place. Jin could almost hear the enthusiastic lectures about parallel processing and quantum computing, delivered with that characteristic Spanish lisp and wild hand gestures. The way the purple light cascaded through the geometric networks reminded Jin of the professor's diagrams showing data flow through server clusters.

But this was different. Where modern servers hummed with fans and electricity, this chamber pulsed with something deeper—mathematical rhythms that felt both ancient and advanced. The hexagonal patterns were not just decorative; they carried information, processing something beyond his understanding.

"Like a computer," Jin muttered, "but not quite."

He traced a line of light with his finger, watching it branch into perfect fractals across the wall. The precision was unsettling—too perfect for organic tools, too complex for simple machinery. Professor Martinez had always said the future of computing would look nothing like their current systems. Jin wondered if this was what he had meant, though he doubted even Martinez had imagined anything this alien.

The crystalline construct continued its silent observation as Jin studied the patterns, its compound eyes reflecting the cascade of purple calculations spreading through the chamber. Each new sequence felt familiar yet impossible, like reading code written in a language that should not exist.

The shard in Butch's pocket grew warm against his thigh. Not burning, but insistent, like a phone left charging too long. He pulled it out, purple light spilling between his fingers as the crystal pulsed in rhythm with the chamber's awakening systems.

Geometric patterns rippled outward from where he stood, each pulse of the shard triggering new sequences of light across the hexagonal walls. The mechanical hum deepened, gaining harmonics that made the metal floor vibrate beneath their feet.

Ara's markings flickered rapidly, shifting through colors he had never seen before. She pressed her palm against a wall panel, then jerked back as if shocked.

"Wrong song," she whispered, her voice tight. "Not meant to echo now."

The construct's crystalline eyes tracked the shard in Butch's hand, its frame adjusting with precise micro-movements to maintain perfect alignment. More panels slid open along the walls, revealing deeper chambers filled with dormant machinery.

Jin watched as purple light spread through previously dark sections of the facility. "It's like the whole place is booting up."

Ahko barked sharp commands to his scouts, who tightened their formation around the group. Their glass-tipped spears caught the spreading purple glow, casting fractured reflections across the geometric floor patterns.

The shard's warmth increased steadily, matching the rising tempo of the chamber's activation sequence. Not hot enough to burn, but alive with energy that pulsed through Butch's palm and up his arm. Each wave triggered new responses from the facility—more systems awakening, more lights igniting, more ancient machinery stirring to life.

The construct's crystalline joints flexed as it processed these changes, its compound eyes reflecting countless purple calculations. The geometric patterns flowing across its frame accelerated, matching the shard's heightened energy signature.

CHAPTER 18

The group squeezed through the narrow fissure, leaving the geometric precision of the Vault behind. Jin's shoulders scraped against rough stone as they climbed upward through the natural break. The air changed from sterile and mathematical to something thick with organic decay.

Butch emerged first, crowbar leading the way. He squinted as alien sunlight struck his face, the pale blue sky harsh after hours underground. The light felt wrong, too sharp, too precise, like being under surgical lamps.

The canyon basin sprawled before them, a twisted mockery of nature. Massive roots burst through cracked earth at impossible angles, their surfaces covered in pulsing fungal growths that shifted between purple and green. The ground itself seemed diseased, with patches of soil that looked almost crystallized.

Ara's silver markings dimmed in the daylight as she pulled herself from the fissure. Her usual grace faltered as she took in their surroundings, her body tensing at the warped landscape.

"Grove-song is weak here," she muttered, pressing her palm against a gnarled trunk. "Trees remember wrong."

Jin stumbled on emergence, caught off guard by how the terrain seemed to ripple beneath his feet. What looked like solid ground turned out to be layers of decomposing vegetation and crystal formations. The air carried too many scents: sweet rot, metallic tang, and something else that burned his nose.

Jin glanced back, even though the Vault was no longer in view. The shard's warmth had faded, but the memory of the light, sharp and alive, still hummed in his bones.

"It wasn't just machines down there," he murmured. "Felt like something watching. Like it knew us."

Butch didn't answer at first. His boots crunched over the stone as he climbed. Then, quietly, he said, "Place like that? Feels like it's waiting for a reason to wake up."

Ara slowed just enough to glance back at them. Her silver markings had dimmed to faint flickers.

"It remembers," she said. "Even in sleep. And it does not forget who walks its halls."

Ahko and his scouts spread out in defensive formation, their spears ready as they scanned the hostile environment. One scout prodded a fungal mass with his weapon. The growth recoiled, releasing a cloud of spores that glowed briefly before dissipating.

The basin walls rose around them like broken teeth, their surfaces scarred by deep fissures and overgrown with twisted vegetation. Nothing moved naturally here; even the wind seemed to curl wrong through the warped branches above.

Ara knelt beside the fissure they had emerged from, her markings pulsing as she pressed both palms against the stone. The harmonics she produced were deeper than usual, traveling through rock rather than air. After several moments, she lifted her head.

"It sleeps. They do not." Her voice carried no emotion, only cold certainty.

The scouts shifted uneasily at her words, their glass-tipped spears catching the harsh sunlight. Even Ahko's stoic demeanor cracked slightly as he gazed back at the sealed entrance.

Jin hung back from the group, one hand trailing against the rough canyon wall. "Mina," he whispered, the name almost lost in the twisted wind. His fingers traced the geometric patterns that had followed them up from the Vault, now fading as the facility powered down.

Butch watched Jin for a moment, then moved with deliberate purpose. His boots scraped against crystallized earth as he kicked dust and debris over the Vault's entrance. Each movement was precise and methodical, like burying something that should stay hidden. The purple glow from below dimmed further with each layer of soil and stone.

The shard in his pocket had gone cold, no longer pulsing with the facility's alien rhythm. He kept kicking until the entrance was completely obscured, leaving only natural rock visible among the twisted roots and fungal growths.

* * *

The group climbed a rocky rise, their boots finding uncertain purchase on the crystallized terrain. Butch led with his crowbar, testing each step before committing his weight. The scouts moved in practiced formation while Jin struggled with the steep incline, his borrowed spear serving as a walking stick.

At the crest, Ara froze. Her markings flickered as she pointed toward the horizon, where four distinct columns of smoke rose against the pale sky. The dark pillars twisted unnaturally in the alien wind, carrying an acrid scent that made Jin's stomach turn.

"Scorched meat," Butch muttered, his grip tightening on the crowbar. The smell triggered memories he'd rather forget, combat zones where the air carried similar hints of flesh and fat.

Ahko moved forward in a low crouch, examining the ground with practiced precision. His fingers traced deep grooves in the crystallized soil, drag marks where multiple bodies had been pulled across the terrain. Some tracks showed signs of struggle, while others suggested unconscious victims.

Ara knelt beside a particularly clear set of prints. "Hobgoblin," she whispered, her voice carrying both fear and hatred. The massive footprint dwarfed the surrounding goblin tracks, its depth indicating significant weight and authority. Around it, dozens of smaller

264

clawed prints moved in coordinated patterns, showing military-like organization unusual for normal goblin packs.

Jin stared at the drag marks, his throat tight. Each groove represented another victim, someone's sister, daughter, or friend. He touched one of the deeper tracks, wondering if Mina had left this trace of her passage.

The scouts spread out, mapping the trail through practiced hand signals. The tracks told a clear story, a large group moving north, dragging captives, led by at least one Hobgoblin who kept the goblins in strict formation.

Ara's markings pulsed with muted colors as she traced the drag marks with her fingertips. Her shoulders tensed as she processed the information carried in the crystalline soil.

"They keep them." Her words came slow, deliberate. "Trade value. Breeding stock." She paused, searching for the right English phrases. "Not food. Never food."

Butch's weathered face hardened at her words, but he kept his reaction controlled. His fingers flexed around the crowbar's grip as he studied the horizon where the smoke columns twisted.

"Goblins trade with other tribes," Ara continued. "Keep captives healthy. Strong." Her silver markings shifted to a deep blue. "But not kind. Never kind."

Jin knelt in the crystallized dirt, his hand hovering over one of the deeper grooves. His voice came out barely above a whisper.

"Then she's still alive." The words carried equal parts hope and horror as he processed the implications of Ara's explanation.

Ahko maintained his distance, watching the exchange while keeping guard. His posture revealed his discomfort with the topic, but his tactical focus never wavered from scanning their surroundings.

"Hobgoblins organize," Ara added, her tone carrying ancient knowledge. "Build camps. Keep order." She touched Jin's shoulder.

The crystalline ground reflected purple light from the shard in Butch's pocket, casting strange shadows across their faces as they absorbed this new understanding. The acrid smoke continued to twist overhead, carrying the weight of countless stolen lives in its dark coils.

***

The group made camp beneath massive crystallized roots that arched overhead like ancient ribs. The grotto's collapsed ceiling provided natural cover while allowing enough ventilation to prevent smoke signals. Butch arranged the supplies, their dwindling rations spread thin across a worn cloth.

"Three days," he muttered, dividing dried fungi and berries into careful portions. The Grove's preserved food looked alien but kept well, though they hadn't planned for such an extended pursuit.

Ahko sat cross-legged on a flat stone, his fingers tracing patterns in the dirt. His map took shape with military precision, each mark representing confirmed goblin movements. Lines connected sighting points, showing clear migration routes that formed deliberate patterns.

Ara watched over his shoulder, her markings pulsing with recognition. "Not random," she whispered, touching one of the converging paths. "They move like soldiers now."

The map revealed what they'd feared. The scattered goblin tribes were being coordinated. Their raids followed strategic patterns, hitting vulnerable targets while avoiding Grove defenses. Supply lines emerged in the dirt sketch, along with fallback positions and staging areas.

"Someone leads them," Ahko said through harmonics that Ara translated. His tone carried grudging respect for the tactical efficiency. "One mind. One purpose."

The patterns showed a spider web of movement, all threads leading toward a central point in the northern wastes. Each raid, each abduction fed back to this hub of activity. The goblins weren't just stealing victims, they were building an army.

Jin studied the map from his position by the roots, absently touching the spear he'd used to make his first kill. The organized nature of the abductions made them more terrifying, not less. Someone was directing these creatures with purpose and intelligence.

Ahko added another mark to the dirt map, their current position relative to the goblin movements. Their own supplies might be low, but they were closing the distance. The central force controlling the goblins was somewhere ahead, hidden in the wasteland's twisted geography.

Ara's markings shifted to a deep crimson as she studied the converging lines on Ahko's map. Her fingers traced the paths, stopping at intersections where the trails merged.

"Here," she said, tapping a point where multiple routes connected. "Old stones. Sacred ground." Her voice carried both certainty and dread.

Jin leaned forward. "What kind of sacred ground?"

"Blood magic." Ara's markings pulsed darker. "Hobgoblin ritual place. They believe power flows from death."

Ahko produced a series of sharp harmonics that made the crystallized roots vibrate. Ara nodded at his assessment.

"Ahko says tracks show many tribes moving together. This only happens when Hobgoblin Warlord commands." She pointed to specific marks on the map. "These patterns, military formation. Too organized for normal goblins."

Butch gripped his crowbar tighter. "How long before they move the captives?"

"Three days, maybe less." Ara's markings flickered with urgency. "When moon aligns, ritual begins. Must reach them before."

"Can we intercept?" Jin asked, his voice tight with concern for Mina.

Ara traced a route through the dirt map, cutting across several goblin paths. "Here, narrow pass leads to ritual ground. If we move fast, might catch them gathering." She glanced at Ahko. "Dangerous. Many guards."

Ahko's responding harmonics carried grim agreement. The elite scout understood the tactical challenge they faced, a small group attempting to disrupt a massive tribal gathering.

"We go now," Ara said, rising to her feet. "Longer we wait, more tribes join. More guards protect ritual."

The others nodded, gathering their supplies with practiced efficiency. Time was running out, and somewhere ahead, a Hobgoblin Warlord was assembling his forces for a dark purpose.

Jin surged to his feet, fingers tight around his borrowed spear. "We can't wait. If they're gathering for some ritual, Mina could-"

"Running blind gets us killed," Butch cut in, his voice low but firm. The crowbar rested across his knees as he studied Ahko's dirt map. "Need to know guard positions, entry points."

"While we scout, they could move her!" Jin's voice cracked with frustration.

Butch shook his head. "Can't help anyone if we're dead."

Ara's markings flashed silver as she stepped between them. Her harmonics cut through their argument like a blade, silencing both men instantly.

"We move tonight," she said, each word precise and measured. "Quiet. Fast. Before the exchange begins."

Her tone left no room for debate. Even Ahko straightened at the authority in her voice, recognizing the shift from guide to commander. The elite scout's fingers moved in quick patterns, sketching final details into the dirt map before brushing it away with practiced efficiency.

Jin subsided, though tension still radiated from his shoulders. Butch gave a single nod, already checking his makeshift weapons and adjusting the crystal shard secured in his pocket.

The rest of the scouts began breaking down their temporary camp, moving with the silent precision of experienced warriors. No trace would remain to mark their passage through the crystallized grotto.

The crystallized grotto dissolved into darkness as they dismantled their camp. Above, alien constellations pierced a pale sky that seemed to mock their preparations with its cold indifference.

Butch methodically checked his gear, each movement deliberate and controlled. The familiar weight of the crowbar grounded him as his muscles remembered other nights of waiting. Different place, different enemy, same hollow quiet before violence began. He pushed those thoughts aside, focusing on the present moment.

Jin sat against a twisted root, fingers tracing the dead phone in his pocket. The black screen reflected nothing back, useless in this strange world. His father's last moments replayed in his mind, the golf club arcing through the air, defiant until the end. Now Mina waited somewhere ahead in the darkness. The thought of failing her, of failing them both, made his hands tremble.

In the shadows where crystal met stone, Ara knelt alone with her ritual pouch. Her fingers moved with practiced grace, applying luminescent sap in precise patterns across her face. Each stroke carried meaning, position, rank, lineage. The markings she'd worn for decades took shape with fluid certainty. First the curved line beneath her left eye, then the ascending arc that proclaimed her status as Hollow. The small dots along her temple spoke of years served, while the swooping pattern near her jaw marked her as guardian and guide.

The bioluminescent designs began to glow as they dried, pulsing faintly with her breath. In their light, her expression remained carefully neutral, but her hands moved with the surety of one who had performed this ritual countless times. The markings were more than decoration, they were identity, purpose, and belonging made visible on skin.

The pale sky offered no warmth, no guidance, no promise of dawn. Only the cold light of unfamiliar stars watched as they prepared for what lay ahead.

CHAPTER 19

Moonlight filtered through twisted crystal formations, casting strange shadows across the narrow gully as the group moved in single file. Ahko led the way, each step a calculated dance between loose stones and treacherous footing. His glass-tipped spear reflected brief glints of starlight, a silent beacon for those who followed.

Ara moved three positions back, her fresh markings pulsing with subdued silver light that matched her careful breathing. She kept her harmonics tightly controlled, the barest whisper of sound to map the path ahead without alerting watchers in the dark.

Between two scouts, Jin picked his way forward with the measured pace of someone fighting the urge to rush. The borrowed spear stayed close to his body, minimizing its profile against the pale sky above. His boots found purchase where others stepped, trusting the path chosen by those ahead.

Butch brought up the rear with two scouts, his crowbar a familiar weight against his thigh. The shard in his pocket remained cold and silent, offering no guidance through the shadowed passage. His movements carried the weight of experience, each foot placement deliberate, each pause timed to the group's rhythm.

The gully walls pressed close on either side, forcing them to angle sideways at the narrowest points. Loose gravel threatened to betray their passage with the slightest misstep. No one spoke. Even breathing seemed too loud in the confined space.

When Ahko froze at point position, the entire line stopped as one. Seconds stretched into minutes as the scout commander tested the air with barely audible harmonics. Only after his all-clear signal rippled back through the group did they resume their careful advance.

The moonlight played tricks with distance and depth, turning familiar shapes alien and casting deeper shadows where the crystal faces met. Each scout moved like liquid shadow, their weapons held close to avoid catching any stray reflection.

Ahko crouched at a junction where three crystal walls met, his fingers tracing patterns in the loose soil. The starlight caught the edges of his glass-tipped spear as he tested the ground's stability. His movements carried the precision of countless night patrols, each gesture born from hard-earned wisdom.

Ara shifted between formations, her silver markings dimmed to match the ambient glow of phosphorescent fungi. She pressed her palm against different rock faces, reading vibrations through the stone. Her harmonics remained tight and controlled, brief pulses that mapped terrain without broadcasting their presence.

Jin kept his eyes fixed on Ara's back, using her measured pace to regulate his own breathing. In through his nose, out through his mouth. One, two, three, four. The counting helped quiet the thunder of his heartbeat and gave structure to the chaos of fear and anticipation. The borrowed spear felt awkward in his grip, but he forced his fingers to stay relaxed.

Butch maintained his position at the rear, crowbar held low and ready. His footsteps fell in perfect silence, decades of muscle memory translating seamlessly to this alien terrain. The shard sat cold against his leg, offering neither warmth nor guidance. His eyes swept the shadows in practiced patterns, tracking movement in the spaces between moonlight and crystal.

The formation moved like a single organism, each member compensating for the others' shifts in weight and balance. When Ahko paused, they froze. When he advanced, they followed. The discipline of their movement spoke of countless hours of training, though Jin's occasional scuff of boot on stone marked him as the outsider he was.

Ara's markings flickered briefly, a warning. The group pressed closer to the crystal wall, melting into the deeper shadows. Above them, something large displaced air with leathery wings, but the sound died quickly in the night. Only after Ara's markings steadied did they resume their careful advance.

The group halted at a fallen stone marker, its carefully stacked rocks scattered across blood-stained ground. Ahko knelt to examine crude symbols carved into the base stones, fresh cuts that gleamed wet in the moonlight.

Ara pressed her palm against the cairn's foundation, silver markings shifting to a deep purple. "Hunter-sign. Grove-made." Her fingers traced older markings beneath the goblin vandalism. "They mock our dead."

Jin's grip tightened on his borrowed spear as he recognized dark stains soaked into the soil, not all of them old. The scattered stones formed a rough circle, like a broken crown in the dirt.

Butch moved to the edge of their position, crowbar ready as he scanned the shadows. The shard in his pocket remained cold, but something else pulled at his senses, a steady vibration through the rock beneath his feet.

"Listen," Ara whispered, her head tilted. Through the crystal formations came the distant pulse of drums, not Grove harmonics, but something darker and more primitive. The rhythm carried through stone and soil, a heartbeat of violence that set the scattered cairn stones trembling.

Ahko straightened from his examination, using precise harmonics to signal his scouts. The drum rhythm grew stronger, bleeding through the rock walls around them. Each beat carried echoes of older songs twisted into weapons.

The fallen cairn stones shifted with each drumbeat, rolling slightly in their own blood-stained hollows. What was once a marker of respected territory had become a testament to desecration. The goblin markings stood out stark and cruel against the weathered stone, claiming victory over another piece of Grove history.

Butch's hand shot up, fingers spread in the universal signal to halt. The group froze mid-step, pressing against the crystal walls as Butch's eyes locked onto something ahead in the gloom.

Suspended between two crystal spires hung a crude net woven from sinew and vine. Bones dangled within its web, too long and too curved to be human. The remains swayed slightly in the night air, clicking together with hollow music.

Ahko moved forward in perfect silence, glass spear angled low as he studied the grisly display. His harmonics probed the darkness beyond the bone curtain, testing for threats.

The bones bore deep scoring marks, teeth, claws, and something else. Clean cuts that spoke of tools and purpose. Trophy and warning combined into a single message: death waited ahead.

Ara's markings shifted to a deep crimson as she traced the patterns of dismemberment. "Not Grove-dead," she whispered. "Not goblin-prey." Her fingers sketched shapes in the air, mapping the skeleton's original form. "Something older."

Jin fought to control his breathing as moonlight caught the bones' polished surfaces. Whatever creature these remains belonged to, it had been massive. The ribcage alone spanned wider than his outstretched arms.

Butch kept his crowbar ready, eyes scanning the shadows beyond the hanging bones. The shard in his pocket remained cold, but the vibration through the stone grew stronger. Each drum beat from the distance set the bones swaying, creating patterns of movement that drew the eye.

The net creaked softly, fibers stretching under the weight of their ancient burden. Warning or trophy, the display had achieved its purpose, marking the boundary between survival and slaughter.

***

The group crouched at the ledge's edge, studying the goblin camp sprawled across the basin below. Moonlight caught the edges of crude tents stitched from leather and stolen cloth, their surfaces stained dark with old blood. Wooden stakes ringed the perimeter, each topped with skulls that reflected dully in the firelight.

At the camp's center loomed an altar of black stone, its surface carved with spiral patterns that seemed to move in the flickering light. Unlike the goblins' crude work, the altar bore precise geometric cuts that spoke of older, more sophisticated builders.

"Count thirty tents," Butch whispered, his eyes methodically tracking movement between the fires. "Guards posted in pairs."

Jin's hands clenched around his borrowed spear as he spotted cages near the altar—metal and wood structures large enough to hold people. The firelight did not reach far enough to see inside.

Ara's markings pulsed with subtle warning as she studied the altar's surface. "Stone remembers wrong songs," she murmured. "Not Grove-made."

Ahko signaled his scouts to spread along the ridge, their glass-tipped spears catching moonlight as they moved into position. Below, goblins prowled between the tents with predatory grace, their weapons crude but deadly: clubs wrapped in rusted metal, spears tipped with sharpened bone.

The camp reeked of smoke and rotting meat, the smell carrying up to their position on the thermal currents. Cooking fires cast dancing shadows across the tents, while larger bonfires marked the cardinal points around the altar.

Butch noted the disciplined positioning of the guards, their movements too coordinated for typical goblin behavior. "Someone's trained them," he observed quietly. "They're organized."

The shard in his pocket remained cold against his chest, but the altar's geometric patterns drew his eye. Like the Vault's architecture, its precise angles suggested builders who thought in mathematics rather than magic.

Ara's markings shifted to a deeper silver as she focused on the darkness beyond the fires. Her head tilted, tracking movement that the others could not perceive.

"There," she breathed, gesturing toward a cave mouth partially hidden by hanging hides. "Behind guards. Reed pens hold your people."

Jin squinted through the gloom, barely making out the shapes of large goblins posted at the entrance. These were not normal sentries;

their bodies bore extensive battle scars, and they had a head wider than their kin. They carried themselves with the confidence of veterans, their crude weapons marked with notches of past kills.

"I see cages," Jin whispered. "But the guards—"

"Elite warriors," Ara confirmed. "Chosen for size, survival. Not hobgoblin-touched, but close in rank."

Beyond the scarred guards, deeper in the shadows, Jin could just detect movement—human forms shifting behind walls of woven reed and stretched hide. The captives appeared to be sitting or lying down, but none showed signs of serious injury.

Butch leaned forward, eyes narrowed as he tried to pierce the darkness. After a moment, he sat back with a frustrated grunt. "Should have brought my glasses," he muttered. "Getting too old for this."

The absurd image of Butch doing battle in his wire-rimmed work glasses caught Jin off guard. A chuckle bubbled up before he could stop it, and he quickly clamped a hand over his mouth. His shoulders shook with silent laughter as the tension briefly broke.

Ara's markings flickered with confusion at their exchange, but her focus remained on the cave entrance and its precious cargo. She continued tracking the guards' movements, memorizing their patterns while the humans collected themselves.

Ara's markings darkened to a deep indigo as she traced patterns in the air, mapping sound waves that bounced off the camp's structures. Her fingers twitched with each echo, reading vibrations human senses could not detect.

"Something changes," she whispered, her voice tight. Below, the goblins' movements shifted—subtle adjustments in posture and spacing that spoke volumes to her trained eye. Their shoulders hunched lower, heads tilted in submission. Even the elite guards at the cave entrance redistributed their weight, weapons angling downward in unconscious deference.

"Fear-scent rises," she continued, silver markings pulsing faster. "Hobgoblin approaches. Not seen yet, but they feel its presence."

The goblins near the altar began clearing a path, their previously coordinated movements now tinged with nervous energy. Those closest to the ground pressed their foreheads to the dirt, while others backed away from the central space with careful, sliding steps.

"Watch their necks," Ara murmured, touching Jin's arm to direct his attention. "See how they bare throat-sides? Sign of submission. Only hobgoblin commands such fear."

Butch noted how the camp's atmosphere had shifted from military precision to religious dread. The goblins maintained their posts but now moved like supplicants in a temple, their earlier predatory confidence replaced by ritualistic caution.

"They don't act like this for normal leaders," Ara explained, her markings reflecting the firelight in troubled patterns. "Hobgoblin is a god to them. Living god that walks, breathes, kills."

Jin's breath caught as his eyes locked onto a strip of fabric tied around one of the posts near the cave entrance. Even in the dim firelight, the hot pink color was unmistakable—a piece of Mina's sweater, the one she'd worn the night of the attack. He remembered how she'd saved for weeks to buy the limited-edition merchandise of her favorite band, proudly showing off the group's logo.

Now it hung there like a piece of rope, dirty and frayed, marking the entrance where his sister was held captive. The sight hit him like a physical blow, memories of that night flooding back—Mina's screams, his father's final stand.

Jin surged forward without thinking, every muscle tensed to sprint down the ridge. Butch's arm shot out, catching him across the chest and yanking him back before he could expose their position.

"Let me go," Jin hissed, struggling against Butch's iron grip. "That's her sweater. They have her in there!"

"I know," Butch whispered firmly, maintaining his hold while keeping Jin pinned against the ground. "But you run down there now, you die. She dies. Everyone dies."

Jin's fingers clawed at Butch's arm, his whole body shaking with desperate need to reach that cave entrance. But Butch held firm, weathering Jin's attempts to break free with grim patience.

"Your sister needs you alive," Butch murmured, his voice low and steady. "We do this smart, or we don't do it at all."

"And we need a plan," Butch added, easing his grip on Jin's shoulder. "Let's go. This has to be done right or everyone is dead."

The group began backing away from the ridge, moving with practiced silence. Ahko's scouts melted into the shadows first, their glass-tipped spears vanishing into the darkness without a sound. Ara's markings dimmed to barely visible silver as she covered their retreat.

Jin's hands trembled around his borrowed spear as he followed, his eyes locked on that strip of pink fabric until the last possible moment. The sight of Mina's torn sweater burned in his mind, feeding a mixture of rage and desperate hope that made his chest tight. She had to be in there. She had to be alive.

Butch kept close to Jin as they withdrew, reading the younger man's turmoil in the rigid set of his shoulders and the white-knuckled grip on his weapon. The crowbar hung ready at Butch's side, its familiar weight a comfort as they picked their way back through the crystal-studded terrain.

Jin wanted to scream, to charge down that ridge and tear through anyone between him and that cave. But Butch was right: they needed a real plan. The memory of his father's stand flashed through his mind—brave, desperate, and ultimately futile. Jin could not make the same mistake. Mina needed him to be smarter than that.

Soon they would have a plan, and he would bring his sister home.

***

"I have no plan." Butch furiously scratched at his hair, his voice carrying the weight of exhaustion and frustration. "Not without most of us dying. Too many of them, too few of us."

He paced the small clearing where they had retreated, his crowbar tapping against his leg with each step. The odds kept spinning in his head: thirty tents meant at least a hundred, maybe two hundred fighters, plus the elite guards, and now a hobgoblin. Their own group barely numbered ten.

Ara watched him from her perch on a fallen log, her silver markings pulsing with what looked suspiciously like amusement. The slight curve of her lips only deepened his frustration.

"What's so funny?" Butch stopped pacing to face her. "Your people will die if we get this wrong. The hostages..." He cut himself off, jaw clenching. "We could try stealth, maybe..."

Ara's expression shifted from amusement to something more knowing. She rose gracefully from the log and pointed toward the dense forest to the west, a smile playing at the corners of her mouth.

***

Through the dense forest canopy, three silhouettes emerged from the western shadows. Their movements carried the fluid grace of seasoned hunters, each step precise and measured against the crystalline ground.

Ahko's hand shot up, halting the group. His chest expanded as he produced a complex series of challenge tones, sharp, aggressive harmonics that cut through the evening air like glass shards.

The response came instantly—not the guttural sounds of goblins or the discordant screech of Iron-Wings, but pure elven war-scout frequencies. The harmonics layered over each other in practiced patterns, each note carrying coded meaning about rank, intention, and allegiance.

Ahko's posture relaxed slightly, though his grip remained firm on his spear. The three figures stepped into the clearing's dim light, revealing the copper-brown skin and tactical gear of Deep Fold scouts. Their glass-tipped weapons caught what little light filtered through the canopy, creating small prisms across the forest floor.

The lead scout stepped forward, a lean figure with ritual scars tracing down his arms. Two warriors flanked him, their faces marked by old battles, glass-tipped spears held with casual expertise.

Ara's markings shifted to a warm silver as she recognized them. She pressed her forehead briefly against the war-singer's in formal greeting before turning to Butch and Jin.

"They come to help," she said, her English careful and measured. "When we left, Council could not agree. Some say help humans, others say stay away." Her fingers traced patterns in the air as she searched for the right words. "No choice made. But those who believe, they send warriors. Volunteers only."

The war-singer produced a series of overlapping tones that made Jin's teeth ache. Ara listened intently, her markings pulsing with each harmonic layer.

"Thirty-one chose to come," she translated, pride evident in her voice. "All warriors of Deep Fold. They track us through crystal-song."

Butch studied the newcomers with tactical assessment. "The Council let them?"

"Council splits now." Ara's expression grew troubled. "Deep divide. Some say helping humans breaks old laws. Others say..." She paused, choosing her words carefully. "Others say time for change."

The war-singer and his companions took defensive positions around the group's perimeter, moving with the fluid grace of veterans. Their presence transformed the small band into something more formidable, a proper strike force.

"They are first," Ara explained. "More follow. All choose freely to come. All know the risk."

Jin watched the elven warriors settle into their positions with practiced efficiency. "Why would they volunteer? They don't know us."

Ara's markings flickered with complex emotions. "Some remember old stories. Some feel Grove-song changing. All believe helping you is right path, even if Council cannot decide."

Butch stepped forward, his weathered face softening as he looked at the three warriors. He placed his hand over his heart and bowed his head slightly. "Thank you." He tapped his chest. "Butch."

Jin moved beside him. "Jin."

The warriors tilted their heads, studying the simple sounds. They attempted to echo the names, their elven vocal cords creating musical variations that turned "Butch" into a layered harmony and "Jin" into a resonant chime, and yet they could hear their name in the tone.

The lead warrior responded with a complex series of overlapping tones that rippled through the air like water. His companions followed with equally intricate harmonic introductions that seemed to blend with the forest's natural sounds.

Butch scratched his head and turned to Ara. "Can I call you Dusty?" He pointed to the lead warrior with squinted eyes. Then to the shortest one, "Ned?" Finally, to the stocky warrior, "Lucky?"

Ara translated through a series of melodic tones. The three warriors exchanged glances, their expressions shifting from confusion to amusement. Their faces brightened with what could only be described as smiles, nodding in acceptance of their new designations.

"They agree," Ara said, her markings pulsing with silver mirth.

Jin looked at Butch with raised eyebrows. "Why those names?"

Butch's face split into a wide grin, his eyes crinkling at the corners. "Cause they're my Three Amigos." He chuckled to himself, clearly enjoying a private joke that no one else understood.

***

More elven warriors materialized from the shadows over the next hour, arriving in small groups of three or four. Each unit followed the same protocol: challenge tones, recognition harmonics, formal greetings. By moonrise, thirty-three volunteers had gathered in the clearing, their glass-tipped weapons catching starlight.

The final group brought troubling news. The war-singer's harmonics carried tension as he reported to Ahko and Ara. Jin watched their markings pulse with concern as the tones painted a darker picture.

Ara turned to Butch and Jin, her voice low. "More goblins gather east. This camp..." She gestured toward the enemy position. "Not final place. Is connection point. Two more camps ahead. Bigger."

"A hub," Butch muttered, his weathered face hardening as he processed the tactical implications. His fingers tightened around the crowbar as a thought struck him. "The hobgoblin here could be the one. The one that led the raid through the portal."

Jin's eyes widened with recognition. "The ones that took Mina..."

"The ones that killed your father." Butch's voice carried no emotion, but his knuckles whitened against the metal of his weapon.

Heat rose in his chest with familiar anger, old rage that wanted to burn everything down.

He closed his eyes. Took a slow breath. Let the fire sink back into ice.

When he opened them again, his expression was calm. Cold. The anger had not disappeared—he had frozen it into something harder. More useful.

The war-singer continued his report, his harmonics painting images of massive gatherings, hundreds of goblins moving with unnatural coordination under their hobgoblin commander's influence.

Ara stepped forward, her silver markings pulsing with command presence. The warriors straightened, responding to her authority through shared harmonics. She positioned herself at the center of their gathering, bridging the gap between the elven forces and her human companions.

"They are mine," she declared in clear tones that needed no translation. "My choice. My command."

The warriors' acceptance rippled through their ranks in waves of musical acknowledgment. Ahko nodded once, deferring to her position.

Butch cleared his throat. "May I suggest something?"

Ara turned to him, head tilted in consideration.

"We can't let them link up with the main force," Butch said, his voice carrying the weight of experience. "Back in the mountains of Mindanao..." He paused, checking himself. "Different time, different war. But we faced larger numbers. The trick wasn't fighting fair."

His eyes took on a distant look as he traced patterns in the dirt with his crowbar. "When you're outnumbered, you hit hard. Hit first. Create chaos." His movements became more precise as he marked positions. "The bigger their force, the more they rely on coordination. Break that coordination."

Ara knelt beside his markings, her fingers hovering over the crude map. Her markings shifted to a deep purple as she processed his meaning.

"I've seen how your people move. How you use sound." Butch tapped specific points in his diagram. "If we combine that with what I know..." He glanced at the gathered warriors, then back to Ara. "This is what we do."

Ara's markings blazed silver as she translated his plan into harmonic language, the musical strategy flowing through the assembled warriors like a rising tide.

CHAPTER 20

Moonlight caught the glass tips of thirty spears as the war party moved like water down the cliff face. No words passed between them, just the faintest whisper of leather on stone and the careful placement of each foot.

Butch descended between two elven warriors, his crowbar secured across his back. The shard in his pocket pulsed with cold energy against his hip. Behind him, Jin navigated the rocky terrain with unpracticed determination.

A goblin sentry lifted its head, nostrils flaring. Before it could sound the alarm, three arrows struck in perfect harmony. The creature collapsed without a sound.

From hidden positions along the ridge, Deep Fold archers released their first coordinated volley. Glass-tipped arrows rained down in precise patterns, each shaft humming a different note as it cut through the air. The combined harmonics created waves of disorienting sound that rippled through the goblin camp.

Two more sentries fell. A third stumbled, clutching its throat where an arrow protruded. The creature's warning cry died in a gurgle.

Ara's markings pulsed once, the signal. No time for elaborate tactics or careful positioning. They had to strike hard and fast before the camp could organize a defense.

The war party surged forward as one entity. Thirty-three warriors plus two humans against hundreds, impossible odds made possible only through perfect coordination and the element of surprise.

Another volley of arrows swept the camp's perimeter. Goblins scrambled for weapons as the first wave of Deep Fold warriors crashed into their lines. Glass spears flashed in the darkness. Battle harmonics shattered the night's silence.

The assault had begun.

Butch's crowbar caught a goblin under the jaw, shattering bone. The creature dropped its rusted blade and collapsed. Blood sprayed across Butch's arms as he yanked the weapon free.

Jin thrust his borrowed glass spear through a charging goblin's chest. The creature's momentum carried it forward, nearly ripping the weapon from Jin's grip. Ara's hand steadied his arm, helping him wrench the spear free.

They moved as one unit: Butch's brutal strength, Jin's desperate precision, and Ara's fluid grace. When a goblin pack tried to flank them, Ara's harmonics scattered their formation. Jin's spear found gaps in their defense while Butch's crowbar crushed skulls and broke limbs.

"Left!" Butch barked. His crowbar swung in a deadly arc, catching a leaping goblin midair. The impact splattered gore across his chest. The metal gleamed wet and dark in the moonlight.

Jin pivoted, driving his spear through another attacker's throat. The glass tip emerged red from the back of its neck. Ara flowed around him, her blade opening a goblin from collar to hip.

Three more creatures rushed their position. Butch met them with mechanical efficiency. The crowbar rose and fell. Blood dripped from its curved edge as bodies crumpled at his feet.

Ara's markings pulsed with battle light, casting silver shadows across their tight formation. Her harmonics kept the trio synchronized, moving together through the chaos like a single deadly organism.

Goblins erupted from between the tents, shields locked in ragged formation. Crude plates of wood and bone clattered together as they advanced, spears bristling between the gaps. Their unified movement betrayed the Hobgoblin's influence. No ordinary raid party showed such discipline.

Ara's silver markings pulsed with battle light as she signaled her squad. Six Deep Fold warriors fell into position behind her, glass spears catching the moonlight. Her blade hummed a single pure note that resonated through their bones.

The shield wall surged forward. Ara's harmonics rippled through the air, a complex pattern of sound that made the wooden shields vibrate. Splinters flew as the crude barriers shook apart under the sonic assault.

The Deep Fold warriors struck in perfect synchronization. Glass tips punched through gaps in the breaking formation. Goblins screamed as crystal blades found throats and hearts. Their line buckled but held.

Ara flowed through the chaos like quicksilver. Her blade opened arteries and severed tendons with surgical precision. Two goblins fell before they could track her movement. A third lost its shield arm at the elbow.

The squad pressed the advantage, exploiting every crack in the enemy's defense. Where three warriors struck high, three struck low. Glass spears wove deadly patterns through the air. The shield wall crumbled under their coordinated assault.

More goblins poured from the darkness, trampling their fallen to plug the gaps. They fought with desperate savagery now, abandoning formation for brute force. Blood sprayed as crude axes met crystal edges.

Ara's harmonics shifted pitch. Her squad responded instantly, falling back half a step before surging forward as one. Their combined strike shattered the remains of the shield wall. Goblins sprawled in the dirt, weapons scattered.

The Deep Fold warriors pressed through the breach, cutting down anything that moved. No wasted motion, no hesitation, just the efficient application of lethal force. Where they passed, only bodies remained.

Ahko moved like a dancer through the carnage, his glass-tipped spear tracing lethal arcs through the air. Two goblins charged him from opposite sides, their crude weapons raised high. His body twisted in a fluid spin, the spear's edge opening both creatures' throats in a single graceful motion. They collapsed, gurgling their last breaths into the blood-soaked earth.

Deep Fold scouts identified gaps in the goblin lines and struck with precision. Their glass blades found the spaces between makeshift armor, punching through leather and flesh. Each kill created new openings for the warriors behind them.

The goblins surged back with savage fury. Sharpened poles thrust forward like wooden fangs. Hooked blades swept low, seeking ankles and knees. Crude axes hammered against crystal weapons, sending discordant notes ringing through the night air.

A particularly large goblin lunged at Ahko, its jagged sword missing his throat by inches. Without breaking stride, Ahko spun into the attack, stepping into the motion just beside the goblin's head. His throat constricted as he produced a complex harmonic tone, not music, but a weaponized frequency that cut through the creature's brain.

The goblin's eyes bulged. Blood trickled from its ears and eye sockets as the harmonic attack shredded its nervous system. It dropped its weapon, body convulsing, before collapsing into a twitching heap at Ahko's feet.

***

A goblin's club smashed into Butch's side. The impact drove the air from his lungs and sent lightning bolts of pain through his ribs. He staggered but kept his feet, muscle memory from old fights taking over.

The goblin pressed its advantage, swinging again. Butch caught the blow on his forearm and let the force slide past him. His crowbar snapped up, catching the creature under its chin. Bone crunched. The goblin sprawled backward.

Pain flared with each breath, but Butch pushed through it. Another attacker charged. He stepped into its guard and hooked the crowbar behind its knee. A sharp pull sent the goblin face-first into the dirt. The curved metal came down hard on the back of its skull.

Ahead, goblins had piled crates and broken furniture into a crude barricade. Spears bristled between the gaps, jabbing at anyone who came close. Bodies of fallen warriors lay scattered around its base.

Butch planted his feet and ignored the stabbing protest from his ribs. The crowbar's weight felt right in his hands, a solid tool meant for leverage and breaking things. He had done this before, in another life, with different barriers.

He charged forward, keeping low. A spear thrust caught his sleeve, tearing fabric but missing flesh. The crowbar's hook caught the edge of a crate. Butch threw his weight backward, muscles burning. Wood splintered. The barricade shifted.

Goblins scrambled to brace the weakening structure. Butch struck again, targeting the same spot. The crowbar bit deep into weathered wood. He twisted, using the tool's length for maximum leverage. More crates toppled.

A gap opened. Butch rammed his shoulder into it, grinding his teeth against the pain in his side. The barricade groaned. Pieces of furniture shifted and lost their precarious balance. The whole structure began to collapse.

Goblins abandoned their positions as the barrier came apart. Butch's crowbar found flesh instead of wood, crushing limbs and skulls. He fought through the pain and exhaustion, breaking bodies as efficiently as he had broken the barricade.

Jin spotted the fallen elf warrior through the chaos, silver markings dim, glass spear shattered beside him. An elite goblin loomed over the prone figure, its armor decorated with bones and crystalline shards. The creature's movements were not frenzied like its lesser kin. It advanced with practiced menace, curved blade raised for a killing blow.

Jin's borrowed spear felt slick in his sweating palms. His heart hammered against his ribs as he remembered Ara's lessons in the grove. The basic forms they had practiced between meals and rest stops flooded back.

The elite goblin sensed his approach. It turned, yellow eyes narrowing as it assessed this new threat. Jin did not give it time to finish. He thrust the glass-tipped spear forward, just as Ara had shown him. The goblin deflected the strike with its blade.

Jin stepped back, creating distance. *Keep the point between you and them,* Ara's voice echoed in his mind. The elite goblin pressed forward with a series of quick slashes. Jin retreated, spear tip tracking the creature's movements.

Another thrust, this time the glass tip scored along the goblin's arm. Dark blood welled from the cut. The creature snarled, its calculated demeanor cracking. It lunged, trying to get inside Jin's reach.

Jin backpedaled, nearly tripping. The spear's length kept the goblin's blade from finding flesh. Thrust and step back. The simple pattern steadied him. His next strike caught the elite goblin in the shoulder, puncturing its leather armor.

The creature staggered. Jin drove the spear forward one final time, putting his weight behind the thrust. The glass tip punched through the goblin's chest. Its yellow eyes widened in surprise, then dulled. The body slumped to the ground.

Jin's hands shook as he retrieved his weapon. The fallen elf was already being helped up by fellow warriors. Their silver markings pulsed with approval as they nodded to Jin.

Ara's markings flashed bright silver as she lifted her arm, signaling through the chaos. The northern squad responded instantly, breaking right in perfect formation. Their glass-tipped spears caught the firelight as they moved as one unit, cutting through the goblin lines with lethal precision.

The war party drove deeper into the camp, leaving broken bodies and shattered defenses in their wake. Harmonics rippled through the air as Deep Fold warriors coordinated their attacks. Each burst of sound found gaps in the goblins' crude armor, dropping them with surgical accuracy.

Ara moved with fluid grace between the fighting groups, her markings pulsing in rhythm with the battle harmonics. Her glass blade claimed three goblins in quick succession: throat, heart, spine. No wasted movement, no hesitation.

The northern squad's flanking maneuver caught a group of goblins. Glass spears struck. The squad maintained perfect spacing as they advanced, each warrior covering the others' blind spots. Their harmonics wove together, creating a wall of sound that staggered any goblins that came too close.

Deeper into the camp, tents burned and supplies scattered. Goblins broke ranks, their usual pack tactics falling apart under the coordinated assault. The war party's advance was methodical and unstoppable. Each step claimed more ground. Each harmonic burst weakened enemy resistance.

The northern squad reached a row of storage huts, securing the position with practiced efficiency. Their spears formed a bristling wall as they established a defensive line. Ara's markings shifted to deep blue as she assessed their progress through the camp. The war party had cut nearly halfway to their objective, leaving chaos in their wake.

Horns shrieked through the night, their harsh notes cutting across the battlefield. The goblins' scattered forces coalesced, responding to the signal with practiced discipline. They formed tight clusters, shields locked, spears bristling outward like thorns.

Ara's markings pulsed rapid silver as she tracked their movements. The enemy adapted faster than expected, transforming from rabble into organized units. Bodies littered the ground, both goblin and elf, their blood mixing with ash and mud.

The main goblin force had pulled back to the cave entrance, forming three defensive rings around the hostage hold. Elite warriors took position at the front, their armor decorated with bones and trophy skulls. Behind them, lesser goblins arranged themselves in overlapping formations, ready to fill any gaps in the line.

Ara's hand slashed through the air, her fingers weaving complex patterns. Silver light rippled across her skin as she issued the command for phase two. The war party responded instantly, breaking into smaller strike teams.

Three squads converged on the goblin center, glass spears held at precise angles. Their harmonics merged into a single piercing note that made the air vibrate. The sound hit the goblin lines like a physical force, disrupting their shield wall.

The elite warriors stumbled, their formations wavering. Ara's strike teams exploited every opening, driving glass tips through gaps in armor. The front rank buckled as warriors fell, but the goblins behind pressed forward, trampling their own dead to close the breach.

Butch's crowbar found skulls and joints, breaking through the press of bodies. Jin moved beside him, keeping goblins at bay with quick thrusts of his borrowed spear. The war party pushed relentlessly toward the cave mouth, even as more horns sounded and fresh goblin units rushed to reinforce the defense.

Blood and ash caked Ara's silver markings as she coordinated the assault. Her glass blade flickered in deadly arcs, opening throats and severing tendons. The strike teams maintained formation despite the chaos, their harmonics never faltering as they carved deeper into the enemy ranks.

***

The war party surged forward as one, their harmonics building to a crescendo that shattered the last goblin defense. Glass spears punched through shields and bodies. The cave mouth swallowed them whole as they drove inside.

Butch's crowbar crushed the skull of a retreating goblin. Jin followed close behind, his borrowed spear dark with blood. The

Deep Fold warriors spread out in practiced formation, securing the entrance with interlocking fields of fire. Their silver markings cast eerie shadows on the rough stone walls.

The stench hit them first: blood, waste, and despair thick enough to taste. Butch's boots splashed through puddles he tried not to identify. Jin gagged but kept moving.

They found the pen in a wider chamber. Crude wooden posts and rope formed a makeshift prison. Bodies pressed against the barriers, women and girls huddled together, clothes torn, faces hollow with fear and exhaustion. Blood stained the dirt floor beneath them.

"Mina!" Jin rushed forward, searching the faces.

Butch swept the chamber with veteran eyes, marking possible threats while Jin called his sister's name. The walls bore scratch marks and dark stains. Discarded bones and scraps of clothing littered the ground around the pen.

Ara's warriors maintained their defensive positions, glass spears ready as harmonics mapped the cave system for approaching threats. Their markings pulsed in rhythm, creating patterns of silver light that pushed back the darkness.

The captives stirred at Jin's voice, lifting their heads. Some reached through gaps in the wooden posts with trembling hands. Others remained curled in on themselves, too broken to respond.

Butch's crowbar made short work of the crude lock. The wood splintered and the gate swung open. The smell of blood and filth rolled out stronger, mixing with the metallic tang of fear.

The women shrank back as the elven warriors approached, pressing themselves against the far wall of the pen. Their eyes went wide at the sight of silver markings and glass spears, alien features sparking fresh terror. One woman screamed when Ara stepped forward, her harmonics meant to soothe only causing more panic.

"It's okay, we're here to help." Jin switched to Korean, calling out names he recognized from missing persons reports. "Mrs. Park? Emily? Sarah?"

Heads lifted at the sound of human speech. A middle-aged woman uncurled herself from the huddle. "Jin?" Her voice cracked.

"We're getting you out," Butch added in his accented English. He gestured at the elven warriors. "They're friends."

The tension eased slightly as more women recognized their rescuers were human. Some began to whisper names back, reaching toward Jin and Butch while still eyeing the elves with fear.

"Tito Butch?" A young Filipina woman pushed forward. "From the warehouse?"

"Maria." Butch's voice softened. "You're safe now."

The sound of familiar names and voices worked like a spell, breaking through the haze of terror. Women started moving toward the gate, supporting those too weak to walk. They flinched when the elven warriors shifted positions, but Jin and Butch's continued presence helped them push through their fear.

"Stay close to us," Jin assured them in English, then Korean. "We'll protect you."

Ara hung back, understanding her presence only complicated things. Her warriors maintained their defensive positions but remained still, trying not to frighten the captives further with sudden movements. Their silver markings dimmed to barely a glow.

Jin knelt beside each body, closing their eyes with trembling fingers. Eleven women and girls lay where the goblins had discarded them against the cave wall. Their skin bore purple bruises and deep cuts. Some showed signs of fighting back, broken fingernails and defensive wounds on their arms.

He recognized Mrs. Chen from the Asian market, her once-proud face now slack and empty. Emily Torres, who'd played volleyball with Mina, lay crumpled nearby. Her team jersey was shredded and stained dark.

Jin whispered their names as he moved from one to the next, giving them this final dignity. His hands shook but his movements remained gentle. They had suffered enough violence.

The elven warriors stood silent watch, their markings casting silver light over the dead. Butch kept his distance, letting Jin complete this grim task while scanning for threats.

When Jin reached the last body, a girl no older than fourteen, his breath caught. For a moment, he thought... but no. The pink sweater was similar to Mina's, but the face belonged to someone else's sister. He closed her eyes too, whispering a prayer his mother had taught him.

Mina wasn't here. The relief of that knowledge twisted in his gut, mixing with shame at feeling grateful when eleven others lay dead. He stood slowly, legs unsteady.

The captive women huddled together, some crying silently as they recognized friends among the dead. One woman clutched a torn photograph she'd found near Mrs. Chen's body, a family portrait that would never be whole again.

***

"Jin!" A scream pierced through the cave's heavy silence. "Jin!"

The voice cut through everything else the wounded, the grieving, the dead. Jin's head snapped up, his heart stopping at the sound he'd dreamed of hearing for so long.

A figure burst from the back of the huddled group. Mina's dark hair flew wild as she pushed through the crowd, tears streaming down her face. Her clothes were torn and dirty, but she was alive. She was real.

Jin's legs gave out as Mina slammed into him. They collapsed together, clinging to each other with desperate strength. Jin buried his face in his sister's hair, breathing in her familiar scent beneath the cave's grime and horror. His shoulders shook as fear and guilt poured out.

Mina sobbed against his chest, fingers digging into his back like she'd never let go. Neither could form words. They didn't need to. Everything that mattered was in the way they held each other, the last pieces of their family finding their way home.

The elven warriors turned away, giving the siblings privacy in their reunion. Even Ara stepped back, her silver markings dimming to barely a glow. Butch kept watch over them all, his weathered face softening at the sight of brother and sister together again.

Around them, other women wept, for joy at this reunion, for grief at those who would never return to their families. But for Jin and Mina, the world had narrowed to this single point of contact. They were no longer alone.

*****

Butch caught movement at the edge of his vision. Three figures huddled in the darkest corner of the cave, pressed against the rough wall. Their skin was pale as milk, their hair a strange silver-white that seemed to absorb the cave's dim light. Unlike the Deep Fold elves with their copper-brown complexions and luminescent markings, these three were ghostly and unmarked.

An elven warrior spotted them and barked out a sharp harmonic. The response was immediate. Four Deep Fold warriors surrounded the pale elves, glass spears raised. The pale ones didn't resist or make a sound as they were quickly separated from the human captives.

"Ara." Butch's voice was low and careful. He gestured toward the pale elves being escorted away. "Who are they?"

Ara's markings flickered with colors Butch had never seen before, deep indigo shot through with threads of grey. Her usual fluid grace turned rigid as she watched her fellow warriors lead the strange elves away.

"Others," she said finally, the word coming out rough and clipped. Her silver eyes tracked the pale elves until they disappeared from view, then she turned away sharply, refusing to elaborate further.

Butch noticed how the Deep Fold warriors handled the pale elves, not roughly, but with a wary distance, as if touching them might be dangerous. The pale ones moved with an unnatural smoothness, their bare feet silent on the stone floor. They kept their eyes downcast, but Butch caught a glimpse of one's face, features similar to Ara's but somehow different, like a painting that had been subtly distorted.

The last pale elf paused at the cave's entrance, head tilting as if listening to something no one else could hear. A Deep Fold warrior prodded them forward with the blunt end of his spear, and they vanished into the darkness beyond.

***

A goblin war cry echoed through the cave entrance. Deep Fold warriors formed a perfect crescent, their glass-tipped spears creating an impenetrable wall. The first wave crashed against them like water on stone.

Three goblins died on Ahko's spear before they realized the futility of their charge. The fourth tried to duck under, but Ahko's harmonics shattered its spine. The creature dropped, twitching, as five more scrambled over its corpse.

"Left side," Butch called out. His crowbar caught a goblin under the jaw, spraying teeth across the stone floor. The creature stumbled back into its companions, creating a brief tangle of limbs that the elven warriors exploited with ruthless efficiency.

Blood slicked the cave entrance. Bodies piled up, forcing subsequent waves to climb over their fallen. The Deep Fold warriors maintained their discipline, coordinating through subtle harmonic tones that made the air vibrate.

A larger goblin pushed through, wielding a crude axe. It managed two steps before three glass spears pierced its chest. The creature's momentum carried it forward onto the spears, but the line held. More goblins pressed in behind it, driven by something beyond normal aggression.

"They're being forced forward," Ara observed, her markings pulsing red. Her blade flashed, opening a goblin from collar to hip. "Something drives them."

The warriors shifted positions with practiced ease, rotating fresh fighters to the front while those who needed rest fell back. Not a single goblin made it past their defensive line. The cave entrance became a killing ground, the stone walls amplifying the sounds of death into a terrible chorus.

Another wave formed up outside. Through the gaps between warriors, Butch glimpsed the goblins' eyes, wide with fear but unable to retreat. They charged forward anyway, straight into the waiting spears.

Butch leaned against the blood-streaked wall, his chest heaving. The crowbar hung loose in his grip, its surface dark and wet. His arms burned from the endless strikes, but the familiar weight kept him grounded.

Jin approached with Mina close behind, still gripping the glass spear like it might shatter. Her eyes darted between the fallen goblins and the elven warriors, trying to process the impossible scene before her.

Mina broke away from Jin and wrapped her arms around Butch in a fierce hug. "Thank you. Thank you for coming." Her voice cracked with exhaustion and relief.

"No sweat," Butch mumbled, patting her shoulder awkwardly. His Filipino accent slipped through stronger than usual, betraying his emotional state. "Just glad you safe."

Ara stepped over the bodies, her silver markings casting shifting patterns across her skin. Jin gestured between them. "Mina, this is Ara. She helped us find you."

"Welcome," Ara said carefully, each syllable precise and measured as she bowed. Her attempt at a formal greeting came out stiff but sincere.

CHAPTER 21

Deep Fold warriors guided the captives deeper into the cave, their glass spears casting fractured light across tear-stained faces. The women huddled together, sharing sips of precious water from crystal flasks while elven healers checked wounds with gentle hands.

Ahko positioned Dusty near the western curve of the entrance, where shadows provided better cover. Lucky took the opposite side, his stocky frame a stark contrast to the lean elven warriors around him. The rotation continued with mechanical precision, three minutes at the front line and five in reserve, ensuring fresh defenders always faced the darkness beyond.

"Movement's different," Dusty whispered, his squinted eyes tracking shapes in the gloom. The goblin masses remained visible through gaps in the rock, but their usual frenzy had transformed into an unnatural stillness.

Ahko released a series of short harmonic bursts, testing the air. The responding echoes painted a grim picture, hundreds of bodies pressed together, waiting. Just waiting.

Lucky shifted his grip on his spear. "Never seen them hold formation this long."

Blood cooled on stone as minutes stretched into an hour. The cave entrance, so recently a storm of violence, now stood silent except for the quiet harmonics of rotating guards and the muffled sobs of the rescued deeper within.

The goblins maintained their vigil, an ocean of yellow eyes reflecting what little light reached them. Their weapons remained ready, but no war cry came. No surge forward. They simply watched, as if waiting for a signal that had not yet been given.

Ahko's jaw tightened as he tracked another rotation. The warriors moved like water between positions, but tension rode their shoulders. This was not the chaos of battle anymore. This was the calm of a predator sizing up its prey.

Jin sat cross-legged beside Mina in a quiet corner of the cave, their shoulders touching as they spoke in hushed tones. The phosphorescent fungi cast a pale glow across their faces, creating shadows that danced with each subtle movement.

Mina pulled her knees to her chest, the remains of her pink sweater wrapped tight around her shoulders. Her eyes widened as Jin described his journey through the portal, the alien landscape, and the creatures they had encountered. When he mentioned their father's final moments, she covered her mouth with trembling fingers.

Jin's voice cracked as he continued, his words too soft to carry beyond their small bubble of shared grief and relief. Tears tracked down Mina's cheeks, but she did not look away from her brother's face. Her fingers found his hand and squeezed, anchoring them both in the present moment.

Around them, the cave hummed with the quiet activities of the rescued women and their elven protectors. Medical attention continued in whispers and gentle movements, creating a backdrop of controlled urgency that seemed distant from the siblings' intimate conversation.

Butch lowered himself beside Jin and Mina, his muscles aching from the earlier fight. His eyes tracked across the cave until they settled on three figures huddled in a far corner. He nudged Jin's shoulder and pointed.

"Look at those three. Different from the others."

Jin studied the pale elves through the dim cave light. Their features stood out in stark contrast to the Deep Fold warriors: lighter skin that seemed to glow in the phosphorescent light, straight silver-white hair instead of the typical brown or black, and most notably, no trace of the familiar facial markings that adorned their captors.

Ned stood near them with another scout, spears held at ready positions. The pale elves kept to themselves, heads bowed in quiet conversation, their movements fluid but guarded.

"They were here before us," Mina said, her voice barely above a whisper. "When they brought us in, those three were here."

The scrape of boots on stone announced Ara's approach. She settled beside Butch, her silver markings pulsing with subdued light. Her eyes followed their gaze to the pale elves.

"Others," Ara said simply. "Not all elves are Deep Fold." Her tone carried a weight of finality that made it clear no further questions about these strangers would be answered.

Butch opened his mouth to ask more but caught himself. He had learned to read Ara's signals well enough by now. When she chose silence, pressing for details would only lead to frustration.

Jin carefully cleaned the gash on Ara's forearm while she sat motionless, her silver markings dulled by dried blood and grime. As he wiped away the mess, streaks appeared in the luminescent patterns that decorated her skin.

"They're not permanent?" Jin asked, noticing how the markings smeared beneath his touch.

Butch glanced over from where he was checking their supplies but remained silent, his expression thoughtful.

"What are they for?" Jin asked, dabbing at another wound.

Ara's remaining markings pulsed softly as she spoke. "They show name, status, feelings. Change with voice, with heart." She touched one of the brighter patterns near her wrist. "These glow when we speak, when we feel."

"How do they glow like that?" Jin leaned closer to examine the subtle shimmer.

"Made from light-fungi. Same as what you see here." Ara gestured to the phosphorescent growths on the cave walls. "They hear our song, our harmonics. React to voice."

Butch let out a quiet laugh. "It's makeup."

Ara tilted her head, confusion evident in her expression.

"Never mind," Butch waved his hand dismissively, giving up on the explanation.

Jin shook his head, equally unsure how to describe the concept, but Mina spoke up from where she sat nearby.

"Like lipstick, foundation, things humans wear to look more beautiful," she explained.

"Ah." Ara nodded slowly. "Yes, to look prettier. But different." Her markings shifted color as she considered the comparison. "We show what we carry inside. You hide it."

***

The cave walls trembled as drums thundered outside, each beat rattling loose stones from the ceiling. Jin pulled Mina closer to his side while Butch gripped his crowbar with white knuckles. The goblins' war songs pierced the air, not the random shrieks they had heard before, but organized chants that rose and fell in precise rhythm.

Ara's markings flickered erratically as she pressed her palm against the stone wall. Her face tightened with concentration.

"Many voices. Too many." She shook her head. "They wait for something."

The Deep Fold warriors maintained their positions at the cave mouth, glass-tipped spears ready. Ahko moved between them, coordinating defensive positions through quick bursts of harmonics. The rescued women huddled deeper in the cave, some covering their ears against the thunderous noise.

"Why don't they attack?" Jin whispered.

Butch studied the cave entrance, his expression grim. "They're putting on a show. Trying to break us down first."

Another drum joined the cacophony, deeper and slower, its vibrations powerful enough to make the fungi on the walls pulse with each beat. The three pale elves in the corner lifted their heads at the sound, their faces showing the first real emotion anyone had seen from them: recognition.

The war songs grew louder, hundreds of goblin voices merging into a single chant that echoed through the stone. Yet still they held back, content to wage their assault through sound alone.

Ara's markings shifted to a dark crimson as she caught something in the noise. She turned to Butch, her voice tight. "They sing of blood magic. Of power through pain." She paused, struggling to translate. "They wait for their... king? No. Warlord."

The drumming continued its relentless assault on their nerves, each beat a reminder that the goblins could afford to wait. They had the cave surrounded, and time was on their side.

Ara tilted her head, listening intently to the rhythmic chaos outside. Her silver markings pulsed with each drum beat as she decoded the patterns hidden in the noise.

"This waiting is not fear," she said, her English careful and measured. "They count. They plan." She touched the wall again, reading vibrations through stone. "More come. Always more."

Butch shifted his grip on the crowbar. "How many more?"

"Enough to break through." Ara's markings darkened. "Their leader walks among them now. Listen."

A new sound cut through the drumming, not a goblin's guttural shriek, but something deeper, more controlled. The sound carried authority and intelligence that made the rescued women press further into the shadows.

"He sounds... different," Jin whispered, keeping Mina behind him.

Ara nodded grimly. "Not like others. His voice has power. Command." She struggled for the right words. "He shapes them. Makes them more than beasts."

The Hobgoblin's voice rose again, and the surrounding goblin army responded with perfect synchronization, thousands of voices united into a single war cry that shook dust from the cave ceiling.

Ahko's scouts tightened their defensive formation at the entrance, glass spears glinting in the dim light. Through quick harmonics, they reported the growing numbers outside, each update more concerning than the last.

"The delay gives him time to gather strength," Ara explained. "When he has enough, they will come." Her markings flickered with certainty. "All at once."

The three pale elves watched this exchange silently, their unnaturally smooth features betraying no emotion. Yet something in their stillness suggested recognition, as if they had seen this tactical patience before.

A haunting melody drifted through the cave, carried on the wind. The Deep Fold warriors cocked their heads in unison, receiving the message hidden in the breeze. Ara's markings shifted to a dull grey as she translated the harmonics.

"Reinforcements," Butch said, recognizing the tension in her posture.

"Yes." Ara's voice was tight. "But not ours. Theirs." She pointed toward the goblin army massed outside.

One of their scouts, left to watch the surrounding territory, had woven an urgent warning into the wind. The other goblin camp, far to the north, had mobilized.

"We have some time," Ara said, her markings pulsing faster. "But they come."

The drumming outside intensified, as if responding to the approaching reinforcements. The rhythm grew more complex and demanding, until the very air seemed to vibrate with savage anticipation.

Butch adjusted his grip on the crowbar, planting his feet in a fighting stance. Beside him, Ara drew her glass blade while Ahko positioned himself with his spear at the ready, coordinating the defensive line through quick bursts of harmonics.

Jin rose from where he had been crouching with Mina, his borrowed spear in hand. He turned to his sister, face set with determination.

"Go back with the other women," he said firmly. "Stay with them."

CHAPTER 22

Butch leaned against the cave wall, his crowbar tapping against his leg as he listened to the translated suggestions from the warriors. Ara's voice remained steady despite the mounting tension.

"They say we could rush them," she explained, her markings shifting to a dull grey. "Break through their lines before more come."

"Not enough of us," Butch shook his head. "They'd cut us down before we made it fifty feet."

Ahko spoke in quick, sharp harmonics that made the fungi on the walls quiver. Ara translated his tactical assessment. "He agrees. Their numbers are too great for a direct assault."

The discussion continued in circles, each suggestion meeting the same dead end. The warriors grew restless, their harmonics taking on an edge of frustration as Ara relayed each failed plan to Butch.

Ned appeared from the shadows, his movements quick and urgent. He gestured toward one of the pale elves who had separated herself from her companions. Through clipped tones, he indicated she wanted to speak.

The pale elf approached Ara, her voice carrying strange, high-pitched harmonics that seemed to float above normal elven speech. Jin caught fragments of the sound, but barely, like trying to hear a dog whistle at the edge of human perception. Butch heard nothing at all.

Ara's face tensed with concentration as she attempted to communicate with the pale elf. Their exchange grew halting, filled with repeated phrases and confusion. Even Ara, fluent in multiple harmonic dialects, struggled to bridge the gap.

Finally, Ara pressed her forehead against the pale elf's. The contact lasted several seconds, both of them perfectly still. When Ara pulled back, she swayed slightly, her markings dim and flickering.

"Ara!" Jin stepped forward, steadying her arm.

"Are you alright?" Butch's grip tightened on his crowbar.

"Yes," Ara straightened, though her voice sounded drained. "Just tired. The connection with them… it takes strength."

Jin studied Ara's face as she recovered from the mental connection, wondering if there was more to the pale elves' different harmonics than just dialect. The way Ara struggled to communicate with them suggested something deeper, more fundamental in their separation.

Ara's markings shifted to a deep blue as she began translating what the pale elf had shared. "She was prisoner with goblins for over thirty star cycles. First of her kind they caught." Her voice grew tight with controlled anger. "Three pale ones taken. Hundreds of goblins died to capture them."

She paused, collecting the fragments of memory. "Goblins fled here because they fear pale ones' revenge. Lost many breeding slaves to them in battles." Her silver markings pulsed with each translated word. "They ran, split apart, ran more until reaching these lands."

Jin felt his stomach turn as Ara continued. "Here, goblins planned to grow numbers. But land had no breeding stock." Her eyes met Jin's. "Until they brought your women from somewhere. They did not know. Breeding season was to begin soon." She placed a hand on Jin's shoulder. "We came in time."

Butch's knuckles whitened around his crowbar as the implications sank in. The timing of their rescue hadn't just been fortunate. It had prevented something monstrous.

Ara's voice grew solemn as she continued translating the pale elf's words. "She offers herself as sacrifice. Says if goblins see her die, they will lose control." Her markings flickered with unease. "They believe she holds power to birth more hobgoblins. Keep her as prize for breeding season."

The pale elf's eyes remained steady, accepting, as Ara translated her willing martyrdom. "She wants to save her sisters. Says goblins never managed to breed with her kind, but their belief in her power drives them."

"No." Butch's voice cut through the cave like steel. "We're not killing anyone." His hand trembled slightly on the crowbar, eyes distant with shadows of memory. "No sacrifices. Not like that."

"We have no choice," Ara's markings dulled to ash grey. "Her death would create chaos among them."

"There's always a choice," Butch's words carried the weight of experience, of decisions that still haunted him.

Jin's face suddenly lit up with an unexpected grin. "Maybe we can..." he started.

Butch turned to him, shock and disappointment etched across his features. "You can't seriously be considering..."

"No, no," Jin's grin widened. "Trust me, you'll like this." He glanced between Butch and Ara, eyes bright with inspiration. "Hey Butch, did you ever play with toy swords as a kid?"

***

Butch traced lines in the dirt with his crowbar, demonstrating positions while Ara translated his instructions into harmonics. The warriors crowded around, studying the crude battle diagram. Their silver markings pulsed with understanding as Ara conveyed each detail of the strategy.

"Like boxing match," Butch's accent thickened as he explained. "When opponent rush forward." He stepped back, mimicking the movement. "You let them come. Then." His crowbar swept forward in a controlled arc. "Counter hard when they off balance."

Ara's markings brightened as she grasped the concept, transforming Butch's boxing metaphor into precise harmonic commands. The warriors nodded, their own markings synchronizing with hers as they absorbed the tactical pattern.

"Remember, ok?" Butch pointed at the diagram with his crowbar. "When they punch straight at us, we pop back just out of their reach. Then counterpunch." He grinned. "Manny Pacman style."

The Deep Fold warriors took positions loosely in the center, a large target for the goblin mass, but loosely enough to pull back to the cave walls, glass spears ready. Their markings dimmed to barely visible silver threads as they waited in perfect stillness. Butch gripped his crowbar, noting how the elves had instinctively grasped his strategy, positioning themselves exactly as he'd shown.

Ara turned to Jin, her markings pulsing with quiet confidence. "You're up. We're ready."

***

Jin dragged the pale elf toward the cave entrance, making sure the goblins could see her clearly. His hands trembled with rage as he gripped her arm.

"You took my father!" His voice cracked with genuine fury, tears streaming down his face. "You'll all die for what you did! Everything you have will be mine!" The words ripped from his throat, raw and filled with the pain he'd carried since watching his father fall.

The goblin drums faltered.

Jin spun the pale elf sideways, positioning her so the goblins had a perfect view. He drew back his spear and thrust it forward. The leather bag of goblin blood and water she held to her side burst, dark liquid spilling down her front.

The pale elf stood frozen, confusion flickering across her features. She had expected real sacrifice, not theatrics. The spear hadn't touched her, but blood soaked her clothes as planned.

"Down," Ara whispered urgently in harmonics. "Down!"

Jin's eyes darted meaningfully toward the ground. Warriors around them made subtle downward gestures. Understanding finally dawned on the pale elf's face, and she collapsed in a convincing heap.

The goblin drums stopped completely. For a heartbeat, absolute silence filled the air.

Then the silence shattered. Howls of bloodlust erupted from hundreds of throats. The ground trembled with the sound of their frenzy.

The pale elf scrambled to her feet and retreated to join her companions while Deep Fold deWarriors rushed to barricade the entrance. The cave filled with the sounds of preparation - glass spears clicking into position, harmonics humming through the air.

Butch gave Jin a sideways glance as the goblin screams grew louder. "I think you really pissed them off."

***

The first wave of goblins crashed through the cave entrance like a tide of teeth and claws. Their bodies twisted and writhed over each other, yellow eyes blazing with bloodlust. The air filled with their shrieks, not animal sounds, but something older, something that spoke of ancient hunger.

Deep Fold warriors held their positions along the cave walls, glass spears ready. Their silver markings pulsed with battle-light as the goblins poured through the choke point.

The creatures moved with horrible grace, each step precise despite their frenzy. Their weapons glinted, crude spears wrapped in rusted metal, clubs studded with broken crystal. The lead goblin's face contorted into a snarl as it spotted Jin.

Butch's crowbar caught the first attacker under the jaw, shattering bone. The body dropped, but three more scrambled over it. An elite warrior with ritual scars carved across its chest lunged at Jin with a glass-tipped spear, stolen Deep Fold weaponry.

Ara's harmonics cut through the chaos, directing warriors to maintain their positions. The cave amplified her battle-song, making the very air vibrate. Two goblins clutched their heads and stumbled, leaving gaps in their charge.

The warriors struck from both sides, glass spears finding vulnerable points with surgical precision. Goblin blood sprayed across crystal walls. But still they came, climbing over their dead, driven by something beyond reason or survival.

A particularly large goblin broke through, its shoulders scraping the cave ceiling. It grabbed a Deep Fold warrior's spear and snapped it, pulling the elf forward. Before it could strike, Ahko's blade opened its throat. The body fell, but five more replaced it.

The entrance became choked with corpses, yet the goblins kept coming. Their eyes held no fear, no hesitation, only killing hunger. They clawed their way forward, using their dead as shields and stepping stones, shrieking war cries that echoed through the crystal passages.

The Deep Fold warriors maintained their defensive arc until the precise moment Butch signaled. Their silver markings flashed in unison as they executed the planned retreat, glass spears withdrawing from the front line in perfect coordination.

The goblins surged forward, sensing weakness. Their bodies pressed through the gap, shoving and climbing over each other in their frenzy to reach Jin. Yellow eyes blazed with hatred as they poured deeper into the cave, weapons raised high.

Ara's battle-song shifted tone, guiding the warriors' controlled collapse. The defensive line bent inward like a bow string, drawing the goblin mass forward. More creatures squeezed through the entrance, their crude weapons scraping crystal walls as they pushed toward what they thought was victory.

Ahko pulled his squad back step by step, maintaining just enough resistance to keep the goblins' attention. The creatures followed, drunk on bloodlust, forgetting everything except their need to kill. Their war cries echoed off the cave walls as they pressed deeper into the darkness.

Butch held his position near the center, crowbar ready. His steady presence anchored the retreating lines as the goblins flooded past the cave mouth. The creatures' scaled bodies packed the entrance, blocking their own escape route in their eagerness to reach their prey.

The warriors continued their calculated withdrawal, drawing more goblins into the trap. The creatures' momentum carried them forward, their mass of bodies filling the cave's throat like water rushing into a vessel. Their own numbers became their weakness as they pushed and clawed deeper into the confined space.

Ara's markings flashed silver-bright as she released a piercing harmonic that echoed through the cave. The Deep Fold warriors responded instantly, their glass spears plunging into the mass of goblins from all sides. The creatures, packed tight in the confined space, had nowhere to dodge.

Blood sprayed across crystal walls as spear points found throats and hearts. The goblins thrashed and clawed, but their own numbers trapped them. Bodies pressed against bodies, limiting their movement as glass blades struck again and again.

Butch's crowbar whistled through the air, catching a goblin's temple with a wet crack. The creature's skull caved inward as it dropped. Another lunged past its falling companion, teeth bared. Butch stepped inside its reach and brought the crowbar up in a vicious uppercut that shattered its jaw.

Jin drove his spear into the writhing mass of scaled bodies. The glass tip punched through a goblin's leather armor and into its chest. The creature's yellow eyes went wide as it tried to grab the shaft. Jin twisted the blade and yanked it free, already seeking his next target.

The warriors' silver markings pulsed in rhythm as they tightened their circle. Glass spears rose and fell in deadly precision, turning the cave into a killing ground. Trapped goblins screamed and died, their bodies piling higher as the Deep Fold warriors closed ranks like a deadly fist crushing vermin.

Ara's battle-song guided the warriors' movements, her harmonics weaving through the chaos. Each note directed another thrust, another kill, as the Deep Fold forces executed their trap with mechanical efficiency. The goblins' earlier bloodlust turned to panic as they realized too late they had charged into their own grave.

***

The goblins thrashed in the confined space, their scaled bodies pressed together as the Deep Fold warriors closed the circle. Glass spears flashed in the crystal-lit darkness, finding gaps between leather armor and exposed throats. Blood sprayed across cave walls as the warriors struck with surgical precision.

Ara's silver markings pulsed with each kill, but she kept her harmonics contained. In such close quarters, sonic attacks would harm allies as much as enemies. Instead, she wielded her glass blade like the others, letting skill and precision do the work.

A goblin lunged at Jin, yellow eyes blazing with desperate fury. Jin sidestepped and drove his borrowed spear through its chest. The creature's claws raked his arm as it fell, but Jin barely noticed the pain. Another took its place, and another after that.

Butch's crowbar found a goblin's temple with a wet crack. The creature dropped, revealing two more climbing over its body. Butch caught one under the jaw, feeling bone shatter on impact. The second slashed at his face with rusted metal. He ducked and brought the crowbar up into its throat.

Ahko led his warriors in a coordinated advance, glass spears stabbing in perfect rhythm. The goblins tried to retreat but found only walls of crystal and more blades waiting behind them. Bodies piled higher as the trap squeezed tighter.

The creatures fought with desperate savagery, but their own numbers worked against them. Packed together, they couldn't dodge or properly swing their weapons. The warriors' spears found vulnerable points with mechanical efficiency, turning the cave into a killing ground.

Blood ran in rivulets down crystal walls as the Deep Fold forces maintained their deadly circle. The goblins' earlier battle fury gave way to animal panic as they realized there was nowhere left to run.

The warriors dragged fallen goblins aside, resetting their positions along the crystal walls. Blood-slick spears gleamed as they readied for the next wave. Ahko's harmonics directed his squad with precision, each warrior finding their mark in the shadows.

The barricade at the entrance pulled back. Goblins poured through the gap like water through a broken dam, their scaled bodies pressing forward with mindless aggression. Yellow eyes blazed in the darkness as they charged deeper into the cave.

The trap snapped shut again. Glass spears found throats and hearts while Butch's crowbar cracked skulls with mechanical efficiency. Jin's borrowed weapon pierced scaled hide as easily as the first time. Bodies dropped, adding to the growing pile.

Ara's markings pulsed with each coordinated strike as the warriors maintained their deadly circle. The goblins' war cries turned to gurgling screams as they discovered too late they'd rushed into another slaughter.

The barricade pulled back once more. Another wave surged forward, trampling their fallen kin in their battle frenzy. The warriors reset their positions, glass weapons catching purple light from the crystals above.

Again the trap closed. Again the spears found their marks. Again the cave floor ran red with goblin blood. The Deep Fold forces moved like a single organism, their attacks synchronized through subtle harmonics that guided each lethal thrust.

The efficiency of their kills grew with each reset. Bodies piled higher as wave after wave of goblins rushed to their death in the crystal-lit darkness.

The warriors shifted positions, spears dripping with fresh blood as the last of the common goblins fell. Butch wiped gore from his crowbar while Jin retrieved his weapon from a fallen creature's chest. The cave floor was slick with death, bodies stacked against crystal walls like cordwood.

The barricade at the entrance suddenly exploded inward. Three Deep Fold warriors flew backwards, their silver markings flaring in alarm as they hit the ground. Ten massive elite goblins burst through the gap, their muscled frames towering over their fallen kin. Unlike the others, these wore proper armor, crude plates of metal and bone strapped to thick hide. Behind them stood two Hobgoblins, their presence commanding absolute obedience from their elite guard.

But they did not charge.

The elite goblins formed a shield wall at the entrance, weapons held with disciplined precision. The Hobgoblins positioned themselves behind their guards, watching the carnage with cold intelligence. Their stillness was more unnerving than any attack.

Ara's markings shifted to deep crimson. Her harmonics cut short as a new sound filled the cave, heavy, measured footsteps approaching from beyond the entrance. Each impact resonated through the crystal walls, making the purple light pulse in rhythm.

The Deep Fold warriors tightened their formation. Ahko's spear tip tracked the entrance while blood continued to pool around their feet. The footsteps grew closer, deliberate and unhurried.

***

The Warlord ducked through the entrance, his massive frame appearing to fill the space. Dancing cave firelight caught the ridges of scar tissue that covered his chest and arms, thick plates of muscle that moved like living armor. His right lip curled oddly, evidence of an old wound that had healed badly.

In his left hand, he gripped a cruel weapon fashioned from a creature's thigh bone, its joint forming a natural handle while the shaft had been studded with shards of rusted metal. His right hand held something even worse, a length of spine stripped clean and wrapped in razor wire, each vertebra modified into a killing edge.

Blood from the fallen goblins soaked his bare feet, but he paid it no attention. His presence filled the cave like a physical weight, demanding absolute focus from predator and prey alike. The elite guards shifted their shield wall wider to accommodate him, moving with practiced precision that spoke of long conditioning under his command.

The Warlord's gaze swept across the carnage, taking in the piles of dead goblins with cold indifference. He assessed the Deep Fold warriors, Ahko's defensive formation, and the humans who had helped slaughter his forces. His expression remained unchanged, but something stirred behind his eyes, not anger or bloodlust, but calculation—the tactical assessment of a commander who had seen countless battles.

He stepped forward, weapons held loose but ready at his sides. The bone club dragged through pooled blood, leaving crimson trails across crystal stone. His movements carried the fluid grace of a natural killer, each step placed with deliberate care despite his imposing size.

The elite guards maintained their shield wall, awaiting his command. The two Hobgoblins flanked him like honor guards, their own weapons held with rigid discipline. The Warlord's presence had transformed the savage goblins into an organized force.

CHAPTER 23

Butch tightened his grip on the crowbar, studying the Warlord's imposing frame. Despite the creature's bulk, there was nothing slow or clumsy in how he carried himself. Each scar told its own story of survival, a ragged tear across his abdomen, thick rope-like tissue along his shoulders, the mangled right lip that pulled his mouth into a permanent snarl. This was not some beast that relied on brute strength alone.

The scars were not random battle damage. They formed patterns of deliberate violence, the kind you survived only by being faster, smarter, and more ruthless than whatever tried to kill you. The Warlord's muscles moved with coiled precision beneath his marked skin, ready to unleash devastating force in any direction.

Butch recognized the look in those eyes, the cold calculation of someone who had mastered the art of dealing death. No rage, no hesitation, just pure killing efficiency. The way the Warlord held his weapons loose but ready, how he kept his center of gravity perfectly balanced, this was a fighter who had earned his position through countless battles.

A chill ran down Butch's spine, but he forced it aside. Fear was a luxury they could not afford right now. The crowbar felt solid in his hands as he settled into a defensive stance, matching the Warlord's steady gaze. Young or not, this Hobgoblin had survived enough fights to make him deadly beyond his years.

The Warlord's hand twitched, a subtle gesture that sent his elite guards surging forward like a coordinated machine toward the center. Their shield wall split into precise attack formations, weapons raised with practiced efficiency.

The two Hobgoblins moved with shocking speed toward Ara's position. Ahko and Lucky stepped forward to meet the threat, glass spears catching the dim light. The Warlord himself advanced with measured steps directly at Butch, the bone club dragging across stone with a hollow scrape.

Butch shifted his stance, crowbar held low. "Jin, get back to Mina. Get everyone out while you can."

"No." Jin's voice was quiet but firm as he gripped his borrowed spear. "I'm not leaving you."

"Your sister needs you alive." Butch kept his eyes locked on the approaching Warlord. "This is not your fight."

"It became my fight when they killed our father." Jin moved to Butch's side, spear ready. "I'm staying."

The Warlord's massive frame cast a shadow over them both as he closed the distance. His weapons hung loose at his sides, the bone club and spine-wrapped wire somehow more menacing for their casual grip. Each deliberate step brought him closer, muscles coiled and ready beneath his scarred skin.

Butch wanted to argue further, to force Jin to retreat with the others. But there was no time. The Warlord's cold eyes fixed on them both as he raised his weapons with fluid grace. Behind them, the sounds of battle erupted as elite goblins clashed with Deep Fold warriors. The air filled with the ring of metal on glass and the sharp crack of breaking spears.

"Together then," Butch said, adjusting his grip on the crowbar.

Jin nodded once, determination hardening his features as he settled into the fighting stance Ara had taught him. The Warlord's ruined lip pulled back in what might have been a smile as he launched his attack.

***

The hobgoblin's spear thrust toward Ara's throat with crushing force. She twisted away, glass blade flashing as she deflected the strike. Her silver markings pulsed with battle-light, casting sharp shadows across the cave walls.

Her opponent moved with unnatural speed for his size, each attack flowing into the next with practiced efficiency. The hobgoblin's muscles rippled as he brought his weapon around in a sweeping arc. Ara dropped and rolled, the spear tip missing her by inches.

She came up inside his guard, blade seeking vulnerable flesh. The hobgoblin shifted his weight, turning the failed attack into a shield bash that forced her back. His fighting style carried none of the savage sloppiness of regular goblins. Every movement served a purpose, each stance ready to transition into offense or defense.

Ara's markings flickered through shades of crimson and silver as she wove between his strikes. Her blade found purchase along his arm, drawing first blood. The hobgoblin did not flinch, using the moment of contact to drive his knee toward her ribs.

She caught the blow on her forearm, harmonics rippling out to disrupt his balance. The hobgoblin staggered but recovered instantly, spear whirling to keep her at a distance. His fighting instincts adapted to her style with frightening speed.

Their weapons clashed again and again, neither able to land a decisive blow. Where the hobgoblin relied on power and precision, Ara countered with fluid grace and calculated strikes. Her blade traced silver arcs through the air as she probed his defenses, each exchange a deadly dance of steel and glass.

The hobgoblin pressed forward with a series of brutal thrusts. Ara flowed around them like water, her movements precise and economical. No energy wasted, no opening left unexploited. Her markings pulsed brighter with each near miss, reading his rhythm and adjusting her own.

Ahko's glass spear flashed as he struck, its edge opening the hobgoblin's shoulder in a spray of dark blood. Lucky flanked from the opposite side, his movements synchronized with Ahko's attack pattern through years of patrol work.

The hobgoblin absorbed the wound without slowing. Its muscles bunched as it countered, bone club sweeping in a devastating arc. Ahko dropped beneath the strike while Lucky drove his spear toward the creature's exposed flank.

The hobgoblin twisted with impossible speed, deflecting Lucky's thrust with its bracer. The movement carried through into a kick that caught Ahko in the chest. He rolled with the impact, coming up in perfect fighting stance.

Lucky pressed the advantage, glass blade singing through the air. The hobgoblin matched his pace, blocking and striking with mechanical precision. Each exchange rang through the cave like hammer strikes on an anvil.

Ahko circled behind, spear held low and ready. His steps made no sound on the blood-slick stone. The hobgoblin tracked both warriors, its inhuman reflexes keeping pace with their coordinated assault. When Lucky feinted high, Ahko struck low, but the creature read their pattern, stomping down on Ahko's spear while backhanding Lucky across the jaw.

Blood ran down the hobgoblin's shoulder, but its movements showed no sign of slowing. If anything, the wound made it more focused, more deadly. Its attacks flowed with cruel purpose, forcing Ahko and Lucky to spend more energy defending than striking.

The two elves moved like mirror images, years of shared combat experience evident in every step. Where Lucky attacked, Ahko covered. When Ahko drew the hobgoblin's attention, Lucky exploited the opening. Their glass spears wove complex patterns through the air, seeking flesh, finding only steel and bone.

But the hobgoblin matched their rhythm, its superior strength and speed turning defense into brutal counterattacks. What should have been a swift execution became a grinding war of attrition against an opponent that refused to tire or die.

The Warlord's bone club crashed against Butch's crowbar with bone-jarring force. The impact shot through Butch's arms, nearly tearing the weapon from his grip. His muscles screamed as he absorbed the blow, feet sliding back on the blood-slick stone.

The Hobgoblin towered over him, scarred muscles rippling as it brought its weapon around for another strike. Its movements carried deadly grace despite its size, each motion flowing into the next with practiced efficiency. The razor-wire spine in its off-hand whirled in complex patterns, forcing Butch to divide his attention.

Butch's arms trembled from that first exchange. The creature hit harder than anyone he'd ever faced, its raw power amplified by expert technique. He adjusted his grip on the crowbar, knuckles white against the steel. The familiar weight felt inadequate against the Warlord's arsenal.

His breath came in controlled bursts as he settled into a fighting stance. The lighter gravity of this world usually made him feel stronger, but against the Warlord's crushing strength, that advantage meant little. Sweat ran down his back as they circled each other in the cramped cave.

The Warlord's yellow eyes tracked Butch's movements with predatory focus, assessing weaknesses, reading patterns. There was nothing primitive about its gaze, only cold calculation and ancient battle wisdom. Its weapons moved like extensions of its body, each twitch a potential death sentence.

Jin moved in from the side, glass spear held low and ready. His grip adjusted on the unfamiliar weapon as he watched Butch trade devastating blows with the Warlord. The spear felt light in his hands, its balance perfect despite its alien design.

He circled carefully, searching for an opening. The Warlord's reach was longer, its weapons more deadly, but the cave's cramped space limited its mobility. Jin kept close to the wall, using the rough stone to guard his flank while he looked for a chance to strike.

The glass blade caught firelight as Jin jabbed experimentally at the Warlord's leg. The creature shifted its weight, easily avoiding the thrust without breaking its focus on Butch. Jin pulled back before the bone club could sweep his spear aside.

He darted in again, this time targeting the Warlord's weapon arm. The spear tip traced a silver arc through the air. The Warlord twisted away, but Jin was already retreating, staying just beyond the creature's reach. Close enough to threaten, not so close he'd be crushed by those massive arms.

Each time Butch engaged, Jin probed the Warlord's defenses. His strikes came faster as confidence grew, the spear becoming an extension of his body. He could not match the creature's power, but he could force it to divide its attention, create openings for Butch to exploit.

The cave walls pressed in around them, limiting Jin's movement but also preventing the Warlord from bringing its full strength to bear. Jin used the confined space to his advantage, keeping his strikes economic and precise. No wasted motion, no overextension, just quick thrusts followed by immediate withdrawal.

Ara's markings flashed silver as she spun away from a hobgoblin's thrust, her glass blade singing through the air. The creature's spear crashed against the cave wall, sending crystal shards flying. Behind her, Ahko and Lucky moved in perfect sync, forcing the second hobgoblin to divide its attention.

Lucky broke left while Ahko circled right, their spears weaving complex patterns that kept the hobgoblin off balance. When it lunged at Lucky, Ahko's blade opened a gash across its shoulder. The hobgoblin whirled to counter, but Lucky was already inside its guard, glass tip seeking flesh.

Ara pressed her advantage, driving her opponent toward a narrow section of cave. Her blade found purchase along its arm, drawing dark blood. The hobgoblin answered with a devastating sweep of its weapon. She dropped and rolled, coming up beside Ahko as he disengaged from his target.

Without a word, they switched opponents. Ara's harmonics rippled out, disrupting the second hobgoblin's stance while Lucky and Ahko converged on the first. Their glass spears struck in alternating rhythms, never giving the creature time to properly counter.

The hobgoblins tried to regroup, but the three warriors kept them separated. Each time one moved to support the other, precise strikes forced them apart again. Ara's blade flashed as she exploited every opening, while Ahko and Lucky's coordinated attacks slowly wore down their target's defense.

Blood ran black in the cave's dim light as more wounds opened on the hobgoblins' thick hide. Yet they fought with mechanical precision, absorbing injuries that would have dropped lesser creatures. Their weapons carved deadly arcs through the air, each strike powerful enough to shatter bone.

Ara slid between the attacks, her movements fluid and precise. When her hobgoblin overextended, she drew it further from its companion. Ahko and Lucky pressed their advantage, glass blades seeking vulnerable points as they maneuvered their opponent into a corner.

The cave echoed with the clash of weapons and the hobgoblins' guttural snarls. Four separate battles merged into one deadly dance as the warriors flowed between opponents, never staying still long enough to become predictable.

***

Ned's glass spear caught an elite goblin's throat as it breached the defensive line. Dark blood sprayed across the cave wall. The creature's armor clinked against stone as it dropped, but three more rushed forward to take its place.

Dusty crouched low, deflecting a rusted blade with his spear shaft. The elite goblins moved with unsettling coordination, their attacks flowing together in practiced sequences. Gone was the frenzied violence of common goblins. These warriors fought with cold precision.

"Hold the line," Dusty called in harmonic tones. The Deep Fold scouts shifted formation, glass spears creating an overlapping barrier of deadly points.

An elite goblin slammed its shield into the defense, forcing a gap between two scouts. Ned stepped into the breach, his shorter stature allowing him to strike up under the creature's guard. The glass blade punched through leather armor, but the goblin barely flinched.

The warriors' silver markings pulsed with each coordinated movement as they fought to maintain their circular defense. Elite goblins probed for weaknesses, testing different sections of the line. When one attack failed, they immediately shifted to another angle.

Blood and sweat made the cave floor treacherous. A scout lost his footing, and three elite goblins surged forward. Dusty and Ned converged on the breach, their spears moving in perfect harmony. One goblin fell, but the others pressed through, forcing the warriors to give ground.

The Deep Fold scouts retreated step by step, maintaining formation even as the elite goblins pushed them deeper into the cave. Each warrior covered their companions' withdrawal, never leaving an opening for the enemy to exploit. Their silver markings cast shifting shadows on the crystal walls as they fought for survival.

Ned deflected a vicious overhead strike while Dusty's spear found a gap in scaled armor. The elite goblin staggered but kept fighting, its movements mechanical and relentless. Around them, the battle devolved into a desperate struggle to hold position as more armored figures pressed into the cave.

Butch's crowbar whistled through the stale cave air. The curved steel connected with the Warlord's shoulder, the impact sending shockwaves up Butch's arms. Bone cracked beneath scarred flesh.

The Warlord staggered back, his massive frame shifting to compensate. His bone club dropped slightly, the first sign of weakness he'd shown. Blood welled up where the crowbar had torn skin.

Copper filled Butch's mouth. His split lip dripped red onto the cave floor, mixing with the dark pools left by fallen goblins. Each breath burned in his chest. His arms felt like lead, muscles screaming from deflecting the Warlord's crushing blows.

The Warlord's eyes narrowed, reassessing the aging human who had managed to wound him. His scarred lip twisted, revealing yellowed fangs. The shoulder injury seemed only to fuel his cold rage rather than slow him down.

Butch spat blood and adjusted his grip on the crowbar. The steel felt slick with sweat and gore, but he couldn't afford to let it slip now. His body protested every movement, yet he forced himself to maintain his fighting stance.

Jin lunged with his glass spear, aiming for the gap between the Warlord's ribs. The Hobgoblin's free hand shot out with terrifying speed, catching Jin across the face. The casual backhand sent him flying as if he weighed nothing.

Jin's body slammed into the crystal wall. His head cracked against the stone, and the spear clattered from his grip. Stars exploded behind his eyes as he slid to the ground, legs giving out beneath him.

The Warlord never even looked at Jin. His cold, predatory gaze remained fixed on Butch, dismissing the younger human as unworthy of attention. Blood from his shoulder wound dripped steadily onto the cave floor, but his stance showed no sign of pain or weakness.

Jin tried to push himself up, but his arms wouldn't cooperate. The cave spun around him as consciousness threatened to slip away. Through blurred vision, he watched the Warlord advance on Butch, bone club raised for another devastating attack.

The Warlord's massive hand clamped around Butch's throat, fingers digging into flesh as he lifted the human off his feet. Butch's boots kicked uselessly in the air for a moment before the Warlord slammed him down. The impact drove the breath from Butch's lungs, his skull cracking against the stone floor.

Pain exploded through Butch's body. The cave ceiling blurred above him as spots danced in his vision. His ribs screamed in protest, and copper flooded his mouth. But his grip on the crowbar never loosened.

The Warlord loomed over him, a mountain of scarred muscle blocking out the crystal light. His yellow eyes held no emotion, just cold calculation as he prepared to crush his prey.

Butch twisted, muscles burning as he swung the crowbar in a tight arc. The curved steel connected with the Warlord's knee joint, striking the exact spot where bone met tendon. The satisfying crunch of impact echoed off the cave walls.

A guttural sound, half growl, half roar, tore from Butch's throat as he put every ounce of remaining strength behind the blow. His arms trembled with the force of it, shoulders straining as he drove the crowbar deeper into the Warlord's flesh.

Ara's glass blade sliced through the hobgoblin's forearm, opening a deep gash that sprayed dark blood across the crystal walls. The creature stumbled back, its spear wavering for the first time since the battle began.

Ahko capitalized on his opponent's momentary distraction, driving his spear point into the second hobgoblin's thigh. The glass tip shattered on impact, sending crystalline shards deep into muscle and bone. The hobgoblin's leg buckled, forcing it to one knee.

Ara's silver markings pulsed crimson as she pressed her advantage. Her harmonics cut through the cave's chaos, disrupting her opponent's balance. The hobgoblin's movements grew sluggish, its previous precision crumbling under her relentless assault.

Blood loss took its toll on Ara's target. The hobgoblin's attacks became desperate, wild swings replacing calculated strikes. Its spear clattered against the cave wall, the sound sharp and discordant.

Ahko kicked his wounded opponent's chest, sending it sprawling onto its back. The hobgoblin rolled away from his follow-up strike, leaving a trail of blood as it scrambled into the shadows beyond the crystal light. Its retreat was awkward and graceless, a far cry from its earlier deadly efficiency.

The remaining hobgoblin facing Ara backed away, yellow eyes darting between opponents as the other two Deep Fold warriors closed in. It snarled once, baring blood-stained fangs, before melting into the darkness of the deeper cave passages.

Lucky moved to pursue, but Ahko's sharp harmonic tone held him back. The wounded hobgoblins were still deadly, even in retreat. The shadows could hide any number of traps or ambush positions.

Ara's markings flashed as she caught movement at the edge of her vision. The elite goblins had forced Ned and Dusty's group back against the walls, their coordinated attacks breaking through the scouts' defensive formation. Blood stained the cave floor where fallen warriors lay.

Dusty deflected a blade with his spear shaft, but the motion left his side exposed. An elite goblin's rusted sword sliced through his leather armor. He staggered, silver markings dimming as pain shot through his body.

Ned tried to cover his companion, but three armored goblins pressed forward at once. Their shields formed an advancing wall that pushed the remaining scouts further into the shadows.

Ahko's harmonic command cut through the chaos. He and Lucky charged toward their embattled companions, glass spears leading the way. Lucky's blade found a gap between armor plates, dropping one elite goblin. Ahko's precise strikes forced two others back, creating space for the scouts to reform their line.

Ara turned toward the Warlord, glass blade ready, but movement near the crystal wall caught her attention. Jin lay crumpled against the stone, blood trickling from his temple where he had struck the rock. His eyes were unfocused, and his limbs trembled as he tried to push himself up.

Without hesitation, Ara changed direction. Her boots slid through goblin blood as she sprinted to Jin's side. Her silver markings pulsed with urgency as she reached him, one hand pressing against his chest to keep him from rising too quickly.

Jin's glazed eyes struggled to focus on her face. His fingers clutched weakly at her arm as she checked his wound, her harmonics probing for signs of serious injury.

***

The Warlord's massive hand clamped around Butch's throat, lifting him off the blood-slick cave floor. Butch's crowbar struck the creature's injured knee again, but the Warlord barely flinched. His scarred face showed no pain, only cold focus as he squeezed.

Butch drove his elbow into the Warlord's forearm, targeting nerve clusters that should have made any normal opponent release their grip. The Warlord's flesh felt like iron beneath his strikes. Dark spots danced at the edges of Butch's vision as his lungs burned for air.

The Warlord slammed Butch against the crystal wall. The impact knocked what little breath remained from his body. His ribs screamed in protest. Still, Butch's fingers maintained their death grip on the crowbar, his lifeline in this nightmare.

Blood from the Warlord's knee wound pooled beneath them both. The creature's breathing came in controlled, measured bursts despite the injury. His yellow eyes bore into Butch's with predatory intelligence as he increased pressure on Butch's windpipe.

Butch's arms felt like lead weights. Each swing of the crowbar grew weaker and less coordinated. The Warlord simply absorbed the blows, using his superior reach and strength to keep Butch pinned.

There was no technique here and no finesse, only raw power against desperate survival instinct.

The cave walls blurred as darkness crept farther into Butch's field of vision. His lungs spasmed. The crowbar struck the Warlord's shoulder, but the blow held no force. The metal felt impossibly heavy in Butch's grip.

The Warlord's other hand seized Butch's wrist and slowly pried his fingers from the crowbar. Butch fought against the pressure, but his muscles would not respond. His body was betraying him, strength fading as the Warlord's grip tightened with mechanical precision.

Jin's head throbbed as Ara helped him sit up. The cave spun around him, crystal walls blurring into streaks of purple and shadow. Her silver markings pulsed with concern as she steadied him.

Through the haze, Jin saw Butch dangling from the Warlord's grip. The massive creature had Butch pinned against the wall, thick fingers crushing his throat. Butch's face turned purple, his strikes with the crowbar growing weaker by the second.

The Warlord raised his bone club, muscles rippling beneath scarred flesh. The weapon cast a twisted shadow across Butch's face as the creature prepared to deliver the killing blow.

"No." Jin pushed away from Ara's support, forcing his legs to cooperate. His body protested, but adrenaline surged through him. He could not watch another person die. Not like his father.

Ara's markings flashed crimson as she registered the Warlord's intent. Her hand moved to her glass blade, her body tensing for action.

Jin stumbled forward, each step steadier than the last. The cave floor felt sticky with blood beneath his feet. Around them, the sounds of battle continued, metal on crystal and harmonics cutting through war cries. But Jin focused only on Butch, on the club about to crush his skull.

Jin surged forward, raw emotion flooding his veins. His glass spear caught the torchlight as he charged. Every loss and every horror since that first violet portal crystallized into a single point of fury. His father's death, Mina's capture, the cave of broken women, and Butch dying in the Warlord's grip.

The Warlord's head snapped toward the sound of Jin's footsteps, but his position against Butch left him no room to dodge. Jin's spear struck true, the glass tip piercing the creature's face.

The monster's hold slackened, releasing Butch, who crumpled heavily onto the ground.

The Warlord's massive hand engulfed Jin's face, fingers digging into his skull as he lifted him off the ground. Blood and spittle sprayed from the creature's mouth where Jin's spear protruded from his cheek, the glass shaft trembling with each breath. Jin's knuckles whitened as he gripped the weapon, refusing to let go even as the pressure on his head intensified.

The Warlord's yellow eyes flickered past Jin, catching movement behind him. Ara materialized from the shadows, her silver markings pulsing with deadly intent. The monster's muscles tensed, but he could not release Jin without losing his advantage.

Time stretched like cold honey. Jin's feet dangled above the bloody cave floor. The Warlord's fingers tightened, bones creaking under the crushing force. Crystals reflected torchlight across Ara's face as she launched herself at the creature's broad back.

Her legs locked around the Warlord's waist, and her arms snaked around his thick neck. The monster stumbled half a step, caught between Jin's weight and Ara's sudden attack. His free hand reached back, trying to dislodge her, but Ara held fast.

She pressed her face against the base of his skull and released a pure, piercing note. The sound cut through the cave's chaos like a blade. The Warlord's body went rigid, but his grip on Jin did not loosen. His jaw clenched, muscles straining against the harmonic assault.

Ara's markings blazed silver white as she pushed deeper into the resonance. The sound built in waves, each one more intense than the last. Crystal walls vibrated in sympathy. Still, the Warlord resisted, his immunity to sonic attacks evident in his continued stance.

Desperation crept into Ara's expression. She drew breath and unleashed everything she had, her voice rising beyond human perception into a frequency that made the very air shudder. Her markings strobed with painful brightness as she forced her power past its limits, refusing to let this monster claim another victim.

The harmonic frequency reached its peak, vibrating through crystal and bone. Inside the Warlord's mouth, the glass spear tip caught the resonance and amplified it. For a split second nothing happened, then the glass exploded.

Crystalline shards ripped through flesh and bone, tearing upward through the Warlord's skull. Blood and fragments erupted from his eye socket in a violent spray. The monster's grip on Jin's head loosened instantly as his massive body went slack.

Jin dropped to the cave floor and scrambled backward on hands and knees. The Warlord's corpse swayed for a moment, blood streaming from the ruined remains of his face, before crashing down with a wet thud.

Ara slid from the creature's back, her silver markings dim and flickering as she collapsed against the floor. The harmonic assault had drained her completely. Her chest heaved with ragged breaths as she stared at the Warlord's broken form.

Shards of glass glinted in the torchlight where they protruded from the monster's skull, dark blood pooling beneath his massive frame. What remained of Jin's spear jutted from the ruin of the Warlord's face like a crystalline banner planted in conquered flesh.

CHAPTER 24

The cave walls trembled as Ahko drove his glass spear through an elite goblin's throat. Lucky and Ned worked in tandem, their coordinated strikes forcing the remaining attackers back toward the entrance. Dusty's spear found gaps in goblin armor with surgical precision.

The Deep Fold warriors pressed their advantage, their silver markings pulsing with battle rhythm. Glass-tipped weapons caught torchlight as they pushed forward, step by measured step. Blood sprayed across crystal walls as each strike landed true.

Then the vibrations hit.

The sound cut through flesh and stone, a frequency beyond hearing that made teeth ache and bones shudder. Combat ground to a halt as warriors and goblins alike turned toward its source.

The Warlord's massive frame swayed, blood streaming from his ruined face. His fingers twitched once, then his legs buckled. The cave floor shook as his body crashed down.

For a heartbeat, silence filled the chamber. Elite goblins stared at their fallen leader, their disciplined formation crumbling. One dropped his shield. Another's weapon clattered to the ground.

Panic spread through goblin ranks like wildfire. Their organized defense dissolved into chaos as they scrambled over each other to escape. Shields and weapons lay abandoned as they fled, pushing and clawing past one another in their desperation to reach the exit.

"Move," Ahko commanded through sharp harmonics. The Deep Fold warriors parted, creating a path for the retreating goblins. It was better to let them flee than risk more casualties in close combat.

The elite guards, once precise and deadly, now ran like frightened animals, their military bearing shattered by the sight of their invincible leader lying dead in a pool of his own blood.

Ahko's harmonics cut through the aftermath of battle. "Secure the entrance. Three scouts, track those creatures." His voice carried command authority despite exhaustion. Warriors moved with practiced efficiency, stepping over fallen goblins to take defensive positions.

"Dusty, Lucky, check the hostages." He gestured toward the cave's deeper chambers where the rescued women huddled. "Ned, gather our wounded."

The cave floor was slick with blood, making each step treacherous as Ahko rushed to where Ara lay crumpled beside the Warlord's massive corpse. Her silver markings had dimmed to a dull grey, but her chest rose with shallow breaths. Relief flooded through him—she lived.

Jin sprawled nearby, blood trickling from a gash above his eye, but his pulse beat steady under Ahko's fingers. The human's reckless charge had helped turn the tide.

Butch lay slumped against the wall, his trusted crowbar still gripped tight. Purple bruises darkened his throat where the Warlord had nearly crushed his windpipe. Ahko pressed two fingers to Butch's neck, waiting. There. A faint but regular rhythm.

"Get me three healers," Ahko called out, his harmonics carrying urgency without panic. "All three are alive, but unconscious."

Warriors responded immediately, their silver markings pulsing with shared purpose as they brought supplies and began tending to the fallen. Ahko supervised their work while maintaining awareness of the secured entrance. They had won, but he would not relax his guard until they were safely away from this blood-soaked cave.

Ara's markings flickered weakly as she began to stir. Ahko knelt beside her, his own markings pulsing with concern as he watched her eyes flutter open.

"Can you hear me?" His harmonics carried the question with gentle resonance.

Ara's lips moved, but no sound emerged. Her throat worked as she tried again, attempting to form the complex tones of their language. Only a whisper of air escaped.

Confusion crossed her face. She pressed her hand against her throat, concentrating. Her markings flickered erratically as she attempted to produce even the simplest harmonic note. The sound caught and died before it could form.

A cough wracked her body. Then another. She covered her mouth as the spasms continued, each one more violent than the last. When she pulled her hand away, dark blood stained her palm.

Ahko's markings dimmed as their eyes met. They both understood what this meant—the price of unleashing such powerful harmonics. The resonance that had helped kill the Warlord had damaged her own ability to produce the harmonic sound of her people.

His hand found hers, squeezing gently as her markings pulsed with fear and realization.

***

Jin's eyes fluttered open to find Mina's worried face hovering above him. His entire body screamed in protest as he tried to move. Every breath sent sharp pains through his ribs.

"Easy," Mina whispered, helping him sit up. "You got thrown pretty hard."

Jin gritted his teeth and forced himself to stand, leaning heavily on his sister. The cave spun for a moment before his vision steadied. Deep Fold warriors moved purposefully through the space, tending to their wounded. The metallic scent of blood hung thick in the air.

He spotted Ara sitting cross-legged near one of the walls, her silver markings dim and subdued. Butch lay unconscious beside her, his neck mottled with dark bruises. Jin limped over with Mina's support.

"What happened?" Jin asked, easing himself down next to them.

Ara turned to face him. Her usual fluid grace seemed diminished, her movements stiffer than normal. When she opened her mouth to speak, the sound that emerged was wrong, raspy and broken, barely above a whisper.

"We won," she managed, her voice catching. "The Warlord is dead."

Jin frowned at the strange quality of her speech. Gone were the musical undertones that usually colored her words.

"Your voice..."

Ara's markings flickered with something like grief. "The harmonics damaged. Cannot make proper sound now." She touched her throat. "Like infant now. Can barely speak to my people."

Her silver markings barely pulsed once, then faded to a dull grey. She looked away, her shoulders tight with tension.

Ahko approached with measured steps, his glass spear still coated in goblin blood. He knelt beside Ara and produced a series of complex harmonics that echoed off the cave walls. Ara's markings barely flickered in recognition, but when she tried to respond vocally, only a pained rasp emerged. Instead, she pressed her forehead against Ahko's, sharing her thoughts directly.

After a moment, Ahko pulled back and addressed the group in careful, halting English. "Scout reports strange thing. Big goblin force from other camp. They stop moving." He gestured with his spear. "Not retreat, not advance. Just wait."

Jin shifted uncomfortably. "Why would they stop?"

"Lost leader," Ahko continued. "But still have one hobgoblin who escaped. Still dangerous." He turned to Ara, switching briefly to harmonics before remembering her condition. His expression softened as she nodded in response to his tones.

"We must leave soon," he said, scanning the cave. "Will carry wounded on Travois, sliding beds made from spears and vines. Deep Fold warriors know how to build fast."

Ara pressed her forehead to Ahko's again, and she translated her projected thoughts. "We take all survivors, all dead. No one left behind."

Several warriors were already gathering materials, stripping vines from their armor and lashing them to their glass spears. The makeshift stretchers would allow them to transport the injured through the difficult terrain ahead.

CHAPTER 25

Butch's eyes cracked open to a sky fragmented by twisted crystal spires. His body swayed with the steady rhythm of movement. He lay on a makeshift stretcher crafted from stripped glass spears and thick purple vines. The ingenious construction distributed his weight evenly across the frame, though every bump in the terrain sent jolts through his bruised body.

His right hand still clutched the crowbar, knuckles white from the death grip he'd maintained even while unconscious. The metal was sticky with dried goblin blood.

Jin walked beside the travois, his face drawn with exhaustion but alert. When he noticed Butch's eyes open, relief washed over his features.

"Thought I was dead for sure," Butch croaked, his throat raw. "Even got the rigor mortis already." He lifted the crowbar-clutching hand with a weak laugh that turned into a cough.

Embarrassment flooded through him as two Deep Fold warriors continued pulling his stretcher. Butch planted his free hand against the frame and pushed himself up, ignoring the protests of torn muscles and bruised ribs. His legs wobbled as he slid off the travois onto unsteady feet.

Ara appeared at his side, her usually graceful movements now carrying a subtle stiffness. When she spoke, her voice emerged rough and damaged, missing its musical qualities.

"Almost there," she rasped, silver markings pulsing dimly. The melodic undertones that normally colored her speech were conspicuously absent, replaced by something raw and painful-sounding.

As they made their way through the twisted landscape, Ara explained the aftermath of the battle in her new, damaged voice. The words emerged rough and stripped of their usual harmonic layers.

"After the Warlord choked you out, Jin got up and charged him with the glass spear."

Butch turned to Jin and held out his fist. Jin bumped it with a shy smile.

"I knew you could do it," Butch said.

Jin's face reddened at the praise.

"That's my big brother," Mina beamed from beside Jin.

Butch noticed her for the first time, giving a slight bow of his head. "Miss Mina."

"But Ara was the one who finished it," Jin added. "She used her harmonics on my spear while it was stuck in his face. The whole thing exploded inside his head."

Butch's eyes widened. "Inside his-" He whistled low. "Remind me never to make you angry."

Ara's markings flickered a dull grey. She touched her throat. "The sound broke something. Can't make proper harmonics anymore."

"The goblins stopped pursuing us after their leader fell," Jin said. "But something weird was happening back there. They all just stopped."

Ara admitted she hadn't been eager to linger and discover the reason.

Butch scanned the group as they moved through the crystalline terrain. The numbers didn't add up. Many of the Deep Fold warriors were missing, including his "Three Amigos." His chest tightened at their absence.

"The others—Dusty, Ned, Lucky. Did they..." He couldn't finish the question.

Jin shook his head. "No, they split off. Most of the warriors headed back to the Grove with those pale elves we found."

"The others," Ara corrected, her damaged voice barely above a whisper. Her silver markings pulsed weakly as she spoke. "They will go home."

Butch counted the remaining group: about fifty-three rescued women walking with Jin's sister Mina, a handful of Deep Fold warriors including Ahko, and their small core team. The warriors maintained a protective formation around the civilians despite their obvious exhaustion. More travois carried wrapped bodies.

"We're taking them back to the tear," Jin explained. "The same one we came through. Ara thinks it's still open."

Butch inclined his head, haunted by their failure to rescue all the captives. The fact that they'd had to leave some of the dead behind weighed heavily on him.

***

The violet tear hung in the air like a jagged wound in reality, its edges no longer flickering wildly as they had during that first chaotic night. The portal's light pulsed with an almost mechanical regularity now, casting steady shadows across the suburban street's broken windows and debris-strewn lawns.

Jin stared at the dimensional rift, remembering how his father had fought here, how Mina had been dragged through screaming. The memories felt distant now, dulled by exhaustion and the weight of what they'd endured since crossing over.

"It's different," Jin said, studying the portal's rhythmic behavior. "More... stable?"

Ara nodded, her silver markings reflecting the portal's steady purple glow. When she spoke, her damaged voice emerged as a rough whisper. "The tear learns. Finds its path."

The rescued women huddled together nearby, many still wearing the same clothes from the night they were taken. Some clutched each other's hands, others wrapped their arms around themselves, all watching the portal with a mix of fear and desperate hope.

Ahko positioned his remaining warriors in a protective circle around the group, their glass-tipped spears catching the portal's light. Their silver markings pulsed in sync with each other as they maintained their guard formation, though their usual harmonic communication was notably absent out of respect for Ara's condition.

Butch gripped his bloodied crowbar tighter, studying the portal's steady rhythm. The crystal shard in his pocket had gone cold and silent, as if it too recognized something had changed in the tear's nature.

"Like a heartbeat now," he muttered, watching the purple light's consistent ebb and flow. "Not crazy like before."

Butch watched the portal's rhythm for several more cycles, then gave a firm nod. "Time to go home."

The women moved forward in small groups, some helping others who could barely walk. Two pairs of survivors carried a travois bearing Mrs. Chen's shrouded body, determined not to leave her behind. Their faces showed grim resolve as they approached the violet tear.

"Careful now," Butch said, positioning himself near the portal's edge. "Step through together."

The first group crossed the threshold, vanishing into the purple light with a soft crackle. Another followed, then another. Some hesitated at the last moment, but the sight of others making it through gave them courage.

Maria Rodriguez paused before entering, clutching Emily Torres's personal effects in a makeshift bag. Her eyes met Butch's. "Thank you," she whispered, then stepped into the light.

The women carrying the travois approached next. They adjusted their grip on the poles, sharing a determined look.

"We'll help," Jin said, moving to support one end while Mina steadied the other. Together, they guided Mrs. Chen's body through the portal, honoring her with this final journey home.

More groups passed through until only a handful remained. Each crossing dimmed the portal slightly, as if its energy was being slowly consumed by their passage.

***

Jin turned to Ara, his throat tight with emotion. "I don't know how to thank you for everything."

Ara raised her hand, cutting him off. Her silver markings were very dim, but still shifted to a determined blue. "I go with you."

Butch let out a quiet chuckle, shaking his head. He had seen this coming from the moment she'd sacrificed her voice to save them.

Ahko stepped forward, his own markings flashing with concern. He spoke in their harmonic language, the tones carrying clear disagreement. The other warriors tensed, their spears shifting uneasily.

Ara faced Ahko directly. Without her voice, she couldn't respond in harmonics. Instead, she pressed her forehead to his, initiating the deeper connection unique to Hollows. Her markings pulsed with intense silver light.

Through their mental link, her thoughts flowed clear and strong: *I am Hollow. This is my duty. Tell the Council I go for everyone's sake.*

Ahko's markings flickered as he received her message.

There is danger coming, she continued. *We need friends. True friends.* Her gaze shifted briefly to Jin and Butch. *I will ensure they are friends.*

Ahko pulled back from the connection, his expression torn between understanding and loss. He studied Ara's face, seeing the unwavering resolve in her eyes. The silver markings along his arms dimmed in acceptance.

Jin stepped toward Ahko, his eyes welling with tears. Without warning, he wrapped his arms around the elf warrior in a tight embrace. Ahko stiffened, his markings flickering with surprise at the unexpected physical contact.

Mina followed her brother's lead, giving Ahko a gentle hug that made his markings pulse with confusion. The other Deep Fold warriors watched with a mixture of curiosity and bewilderment at this strange human custom. After a moment's hesitation, Ahko carefully returned the gesture, his movements uncertain but sincere.

Butch approached next, holding out his bloodied crowbar. "Here, you can have this."

Ahko's markings shifted to deep bronze as he shook his head, producing harmonics that clearly meant refusal. The weapon had proven itself in battle, and surely such a gift was too significant.

"Nah, it's okay. It's just for opening big boxes." Butch pressed the crowbar into Ahko's hands with a casual shrug. "Got more back home."

Ahko gripped the weapon reverently, his markings now glowing with solemn acceptance. In his mind, this was a profound warrior's blessing—the passing of a battle-proven weapon from one fighter to another.

Ara watched the exchange, her faded silver markings dancing with barely contained amusement. Neither man understood the other's words, yet both felt the weight of gratitude in their own way, Butch giving away a tool as thanks, Ahko receiving what he believed to be a sacred honor.

CHAPTER 26

The portal's light pulsed behind them as Jin, Mina, Butch, and Ara emerged into the familiar Fullerton night. Harsh floodlights snapped on, flooding the clearing with artificial brightness that made them squint after the alien darkness they had left behind.

Soldiers in tactical gear formed a perimeter, weapons lowered but ready. Their flashlights swept across the newcomers, lingering on Ara's alien features and dimmed silver markings.

In the field before them, medical teams worked among clusters of rescued women. Emergency blankets gleamed under the floodlights as paramedics moved between patients, checking vitals and treating injuries. Some women sat wrapped in blankets, clutching cups of water or speaking quietly with uniformed officers and doctors. Others lay on stretchers, receiving IV fluids or having wounds cleaned.

Maria Rodriguez spotted them from her stretcher and raised a weak hand in greeting. Mrs. Park was there too, being examined by a doctor while answering questions from a police officer.

Ara's markings pulsed faintly as she took in the organized chaos of the human emergency response. Her head tilted slightly, studying the efficient movements of the medical teams with quiet curiosity.

Mina pressed closer to Jin's side as multiple flashlight beams focused on them. Her brother's arm tightened protectively around her shoulders while Butch stepped forward, positioning himself between the group and the approaching soldiers.

"U.S. Army!" a commanding voice called out. "Stay where you are and identify yourselves!"

Butch moved in front of Ara, his broad shoulders blocking the soldiers' view of her alien features. Camera flashes burst like lightning, casting harsh shadows across his face. Above them, a drone's rotors whined, its red recording light blinking steadily.

Radio static crackled through the night. "Subject identified as male, Asian descent, approximately fifty years—"

"Filipino, sir. M-my name is Alec Xander Hidalgo, sir." Butch's voice cracked, his Filipino accent thickening with each word. "Friends call me Butch... sir... ma'am... sir..."

The hard-edged warrior who had fought through alien worlds vanished, replaced by a nervous immigrant trying to appear smaller despite everything. His hands trembled slightly as he held them up in a placating gesture.

Jin and Mina exchanged shocked glances. In all their time together, they had never heard his full name—Xander. The confident protector who had guided them through battle now stumbled over his words.

Ara's silver markings flickered with confusion as she observed the dramatic shift in Butch's demeanor. Her head tilted, trying to reconcile this anxious man with the warrior who had faced down a Hobgoblin Warlord.

Butch turned to Jin, his eyes pleading. "Alec Xander," he repeated softly, as if apologizing for keeping this secret. Jin wondered, *is this an act...*

A pair of paramedics approached with a stretcher, their practiced eyes assessing Mina's condition. They gently guided her away from Jin's protective embrace, speaking in calm, professional tones about checking for injuries and dehydration.

Jin started to follow, then stopped. He turned back to face Butch and Ara, his shoulders trembling. In three quick steps, he wrapped his arms around them both, pulling them close.

"Thank you... thank you..." Jin's voice cracked, tears streaming down his face as he held them tighter. The words carried the weight of everything they had survived together—the battles, the fear, the desperate rescue of his sister.

He released them reluctantly and hurried after Mina's stretcher. A few steps away, Jin paused and looked back, his expression questioning as he noticed Butch's uncharacteristic nervousness among the armed soldiers.

"Authorities with guns," Butch explained quietly, his accent thicker than usual. "Scares me."

Ara tilted her face toward the night sky, her unmarked skin pale under the harsh floodlights. The vast expanse of stars pressed down on her like a physical weight. Earth's heavier gravity dragged at her limbs, making each movement require conscious effort.

She spread her fingers, testing their resistance against the thick air. The metallic tang of pollution coated her tongue, so different from the pure oxygen of her world. Her shoulders tensed as she adjusted her stance, compensating for the increased pull on her muscles.

"Everything... pulls," she said, the English words coming slow and deliberate. Her voice carried none of its former musical quality, stripped of the harmonics that once gave it depth.

Her hand moved to her throat, fingers tracing where the silver markings had once pulsed with light and emotion. Now her skin remained bare, the sacrifice of her resonance leaving no trace of the warrior she had been.

The simple act of standing required more strength than she had anticipated. Each breath felt heavy, compressed by the density of Earth's atmosphere. She shifted her weight, recalibrating her body's responses to this alien gravity.

Butch kept close to Ara as they followed the soldier through the chaos of emergency vehicles and medical stations. Camera flashes erupted behind them, reporters shouting questions that disappeared into the night air. The aide's fatigues rustled with each precise step as he led them toward a large green military tent.

Ara's movements remained careful, each step measured against Earth's stronger gravity. Her bare skin looked almost luminescent under the harsh floodlights, drawing more camera flashes from the perimeter.

The steady thump of rotors cut through the night. Ara froze mid-step, her head snapping up as a helicopter thundered overhead. The machine hung in the air like an impossible metal beast, its searchlight sweeping across the ground below.

She pointed at the aircraft, her eyes wide with a mix of wonder and alarm. The wind from the rotors whipped her hair around her face as she tracked the helicopter's movement.

"I will tell you about it later," Butch said, his voice still carrying that unfamiliar nervous edge. He gently guided her toward the tent entrance, keeping his broad frame between her and the watching cameras.

The aide held the tent flap open, gesturing them inside with practiced efficiency. The canvas walls dulled the chaos outside, creating a bubble of relative quiet broken only by the muffled sound of the helicopter passing overhead.

***

Helicopters circled the Portal Access zone like hungry vultures, their searchlights cutting through the night. News vans lined the perimeter, their satellite dishes raised high above their roofs. Reporters clutched microphones, jostling for position as military personnel maintained the barrier line.

"This is Christine Chen for Channel 7 News, live at the Fullerton Portal site where survivors have emerged from what authorities are calling a dimensional tear." The reporter's voice carried over the helicopter noise as her cameraman zoomed in on the medical tents. "Among those rescued are fifty-three women who were abducted during that first night."

Across the nation, emergency broadcasts cut into regular programming. CNN's ticker scrolled endlessly: "BREAKING NEWS: PORTAL VICTIMS RETURN - MILITARY MAINTAINS CONTAINMENT - DIMENSIONAL TEAR REMAINS ACTIVE."

Fox News split their screen between live helicopter footage and expert panels debating the implications. MSNBC focused on the human element, showing carefully edited clips of reuniting families while avoiding the more disturbing aspects of the rescue.

The violet glow of the portal painted everything in ethereal light, defying the harsh glare of military floodlights. It pulsed with a steady rhythm now, unlike its earlier chaotic manifestation. Armed guards stood at regular intervals, their weapons pointed outward as scientists in hazmat suits took readings with handheld devices.

"The portal shows no signs of destabilization," a Pentagon spokesperson announced from a hastily assembled podium. "The area remains under strict military control. Citizens are advised to avoid downtown Fullerton until further notice."

Local stations ran footage on repeat: survivors being loaded into ambulances, military vehicles forming protective cordons, and glimpses of strange figures moving through the emergency response teams. One clip captured particular attention: a tall, pale woman with pointed ears walking beside a Filipino man, both escorted by armed soldiers toward a command tent.

The media circus intensified as dawn approached. Morning shows prepared their lead stories while international news outlets picked up the feed. The portal continued its steady pulse, a permanent wound in reality that refused to close.

"Breaking news, we're analyzing footage of the survivors emerging from what scientists are calling a dimensional tear," a reporter announced, her perfectly styled hair whipping in the helicopter downdraft. Behind her, massive screens mounted on news vans played the footage in slow motion, frame by frame.

"Our video analysts are particularly interested in this sequence," another reporter said, pointing to a monitor showing the ghostly violet light. "You can see the survivors emerging in groups of two to three, many helping carry what appears to be a covered body."

The footage played on repeat across multiple screens: disoriented women stumbling through, supported by others, followed by military personnel rushing to assist them.

"We've confirmed fifty-three women were rescued," a field reporter stated into her microphone. "Many are being treated for dehydration and trauma. Several survivors mentioned being held in caves, though details remain unclear at this time."

"What's fascinating is this figure here," a news analyst said, circling a tall, slim shape with his laser pointer. "The proportions seem almost inhuman."

"One of the rescued women, speaking on condition of anonymity, claims she heard the words 'elves' and 'goblins' during a conversation in the cave," another reporter added cautiously. "Though this could be attributed to stress and confusion during their ordeal."

"The military maintains strict control of the area," a correspondent reported from behind concrete barriers. "No official statement has been made regarding the exact nature of the rescue operation or the current status of the dimensional anomaly."

The screens continued cycling through the footage: exhausted faces, tear-filled reunions, medical teams rushing forward with blankets and stretchers. Each network picked apart every frame, speculating about shadowy figures and strange movements caught in the violet light.

"Whatever the full story," a veteran reporter summarized, "this marks an unprecedented event in human history. The question remains: what exactly lies on the other side of that tear in reality?"

***

Outside the medical tents, families rushed forward as survivors emerged. A mother collapsed to her knees, wrapping her arms around her teenage daughter. The girl's hospital gown could not hide the bruises, but they were alive, together.

"Thank you, thank you," a father gripped Jin's hand, tears streaming down his weathered face. His daughter Maria stood beside him, wearing a borrowed military jacket. Jin tried to smile, but his eyes remained distant, haunted.

Near the ambulances, Mrs. Torres knelt beside a black body bag. Her shoulders shook as she identified her daughter Emily. The coroner gently zipped the bag closed while another family held Mrs. Torres as she wept.

"My Sarah isn't here," a woman clutched a photo of a smiling girl in a graduation gown. "They said fifty-three came back. Where is my Sarah?" Her voice cracked as she scanned each emerging face, hope dying a little more with each stranger.

Butch stood awkwardly as parents embraced him, murmuring gratitude in broken voices. He kept his responses short, nodding instead of speaking. A teenage girl who had been in the caves recognized him, pointing out to her parents, "He fought them. He protected us."

Some reunions never came. A young woman learned her mother had died fighting the creatures that first night. She sat alone on a curb, holding her house keys that police had recovered from the scene.

"Dad died trying to save me," a girl told her crying aunt as they hugged. "He fought so hard."

Jin watched it all, his face a mask of exhaustion and grief. When a mother thanked him profusely, calling him a hero, he could only shake his head. The word felt hollow against the weight of those still missing, those who would never come home.

Near the command tent, a wall of photos grew—faces of the missing, the ones who had not emerged from the portal. Family members added new pictures hourly, their desperate hope visible in each carefully taped image. Some contained handwritten notes: "Please help find her" and "Call if you saw her."

Butch drifted away from the crowd of grateful parents and survivors, their thanks weighing heavy on his shoulders. Each handshake felt like another burden, their gratitude raw and real against his calloused palms. He gave short nods, his usual Filipino accent thicker with exhaustion as he mumbled brief responses.

The edge of a white medical tent offered refuge. He leaned against a support pole, the canvas rough against his back. The water bottle trembled slightly in his grip as he took slow sips, letting the cool liquid wash away the metallic taste that lingered from the other world.

His gaze lifted to the California night sky. The familiar smog-tinged blue stretched overhead, so different from the alien atmosphere they had left behind. No crystal formations here. No haunting harmonics. Just the steady drone of helicopters and the distant wail of sirens.

The bottle crinkled in his grip. His forearms still bore marks from the battle—purple bruises where the Warlord had grabbed him, scratches from goblin claws. But it was the invisible weight that pressed heaviest. The memory of Mrs. Chen's body being carried through the portal. The faces of those they could not save.

A news helicopter swooped lower, its rotors chopping the air. Butch did not flinch. The sound was almost comforting in its mundane familiarity. His eyes remained fixed on the sky, finding peace in its vast emptiness.

General Berriman approached Butch with measured steps, his uniform crisp despite the late hour. His weathered face bore the careful neutrality of a career officer assessing a situation.

"Mr. Hidalgo, I want to personally thank you for what you've done here." The general extended his hand.

"Just Butch, sir." Butch shook the offered hand with a firm grip, his stance automatically shifting to parade rest.

"That movement right there." Berriman's eyes narrowed slightly. "Special Forces? Your combat experience was evident in the reports. Which unit—"

"Different time, different country, sir." Butch's voice remained respectful but firm. His usual warm demeanor cooled several degrees. "Best left there."

The general studied him for a long moment, noting the subtle tension in Butch's shoulders, the way his accent thickened slightly. Recognition flickered across Berriman's face. He had seen that same guarded look in other men who carried histories they preferred not to discuss.

"Understood." Berriman nodded, backing off the subject with professional courtesy. "Still, what you managed to accomplish—"

"Just did what needed doing, sir." Butch's tone made it clear the conversation was over.

"Sir," Butch cut in politely, his posture still military-straight. "What day is it?"

"Sunday." General Berriman checked his watch. "Just past 2300 hours. Why?"

"Need sleep. I got work tomorrow, sir." Butch's Filipino accent colored the simple statement. "May I go?"

The general's eyebrows lifted slightly, but a hint of respect crossed his weathered features. Here was a man who had fought creatures from another dimension, rescued dozens of captives, yet spoke of returning to his regular job as if it were the most natural thing in the world.

"Of course. And thank you again, Mr. Hidalgo."

Butch paused, his hand reaching into his pocket. "Thanks for not shooting at my old butt back there."

The shard emerged dull and lifeless in his palm, nothing like the pulsing crystal it had been in the other world. He extended it toward General Berriman.

"You might need that in there." Butch nodded toward the portal's violet glow. The general accepted the crystal, turning it over in his hands with careful scrutiny.

Without waiting for a response, Butch turned and walked away through the maze of medical tents and military vehicles, his tired steps carrying him toward a place to sleep.

EPILOGUE

The television cast blue shadows across the emergency response center's walls. News anchors traded breathless updates, their voices competing with the constant hum of military radios and ringing phones.

"Sources confirm fifty-three women rescued through an interdimensional portal in Fullerton, California." The anchor's perfect hair gleamed under studio lights. "The Pentagon has declined to comment on reports of non-human entities involved in the rescue operation."

The channel changed. A panel of experts sat around a glossy table, gesturing with practiced urgency.

"We don't know if it's permanent," declared a silver-haired physicist, adjusting his wire-rimmed glasses. "The portal's energy signature shows no signs of degradation."

"That's precisely my point," cut in a woman in a crisp blazer. "We must treat this as a global security issue. If one portal opened in California, what's stopping others from appearing elsewhere? The military presence in Fullerton needs to be our model for—"

Click. Another network, another panel.

"And what about the one who came through with them? The woman—Ara." A security analyst leaned forward, his tie slightly askew. "Witnesses describe long ears, unusual skin markings. Are we simply accepting the presence of an extraterrestrial being on U.S. soil without—"

Footage played behind him: a tall, pale figure walking between military vehicles, escorted by armed personnel. The image was grainy, captured from a distance, but her otherworldly grace was unmistakable even in the poor-quality video.

The broadcast cut to aerial shots of the portal site, now surrounded by hastily erected barriers and floodlights. The violet tear in reality pulsed steadily, its glow visible even through the news helicopter's filters.

"The FBI has established a task force," a reporter's voice narrated over the footage. "Officials stress the situation is contained, but sources inside the Pentagon suggest preparations are being made for possible similar incidents in other locations."

Dr. Helena Voss adjusted her glasses, her neat gray suit a stark contrast to the chaos of hastily assembled press lights and microphones. Behind her, screens displayed thermal readings of the portal's energy signature.

"Let's not use fantasy names," she said, her tone carrying the weight of decades in xenolinguistics. "These aren't 'elves.'" Her hand cut through the air, dismissing the term. "What we've seen so far points to an evolutionary offshoot of Homo erectus. Possibly a high-functioning subgroup we didn't know existed."

The camera zoomed in as she reached for a tablet, bringing up comparative skull structures. "Culturally divergent. Possibly isolated until now." Her finger traced the distinctive brow ridge pattern. "The sonic communication alone suggests generations of specialized evolution. Their vocal apparatus shows remarkable adaptation for complex frequency modulation."

A reporter's hand shot up. "Dr. Voss, are you saying they're human?"

"I'm saying they're hominids." She tapped the screen, highlighting bone density comparisons. "Their branch split from ours long ago, but we share common ancestors. This isn't about magic or fantasy. It's about isolated evolution producing remarkable adaptations."

The lights caught the silver in her hair as she leaned toward the camera, her expression stern. "We need to approach this scientifically. The terminology matters. Every time someone says 'elf,' they're adding a layer of mythology that obscures the real significance of what we're dealing with."

The studio lights flickered as a producer rushed onto the set, waving papers at the news anchor. Dr. Voss paused mid-sentence about cranial evolution patterns, her hand frozen over the tablet display.

"I apologize for the interruption, Dr. Voss." The anchor's hand pressed against his earpiece, his professional demeanor cracking. "We're receiving breaking news."

The teleprompter scrolled. The anchor's face drained of color as he read.

"Three new portals have opened in the United States. Four in Europe. Three in the Philippines. Two in Australia." His voice caught. He swallowed hard before continuing. "Unconfirmed reports continue to pour in from across Asia, Africa, and South America."

The papers trembled in his hands. The studio fell silent except for the hum of equipment.

"Military response is underway."

Dr. Voss's tablet slipped from her fingers, clattering against the desk. The comparative skull structures still glowed on the screen, forgotten.

Behind them, the monitors showing the Fullerton portal site switched to a grid of live feeds. Multicolored tears appeared in city squares, remote villages, and dense forests. Each one pulsed with the same steady rhythm as the first.

***

Jin's thumb pressed the power button. The television screen blinked out, plunging the living room into darkness. Only the streetlight filtering through thin curtains cast any illumination, painting weak shadows across the carpet.

He sat motionless on the worn couch, the remote still gripped in one hand. His eyes stared unfocused at the blank screen, glassy and distant. The faint tremor in his fingers made the remote rattle softly against his leg.

The silence pressed in around him, broken only by the hum of the refrigerator from the kitchen and the muffled sound of a car passing outside.

The image of his father flickered in Jin's mind not the quiet man who came home tired from work, but the warrior who had faced monsters with nothing but a golf club. The father who died trying to reach Mina as creatures dragged her away. His chest tightened as memories crashed through him their mother's funeral just last year, his father standing stone-faced in the rain, and now...

A sob broke free, small and choked. Jin's shoulders shook as he tried to contain it, but the dam crumbled. His cries grew louder, ripping from deep in his chest until they became desperate, keening sounds that echoed off the apartment walls. His body curled forward, arms wrapping around his middle as if trying to hold himself together.

Quick footsteps padded down the hallway. Mina's arms encircled him from behind, her chin resting on his shoulder. She said nothing, just pulled him closer as her own tears fell silently onto his shirt.

Their shared grief filled the small room raw, exhausted sounds of two people who had lost everything twice over. Outside their window, traffic continued its endless flow, horns honked, and the city carried on, oblivious to the broken pieces of their world scattered across the floor.